<u>Ahab and Jezebel</u>:
A Love that is Unhealthy

This is book #15 of the Bible-based, historical
romance novel series,
Love God's Way!

LA WANDA BLACKMON

HFT PUBLISHING
Inc

HFT Publishing, Inc.

P. O. Box 1863

Brewton, AL 36427-1863

Email: HFT-Publishing@post.com

Paperback ISBN—979-8-90079-007-7

eBook ISBN—979-8-90079-016-9

Exterior and Interior Design of the book by:

HFT Publishing, Inc.

limited AI text, research, and spell check assistance with extensive editing

eBook conversion by:

HFT Publishing, Inc.

Paperback Book Cover and eBook cover designed by:

HFT Publishing, Inc.

The Cover Photo—Fotor AI Generated by Author

Printed in the United States of America

Dedication

I dedicate this book and the accompanying AI-generated animated video to Janet Crawford, one of my dearest friends. She has been my nurse practitioner, psychologist, counselor, debater, and prayer partner.

Janet, what has made this journey with you over the past few decades so remarkable is that, like you, I am a trauma/critical care nurse. More importantly, I am a minister who was raised in the Assembly of God, while you were raised in a devout Mormon home. We have debated the Bible, and we are still best friends! We have encouraged each other to delve into the Word of God, study numerous prophecies, and conduct extensive research since I returned from the Gulf War era of my life.

I love and appreciate you very much! Keep studying God's word. We are going to make it in the Rapture! God is still working on both of us, and He will continue to do so until the end. However, we must first ensure that we are ready, and then we can help everyone around us get ready too. I love you, my friend!

Table Of Contents

Acknowledgments

I want to extend a special thank you to all the ministers who have planted seeds in my life over the years. Many pastors tolerated my endless supply of questions about the Bible, the "what ifs," and the "why's" that I constantly demanded answers to. I was the young person in the church who was continually "deep diving" into topics. I wanted specifics and the "rest of the story!" This book series is a testament to the endless hours you have spent planting seeds in my life and answering questions!

There are too many to list here, but these are the individuals whom I tormented the most with questions. The first list has already gone to heaven.

Pastor, Sanford Cobb
Evangelist, Janice Knowles
Evangelist & Prophetess, Sis. Burford
AL District Secretary, Roy Creamer

My Father/Pastor, Edward Nall
Prophet & Pastor, Jerry Trotter
Pastor, Glyn Lowery
Youth Pastor, Steve Zepp

May God give you an extra crown that you can lay at Jesus' feet for your patience with me!

Introduction

<u>Ahab and Jezebel</u>: *A Love that is Unhealthy*

"Love God's Way" Series book #15

If you read something and think, "I do not remember ever hearing a preacher say that," or if you are asking yourself, "Where in the Bible is this part of the story?" Do not worry. Everything in this book is Biblical. Many wonderful tidbits of people's lives are hidden in the genealogical chapters of the Old Testament. In the back of this book, you will find all of the scriptures to support each event of this story.

In the 1990s, research was done manually—the internet had not yet been created. Much of what I needed to read was written in Hebrew and Aramaic. So, I found three Rabbis and two Imams who were willing to help me. After so many book publishers turned me down in the 1990s and early 2000s, I gave up trying to get these books published. It was too much for them—there was no way to validate my research. Now that we have the internet, and with many Rabbis and Imams online who are willing to answer questions, conducting this type of research is a breeze in 2025.

I have rechecked all the research, and my publisher has confirmed the accuracy of what I have included. You, too, can check the research, ask questions online, and dig even further than I did when I wrote this book.

So, sit back with your favorite drink or coffee and get ready for the story of the century. Remember, this is a novel. Every word or thought cannot be recorded in the Bible. It would be impossible to contain it in one carry-sized book. I used the "normal" human response as my method for generating dialogue for character interactions when their response is not listed in the Bible or historical records.

Now the story begins..........Approximately 900 years before Jesus Christ was born, the kingdom of Israel (12 tribes) was divided into two parts. Judah (two tribes) and Israel (the 10 northern tribes). During this time, King Omri, the sixth king of Israel, a successful military campaigner, fought, conquered, and expanded the northern part of Israel to include the area from Samaria to Shemer (also known as Shimar in some literature). King Omri made Samaria the capital of the northern 10 tribes of Israel.

King Omri's son, Ahab, was designated as his successor. So, he arranged for the marriage of his son, Ahab, to a Phoenician Princess named Jezebel. She was the daughter of King Ethbaal of the Sidonians. Ahab's marriage to Jezebel was one of political advantage for Jezebel's family, but it was a spiritual disaster for Israel. Jezebel, who was a fervent worshipper of Baal and Asherah, began to promote the worship of these idols to the children of Israel. When Ahab became king, she began to prepare food daily for the 400 Prophets of Baal that she had brought into Israel.

King Ahab and Jezebel, both devout worshippers of Baal, began to antagonize and persecute the prophets of Yahweh, including the Prophet Elijah. During this time, Ahab became obsessed with the vineyard next door to the palace. He became angry and emotionally upset because Naboth would not sell him his vineyard. So, Jezebel had Naboth killed and his vineyard seized for Ahab, simply because he desired it so much. The demonic evil that controlled Jezebel loved feeding Ahab's lust!

The Bible says that he was one of the evilest rulers in the history of the nation of Israel up to that time. Because Ahab and Jezebel were so fervent in their idol worship and persecution of the prophets of Yahweh, they had been successful in turning the majority of their citizens from serving Yahweh to worshipping the idols and groves they had set up throughout the northern part of Israel.

Just like it has always been in the past, when evil comes into power, financial deprivation, and war break out, followed by famine and economic collapse. This historical romance novel will take you on a journey through the arrangement of the "Power Couple Marriage" of the millennium and a reign that includes all of these disasters.

This biblically based novel will reveal what happens when evil individuals lead and control the government and the church. Evil always ensures that those in charge get what they want, when they want it, regardless of the cost to the citizens, including persecution of the opposers and murder!

When it seemed all was lost, God spoke to Elijah, instructing him to gather the people to meet him and the prophets of Baal on Mount Carmel. He challenges them to offer a sacrifice, and if their god answers by fire, the people will serve Baal. If Yahweh answers by fire, then the people will serve Yahweh—everyone agreed—the event began.

At the end of the day, Baal does not respond. But Yahweh does. He not only sends down fire to start the sacrifice, but he also burns up the sacrifice, the altar, and laps up the water around the altar. There was no question who the more powerful God was. So, the people agreed to serve only Yahweh. Elijah, under the anointing of God, kills all 400 prophets of Baal. Before he can make it back to Jerusalem, it begins to rain. When the Israelites turned back to God, he sent the rain to stop the famine. But Jezebel was not happy at all. She put out a contract on Elijah. She wanted him dead!

Here at the main characters that you will meet over the following few chapters:

Ahab: King of Israel, husband of Jezebel, who followed her religious practices.

Athena: Queen of Sidon, wife of King Esthbaal. The Bible and the historical records of the Phoenician Kings do not provide the name of King Eshbaal's wife. It is hard to write a story and constantly say the wife of King Esthbaal. For clarity in telling this story, I have given her the name Athena. It was a popular Greek and Hellenistic name in the ancient world.

Baal: A principal god of the Phoenicians and Canaanites, worshiped by Jezebel.

Elijah: A prophet of Yahweh who confronted Jezebel and championed the worship of the one true God.

Esthbaal: King of Sidon (he merged Tyre and Sidon—modern day Lebanon). He was the father of Jezebel. (King Ethbaal reigned in Sidon for 32 years).

Jehu: A military commander anointed to overthrow the house of Ahab and purge Baal worship from Israel.

Jezreel: A fertile valley and important city in Israel, the location of Naboth's vineyard.

Naboth: An Israelite whose vineyard was unjustly seized by King Ahab at Jezebel's instigation.

Samaria: The capital city of the Northern Kingdom of Israel during the reigns of Ahab and Jezebel.

If I have your attention now—read on!

CHAPTER ONE:

The Phoenician Princess's Legacy

The humid air of Sidon was so thick that you could slice it with your hand and feel the mist drip off before you could move to get a tissue. The briny tang of the Mediterranean, the pungent aroma of curing cedarwood, and the earthy scent of countless spices carried on the Levant winds. Looking out the windows of the palace that morning as the sun rose was a young princess.

Jezebel looked at her servant, "Mona, have you seen the sun so bright that it bleached out the limestone buildings?"

"No," replied the servant as she moved closer to the window to see what the princess was looking at so intently. She had to admit that the azure sea looked like a lake of molten sapphire with the sun reflecting off it this morning.

Mona turned toward her mistress, "Oh, my, look at how that azure reflection from the water mixed with the sun has polished your hair. Enjoy this fresh, crisp sea breeze while you can, mistress, because you know the temple down the street will have the air filled with the pungent smells of animal sacrifices before the day is over!"

The young princess, Jezebel, was so accustomed to the offerings at the temple of Baal (the god of rain and fertility) that she did not pay them any attention. In fact, she loved to watch the priest at work with the animal sacrifices. The service that she enjoyed the most was the offerings made every Friday morning to Moloch of the firstborn children. To her, there was something so special about the devotion of a parent that they would give their firstborn to the god who could provide them with prosperity.

As she stood looking out over this city and down toward the docks, she began to think about how awesome it had been to grow up here, where there were so many people continually coming to their city and bringing so many beautiful things, including their gods, and introducing them to the Sidonians. Her mind was in a grateful frame of mind. She began to think about the gods they served. She was so proud that she could admit that she made a sacrifice at least once per month to all gods in the area, including the ones from the far east, India, Egypt, Mesopotamia, and all of the countries close to the Mediterranean Sea.

Her mind began running through the list of gods that she would need to offer a sacrifice to tomorrow. She laughed because there were so many rituals associated with the long list of gods that she desired to worship that she was glad her dad was the king and rich! Then she began to cite each one.

Baal Hadad—the storm god

Asclepius—Greek god of Medicine

Astarte—goddess of fertility, sexuality, and war

Anat—sister and consort to Baal—also associated with fertility and war—life and death

El—the supreme god of the Phoenicians. He was considered the father of the gods. He was associated with wisdom, fatherhood, and creation.

Melqart—god of kingship, navigation, and colonization

Moloch—fire and child sacrifice—if the child was sacrificed, then prosperity would be granted

Eshmum—god of healing and health—this was the main god for most Sidonians.

Tanit—the goddess of fertility, war, and the moon

As Jezebel started her day, she wondered if her father would return from Egypt that day or the next (Friday). She was hoping he would arrive today so that they could go to the temple of Baal together first thing in the morning. Baal was her father's main god, and he had been good to them. Even though she was mesmerized by all the other gods, especially the goddess, she knew that her devotion also needed to be to Baal. Regardless of who she would marry one day or where she would live, she knew she would always worship Baal.

Then her mind shifted to the people her dad had told her about the previous week. He was talking to a merchant from Magdala, Israel. This merchant had told her dad that they worshipped only one God. He said that this God was the Almighty, who is still in Heaven, but He interacts with humans here on earth. He could bless or curse you, depending on whether or not you served him. She thought that was intriguing and wondered if there was somewhere that god could be worshipped here, since he was so powerful.

However, about halfway through her dad's story, he said the strangest thing. This god is so powerful that they cannot say his name. They are not worthy, so they shorten it to four letters in their language, and it sounds like they are saying Yahweh when they speak those four letters. They say he is the "I AM." This God has ten commandments or requirements of them. The first one is what I find hard to believe. These Israelites cannot worship any other god, only this God Jehovah, Yahweh.

For some strange reason, Jezebel could not stop thinking about this for almost 10 days now—a god who is jealous of all of the other gods. I wonder how that works? I wonder what he does if you worship another god? Do you get sick? Die? What?

15

Jezebel did not know why, but this new god was fascinating to her and would drive her crazy until she could travel with her dad to learn more about him. There had to be a way to control this god and trick him into allowing you to worship other gods as well. She had a new mission.

Thursday Evening:

Jezebel was so happy to see her father approaching the palace. King Esthbaal was a mighty king from the Phoenicians, a culture known for its ancient Semitic heritage. Her dad, like so many of the rich Phoenicians, had acquired his wealth through maritime trade investments. He had been successful in securing an "in" in most markets, but there was one area where he had not been able to infiltrate and control it, yet—Israel. He wanted control of the ports at Magdala, in the northern part of Israel, near Galilee.

"Dad, you are back. That trip was too long! I have missed you so much. Was it successful? Did you bring me something special from Egypt?" Jezebel chirped out as she went running down the palace steps to greet her father.

King Esthbaal (some literature uses Ithoball for the spelling) could not help himself. Jezebel was his crown jewel. She always made him smile. He had never seen a child so full of energy. Looking at her as she ran to him, he could not believe how much she had grown. He was not ready for her to be an adult. He needed a few more years of that smile and her energy.

"Of course, my child! You know that I will always bring you something you want, and then I get you something you need, every time!" With that, she was bear-hugging him.

When she stepped back, something like a stabbing pain hit Esthbaal in his chest. He thought, "Oh, the gods better help me. I am not ready for her to be grown—she looks ready to be a queen today! How will I ever control this energy now that she is maturing?" As quickly as these thoughts flooded his mind, they rushed away, because Jezebel was becoming the life of the party of men around him. He had to take control!

Here was his daughter, dancing around, and he could hear the whispers of her name—Jezebel—on the lips of everyone around. Even her name seemed to evoke something special with these men today. He was going to have to talk with his wife and his chief advisor about this—maybe he had been too free with the liberty he had allowed Jezebel. Now that she was maturing so fast, perhaps he needed to apply restrictions. Then he laughed to himself, "Who am I trying to fool—there is nothing that will tame this wild mare—except a husband!" Then the idea hit him!

Bedtime:

It had been a wonderful day. Jezebel had been so busy with her dad returning home. She was exhausted. After her servants bathed and dressed her for bed, she lay down thinking, I will be gone in a second or two. She had nodded off twice during her bath. As soon as her head hit the pillow, it was like her brain was laid in a room with 1000 candles lit. She was wide awake!

Her mind raced over the memories of the day, and then it quickly turned to the noises outside at the harbor. It was the last day of the work week. Tomorrow was a day of rest and worship at the temple. She could hear the sailors and merchants hollering as they bustled about trying to secure the ships at the harbor, take down the sails, and prepare the ship to rest for a day and a half, then restock to go back out the following week.

The tide was coming in, and she could hear the rhythmic slapped against the sides of the boats and the stone quays. The boisterous cursing of the sailors as they fought with the sails that kept trying to get away with the wind that the tide always brought with them. She remembered that it was these waves that had always helped her as a child to fall asleep. But tonight, it was not working. Then the smells began

17

to rush through her open window. She lay there trying to recognize and name each one. She could smell the cedarwood that had arrived from Lebanon that morning. The shipbuilder here in town loved this wood for making his master pieces. There was a new smell that was so fragrant and beautiful that she would have to track it down the next day. She had never smelled that before. It must be a flower brought in on the ship that arrived from Asia this morning. She heard the servants talking about it and all of the new perfumes that this Maji had brought with him.

Jezebel's Education

Jezebel's education was extensive. Her father spared no expense as he brought in experts from the areas where he wanted his daughter to excel. He wanted to be able to marry her off to a king or prince of a larger nation one day. So, her education was not confined to the quiet contemplation of scrolls within the palace walls.

Her actual schooling happened in the streets, in the marketplace, and on the decks of the majestic ships that her people built. She learned the language of trade, the subtle art of negotiation from her father's merchants, observing them haggle over bolts of Tyrian purple and intricately carved ivory. She absorbed the geography of the world not from maps, but from the weathered faces of sailors returning from distant shores, their eyes filled with the wonder of the unknown. They spoke of Egypt's pyramids, of Mesopotamia's fertile plains, of the wild lands to the north. This immersive education, more visceral than any academic pursuit, honed her sharp mind and instilled in her a keen understanding of the world's complexities and opportunities.

But it was her inner life, her spiritual grounding, that truly defined her. Her parents, King Ethbaal and Queen,[1] were devout adherents to the pantheon of Phoenician gods, and their faith was not a passive inheritance but an active, vibrant force that shaped their lives and the lives of their people. Jezebel's earliest lessons were not of kingship or diplomacy, but of reverence and idol worship. She learned the names of the gods, their stories, their domains, and how to honor them in worship that would bring her fame, fortune, fertility, and all of the other benefits she would need one day as a Queen.

Family/Genealogy Education

One of the most unusual facts concerns Jezebel's father, King Ethbaal, and his education, as well as his previous occupation before becoming the King of Sidon. During the 9th century BC, Ethbaal became a prominent king. He was known throughout the region as the king of political and financial influence, due to his strategic location, proximity to port cities, and extensive international trade relations with numerous countries. It is said that he had a tremendous influence over King Omri and his son, King Ahab, during his reign. Tyre and Sidon were both prosperous coastal cities located along the Mediterranean Sea (Modern-day Lebanon). Both towns were renowned for their production of purple dyes, their extraction of precious metals, and their maritime trade. They had wonderful markets and boasted of being the greatest trading hubs in the entire region.

The royal family of Tyre had been in control of the throne for many decades. However, they could not keep the family conflicts down. So, anyone on the throne was not safe. Jezebel's teachers ensured that she was fully aware of her family's genealogy. Where today, we would want to hide the family scandals, in those days, they worshipped and praised the conquerors and their victories. It was survival of the fittest in a battle worse than the jungle. This is the genealogy Jezebel took with her:

Genealogy

Jezebel's family tree is a prophetic example of what is to come for her children and grandchildren. The impact of satanic evil that possesses a person under the influence of idolatry is overwhelming for a non-ministerial person to understand, much less this 21st-century generation. However, understanding the genealogy, history, education, religious, and political platforms of the Old Testament is crucial to understanding "Love God's Way!"

Jezebel's Great-Great-Grandfather: **King Hiram**—2nd King of Tyre. He had a favorable relationship with King David and his son, King Solomon, during their reigns. He provided the cedar timbers that King Solomon needed for building the temple at Jerusalem from the forest of Lebanon.

Jezebel's Great-Grandfather: **King Baal-Eser**: Also known as (Belezarus/Balazeros)—he lived 43 years and reigned for 7 years. He was 36 years old when he became king.

Jezebel's Grandfather: **King Abdastartus**—who was the son of Baal-Eser and the grandson of Hiram I, the first two kings of Tyre. King Abdastartus was 43 years old when his son, Astartus killed him. King Abdastartus only ruled for almost nine years when his oldest son killed him.

Jezebel's Uncle: **King Astartus** (Ashtart)—Killed his father, Abdastartus. He was the oldest son of King Abdastartus. He was the oldest of four sons that King Abdastartus had with his nurse. He reigned for 12 years. His three brothers ruled after each other. Each one seized the throne and killed the others.

Jezebel's Uncle: **King Delestartus**—Second of the four sons of King Abdastartus by his nurse to seize the throne. He reigned for 12 years.

Jezebel's Uncle: **King Astarymus** (Aserymus)—he was the third of four brothers (all sons of Abdastartus' nurse) to seize the throne. King Astarymus had reigned only eight months when, at 50 years of age, he was killed by his brother Phelles.

Jezebel's Uncle: **King Phelles**—was the last of the four children born to King Abdastartus by his nurse. He killed his Aserymus Phelles was killed by "his brother" Esthbaal. He was the last of the "Dynasty of the Four Brothers." He did not reign but eight months, when he was killed by Esthbaal (Ithobasus), the priest of Astarte, who was thought to be his half-brother.

However, he apparently had half-brothers—we do not know how many wives King Abdastartus had, but it is obvious that the king deemed several of his sons unworthy of the throne. Because he appointed them to various positions of prestige, his son, Eshbaal, was appointed to be the first priest of Astarte in Sidon.

Phelles killed his brother (King Aserymus (Astarymus) and seized the throne.

Then King Phelles met his own Karma when his brother or half-brother, Esthbaal, killed him and seized the throne.

Jezebel's Father: **King Esthbaal**—reigned 32 years. He lived 68 years and was murdered by his half-brother Phelles for the throne. Apparently, he was not happy with being appointed Priest of Astarte. He wanted more—the throne! King Esthbaal was the one who combined the two large regions, "Tyre and Sidon," into one country, Sidon. For many years, the capital was Tyre. Both cities were coastal trade areas.

Jezebel: Daughter of King Esthbaal who married King Ahab of Israel. She was the sister of King Badezorus, who was appointed to the throne when their father died.

Jezebel's Brother:	Badezorus—Jezebel's brother took the throne after her father, King Esthbaal, died. Jezebel was married to King Ahab at this time.

Note that all four brothers sat on the throne as kings. Three of them seized the throne from each other after the death of their father. A family legacy of deceit, cunning, murder, and tyranny. What a legacy!

Religious Education

There were two main gods that King Esthbaal wanted his daughter, Jezebel, to know about. Foremost among them was Baal, the powerful storm god, lord of the sky, the bringer of rain and fertility. She learned of his mighty chariot, his thunderous voice, and his ceaseless struggle against the forces of chaos. She would stand with her mother during offerings, her small hands clutching a delicate alabaster bowl filled with perfumed oil, watching as the fragrant smoke spiraled upwards towards the heavens, carrying their prayers to the divine. She learned that Baal's favor was essential for the prosperity of their kingdom, for the bounty of their harvests, for the safety of their ships upon the treacherous sea. His strength mirrored the strength she was taught a king and a queen must possess.

And then there was Asherah, the great mother goddess, the consort of Baal, the source of life, wisdom, and fertility. Asherah was the embodiment of nurturing love, the protector of families, the weaver of destinies. Jezebel discovered her profound connection to the earth, particularly to the sacred groves where her worship was most potent. She understood Asherah as the feminine counterpart to Baal's raw power, the balance that held the cosmos together. The imagery associated with Asherah — the carved wooden poles, the representations of divine motherhood — resonated deeply within her, evoking a sense of primal connection and a maternal strength that she felt stirring within her soul.

These were not abstract deities, distant and unknowable. They were present in the world around her. The life-giving rain that lashed against the city walls was Baal's arrival. The unwavering light of the sun was a manifestation of his power. The fertility of the land, the burgeoning life in the olive groves and vineyards, was Asherah's blessing. The sacred groves, with their ancient trees and whispered secrets, were places where the veil between the mortal and the divine was thin. Jezebel felt the presence of her gods in the rustling leaves, in the crashing waves, in the very air she breathed. This was not a matter of blind faith; it was an intrinsic part of her understanding of reality, a deeply ingrained certainty that shaped her perception of the world and her place within it.

Her tutors, skilled scribes and priests, reinforced this spiritual foundation. They taught her the hymns and chants that honored Baal and Asherah, as well as the intricate rituals and sacrifices that pleased them. They spoke of the divine mandate that lay upon her family, the sacred duty to uphold the worship of the true gods. This devotion was not merely a personal matter; it was the very bedrock of Phoenician identity, the source of their kingdom's strength and legitimacy.

Yet, even in the sun-drenched splendor of Sidon, a young princess could feel the distant stirrings of other worlds, other beliefs. Occasionally, traders from the east would speak of the strange, singular God worshipped by the tribes dwelling in the arid lands of Canaan. They called him Yahweh. The whispers were often tinged with confusion, even derision. A god with no images? A god who dwelled in a hidden tent, not in grand temples? A god who demanded exclusivity, who saw all other gods as false? It seemed a peculiar, almost barbaric notion to the sophisticated people of Phoenicia, who understood divinity as a vibrant, multifaceted pantheon, interwoven with the natural world.

These distant whispers, however, were like faint echoes from another shore, barely audible above the vibrant chorus of her own familiar faith. Jezebel, immersed in the rich spiritual tapestry of Sidon, could not fathom a world so devoid of the divine presence she knew so intimately. Her gods were not abstract concepts; they were the very essence of life, the forces that governed the cycles of nature and the destinies of men. Her devotion was fierce, unshakeable, a flame that burned brightly within her, destined to cast a long and complex shadow upon the land she would one day call home. The spiritual currents of her Phoenician heritage were not merely a backdrop to her life; they were the very essence of her being, the unwavering compass that would guide — and perhaps misguide — her future path. She knew that she had to know more. Each time she heard one of the servants talk about this Israelite God, she felt something stir deep within her.

Amazingly, King Esthbaal had no loyalty to family, yet he maintained such loyalty to his religious connections and gods. There were two main Gods that King Esthbaal wanted his daughter to know about. Foremost among them was Baal, the powerful storm god, lord of the sky, the bringer of rain and fertility. She learned of his mighty chariot, his thunderous voice, and his ceaseless struggle against the forces of chaos. She would stand with her mother during offerings, her small hands clutching a delicate alabaster bowl filled with perfumed oil, watching as the fragrant smoke spiraled upwards towards the heavens, carrying their prayers to the divine. She learned that Baal's favor was essential for the prosperity of their kingdom, for the bounty of their harvests, for the safety of their ships upon the treacherous sea. His strength mirrored the strength she was taught a king, and indeed a queen, must possess.

And then there was Asherah, the great mother goddess, the consort of Baal, the source of life, wisdom, and fertility. Asherah was the embodiment of nurturing love, the protector of families, the weaver of destinies. Jezebel discovered her profound connection to the earth, particularly to the sacred groves where her worship was most potent. She understood Asherah as the feminine counterpart to Baal's raw power, the balance that held the cosmos together. The imagery associated with Asherah – the carved wooden poles, the representations of divine motherhood – resonated deeply within her, evoking a sense of primal connection, a maternal strength that she felt stirring within her own young soul.

These were not abstract deities, distant and unknowable. They were present in the world around her. The life-giving rain that lashed against the city walls was Baal's arrival. The unwavering light of the sun was a manifestation of his power. The fertility of the land, the burgeoning life in the olive groves and vineyards, was Asherah's blessing. The sacred groves, with their ancient trees and whispered secrets, were places where the veil between the mortal and the divine was thin. Jezebel felt the presence of her gods in the rustling leaves, in the crashing waves, in the very air she breathed. This was not a matter of blind faith; it was an intrinsic part of her understanding of reality, a deeply ingrained certainty that shaped her perception of the world and her place within it.

Her tutors, skilled scribes and priests, reinforced this spiritual foundation. They taught her the hymns and chants that honored Baal and Asherah, as well as the intricate rituals and sacrifices that pleased them. They spoke of the divine mandate that lay upon her family, the sacred duty to uphold the worship of the true gods. This devotion was not merely a personal matter; it was the very bedrock of Phoenician identity, the source of their kingdom's strength and legitimacy.

Yet, even in the sun-drenched splendor of Sidon, a young princess could feel the distant stirrings of other worlds, other beliefs. Occasionally, traders from the east would speak of the strange, singular God worshipped by the tribes dwelling in the arid lands of Canaan. They called him Yahweh. The whispers were often tinged with confusion, even derision. A god with no images? A god who dwelled in a hidden tent, not in grand temples? A god who demanded exclusivity, who saw all other gods as false? It seemed a peculiar, almost barbaric notion to the sophisticated people of Phoenicia, who understood divinity as a vibrant, multifaceted pantheon, interwoven with the natural world.

These distant whispers, however, were like faint echoes from another shore, barely audible above the vibrant chorus of her own familiar faith. Jezebel, immersed in the rich spiritual tapestry of Sidon, could not fathom a world so devoid of the divine presence she knew so intimately. Her gods were not abstract concepts; they were the very essence of life, the forces that governed the cycles of nature and the destinies of men. Her devotion was fierce, unshakeable, a flame that burned brightly within her, destined to cast a long and complex shadow upon the land she would one day call home. The spiritual currents of her Phoenician heritage were not merely a backdrop to her life; they were the very essence of her being, the unwavering compass that would guide — and perhaps misguide — her future path. She knew that she had to know more. Each time she heard one of the servants talk about this Israelite God, she felt something stir deep within her.

This year is drawing to a close, and the fall season is quickly approaching. The servants were rushing into the house as if trying to escape the winds coming in off the Mediterranean Sea. There were many murmurs all through the house. Servants were whispering about King Omri in a distant land called Israel. What was so shocking for the people of Tyre and Sidon was that King Omri was getting ready to retire and pass the baton on to his son, Ahab. King Omri was planning to train and successfully transition his son into his role as King at Omri's death. The physicians had not given King Omri any hope that he would live for much longer.

These tales appeared to be unrealistic, especially for the Phoenicians, who worshipped many gods. What made this such alarming news was how fast this group of Israelites was gaining fame and power. They were giving their God-Yahweh the credit for their victories up to King Omri. Now the Israelites were becoming more tolerant and allowing idols to be set up in specific places in Israel. However, there was still a large group of Pharisees who were consistently trying to get the Israelites to rededicate their lives to Yahweh.

Rumors are circulating that King Omir, a dynamic campaigner and conqueror, is gaining an international reputation. He has just captured Samaria and announced that he will make Samaria the capital of Israel. Most of these rumors were tales that had been brought to Sidon by merchants in caravans and sailors on ships importing goods at their docks. Even though Israel was not very large and definitely did not qualify as an Empire, it was showing promise of becoming a political powerhouse to deal with—their king was forging alliances and solidifying his kingdom on the world stage.

For Jezebel, still a princess steeped in the vibrant traditions of her homeland, these were more than just distant political rumblings. They were fragments of a larger narrative that was beginning to unfold, a destiny that had, in subtle ways, already begun to tug at the threads of her life. She listened intently as her father, King Ethbaal, discussed these reports with his advisors. The kingdom of Israel, he explained, was strategically positioned, a bridge between the great powers of Egypt and Mesopotamia. An alliance with such a burgeoning nation held significant appeal, offering potential trade advantages and a bulwark against the unpredictable currents of regional politics, not to mention the impact on trade that would result from controlling the ports across Northern Galilee, especially Magdala.

But it was not the strategic calculations that truly captured Jezebel's imagination. It was the man himself, this son of King Omri, called Ahab, who sounded like the perfect young man for a dynamic princess. The descriptions of his prowess, his leadership were intriguing. There was a strength in his reported ambition that resonated with her own developing sense of purpose. She imagined him, a figure of authority in a land whose spiritual landscape was so starkly different from her own, a land that, according to the traders, was dominated by the worship of a single, unseen deity. The very strangeness of it sparked a curiosity within her, a flicker of interest that was more than just intellectual.

Over the past few weeks, she had been lying in bed at night, trying to picture Ahab, what he looked like, and what he would look like when he finally became king. She imagined his strengths and found herself wondering if he was this good—what would he be like if he had the power of her gods behind him? These questions, initially abstract, began to take on a more personal hue. The idea of an alliance, so vital from her father's perspective, began to subtly shift in her own mind. It was no longer merely a matter of statecraft; it was a potential pathway to something larger, something that called to the core of her being.

Jezebel overheard conversations about the prophets of Israel, figures who wielded immense spiritual authority, who spoke with the voice of their God, Yahweh. They were presented as fervent, unyielding men, guardians of a strict monotheism.

Jezebel, a devout worshipper of Baal and Asherah, found this concept alien, almost bewildering. How could a single god encompass all that was divine? How could a people prosper without the diverse powers and influences of a rich pantheon, without the visible manifestations of their gods in the natural world? Yet, the very challenge posed by this starkly different religious landscape, and by the powerful figures who championed it, stirred something within her. It was a puzzle, a potentially dangerous one, but also one that invited engagement.

Several months have passed, and Jezebel is smitten by the increasing reports coming from Israel. The declarations this week say that Ahab has been officially "anointed" King of Israel. Now, these whispers of King Ahab were not merely tales of a political ally. They were the first faint stirrings of a path being laid before her, a path that led away from the familiar shores of Sidon, across the glittering expanse of the Great Sea, and towards a destiny that was both grand and fraught with peril. She felt an inexplicable pull, a sense of anticipation that transcended the pragmatic considerations of her father's court. It was as if a part of her, a part that had always yearned for a larger stage, for a greater purpose, was responding to a call from across the sea. The news of this Israelite king, this man who ruled a kingdom of such starkly different spiritual currents, was not just a report; it was the harbinger of her own unfolding fate, a destiny that had already begun to weave its intricate design around the young Phoenician princess.

Jezebel was aware of the intricate dance of diplomacy, a waltz of power and alliance, that she had seen her father use so many times. She needed to have a conversation with her father. She could really help him with this alliance if she could convince King Ahab to marry her. This would also give her a throne and kingdom to control. She was fully aware that her father would choose her brother to be king before considering her for the role of queen. The desire to control a kingdom was so strong on her that she felt that it would crush her if she could not exercise this power that was building inside of her.

Jezebel had to get a meeting with her father. She needed to bring it to his attention that he needed to consider a union/alliance/marriage with the King of Ahab. Her father needed to understand how instrumental she could be in making King Ahab a valuable partner, a growing force in a region often dominated by larger, more established empires. Such an alliance would not only solidify Phoenician influence but also open new avenues for trade and cultural exchange. Now, she needed to get started working on this!

Her father has completed his proposal to the new Israeli king, King Ahab. His proposal had been hand-delivered as he presented it charismatically, along with gifts for the King of Israel. Now all he had to do was sit back and wait for the King of Israel to respond. He knew that he should have talked with Jezebel before making the proposal. He felt sure that she would accept the proposal because Ahab was young and handsome. However, he did not want any drama until he knew this was even an option. King Ahab may have already made a contract with another person.

Waiting was not one of King Esthbaal's assets. He had never had patience. Making the trip to Israel and being told to return home, he (King Ahab) would send his answer and an official contract that would be in compliance with the marriage rules for the Jewish population. He would also outline what would happen and when it would occur. Usually, this would have been fighting words for King Esthbaal. However, he had to be careful not to be overly aggressive, as this was his daughter's future.

Six months have passed since King Esthbaal presented the proposal of marriage of his daughter, Jezebel, to King Ahab. He had convinced himself over the past week that it was a wise decision not to discuss this with Jezebel after he returned from making the proposal. Jezebel was very revengeful. If she thought a king had rejected her, she would be asking the gods to curse him. That morning, as he sat in his favorite chair in the vineyard behind the palace, having his fruit, he promised himself to begin trying to find a husband for Jezebel in the new month, just eight days away.

That Same Afternoon:

A royal caravan arrived in Sidon, accompanied by a group of Israelite nobles. They arrived in town and secured a place to rest and refresh just before the sun was directly overhead (12 noon). Then, around sundown (7 pm), two of the royal guards approached the Palace entrance with a formal request, asking for a few moments to meet with the King in the morning.

The palace guard informed them to wait, and he would ask the king's assistant, Kadesh. The guards were then directed to sit down on the benches outside the Palace courtyard. After approximate one hour, Kadesh, the King's Assistant, came out to meet the two guards. He had a formal written reply from the King for the guards to give to the royal delegation at the inn.

The guards did not know the answer, but they hurried back to the inn. It was less than an hour before bedtime. They knew that they needed to hurry. The message stated that the King would meet with them and share the mid-day meal with them. The King noted that he would be honored to receive the delegation. Instead of going to bed, a late-night meeting was quickly put together in the inn's main entrance.

Completely exhausted from the travels and the late-night planning, the royal delegation all retired to their rooms. Too exhausted to move, praying that sleep would come!

King Esthbaal had taken his bath and was dressed to spend his evening leisurely, while having his night meal in his room, so he could finish reading the scrolls that he had brought back with him from Jerusalem, Samaria, and Galilee about their God, Yahweh. He had paid a high price for these scrolls and the other trinkets that he thought Jezebel would need to know about if she was going to live there sometime in the future. He knew that he would need to help prepare his daughter if the offer was accepted. He was certain that King Ahab would require a marriage ceremony and commitment from Jezebel to accept his God and his customs. However, he kept putting off this task. Something had been reminding him for the past three days that it was urgent to read these scrolls. He told his assistant, Kadesh, not to bother him unless it was a matter of life or death.

When Kadesh came pounding on his door only an hour after he had given him instructions not to disturb him, King Esthbaal was so angry that he called out in response, "Enter Kadesh, but know that if it is not life-or-death, you will die Friday morning as I offer you as a sacrifice before Baal!"

Kadesh responded, "Oh, King, it is more important than life and death!"

King Esthbaal raised his brow and wondered what on earth could be more important than life or death. "Enter at your own risk!" he shouted.

When Kadesh handed him the letter and he saw the Star of David seal on the red wax of the envelope, his heart skipped a beat. Could it be? No, it had already been too long. This must be something else, because it was so small. If it were a marriage proposal, it would be a larger stack of papers wrapped and sealed. This note was only a small single sheet of paper folded and sealed, which could not be read by the individuals who delivered it.

The note read, "This is King Ahab of Israel. I am sending a formal delegation of my most trusted noblemen to Sidon to meet with you and formalize your proposal of marriage. Please have your assistant inform my guards of the time the delegation is scheduled to meet you and where they should present themselves. This can be a meeting at your convenience."

King Esthbaal's heart was beating at least 150 beats per minute by the time he finished reading the note. "Kadesh, can you clear my calendar for tomorrow? Or is there anything on it that I must be present for?"

Kadesh responded, "You have to meet with the accountants first thing in the morning to cover the expenses for the temples, cover the cost of the last two voyages, and determine when the new construction for the additional wing here on the palace grounds. Remember, the one you are having built so that your son and his soon-to-be bride can live there while waiting to become king. I would say that all of that would be finished hours before the mid-day meal."

"Great. That is perfect timing. Call the chief butler and baker, and the resident manager. I need them to prepare a banquet for the Israeli delegation for the mid-day meal. Tell them to prepare to serve at least 50 people. I am certain that there will be at least 12 noblemen, with their assistants, and the royal guard. Plus, I will need my advisory committee and scribes present to record this meeting. My lawyer will need to be present. Oh, you had better make that food for 75. There may be extras."

Kadesh looked at him with a shocked expression on his face. What do I tell the guards?

King Esthbaal took out his official papyrus and quill. He jotted down a quick note for the guard to take back to the delegation. Stamped and sealed it and sent Kadesh on his way.

As soon as Kadesh delivered the message to the guards, he ran back to the king's quarters. "Your honor, what do you need me to do besides order the banquet. Are there any dietary restrictions? We do not want to offend the noblemen. I know that pork is off limits. Do you know about anything else?"

King Esthbaal, with a horrified look on his face, said, "Oh, my, I had not even thought about that. Hand me those scrolls, and I will start reading. I must read these before morning. Send a messenger to the chief Priest of each temple. Ask each one the same question you just asked me. Then bring me their responses as soon as the messengers get back with them. In the meantime, tell the baker, butler, and resident manor to prepare meat of all types except pork, vegetables, and fruit. Ensure there is plenty of pure water and our finest wines are ready. Have them make hot and cold desserts. I know that we will need dates and olives, plus that fabulous bread that comes from Galilee that he gets at the souk near the docks. They also need items familiar to them on the table. Now, go! Too much to do, and I have all of this reading."

Kadesh was out the door in a flash, heading to the front entrance courtyard to deliver the invitation to the guard.

The Marriage Delegation from Judah arrives at the palace and is admitted to the library to wait for the noon meal to be served and the King to come from his study.

The formal proposal of marriage arrived in Sidon, carried by a delegation of Israelite nobles, their attire and bearing speaking of a people carving their own identity from the ancient lands.

For Jezebel, the news of the betrothal was a complex tapestry of emotions and a profound affirmation of the subtle call she had felt. She was aware, of course, of the political implications. She understood that her hand in marriage was a significant offering, a cornerstone upon which this crucial alliance would be built. Her father, ever the astute ruler, saw the immense strategic value in binding his daughter to the throne of Israel. It was a masterful stroke of statecraft, securing Phoenicia's interests and extending its cultural reach into a land ripe for influence.

Yet, beneath the weight of political calculation, a deeper current stirred within Jezebel. This was not merely a duty, a sacrifice for the good of her kingdom. It was also a step towards that grander, albeit perilous, destiny that had begun to beckon her. The prospect of leaving her beloved Sidon, the sea that had been her lifelong companion, her familiar gods, and her people, was undoubtedly a somber one. However, it was tempered by an undeniable sense of anticipation —a burgeoning feeling of purpose that resonated with the very core of her being.

Jezebel found herself wondering how the betrothal ceremony would proceed without King Ahab present. She hoped her dad did not give up on negotiating for King Ahab to come here for a betrothal ceremony, even if one was required at a later date for Jerusalem. Jezebel knew that to her, a ceremony here in Sidon was not negotiable.

The betrothal ceremony here in Sidon was a spectacle of Phoenician grandeur, a fitting prelude to the queen she was destined to become. Royal advisors and priests would gather to discuss, review, revise, and add to the marriage contract as they saw fit. Once the political pomp and stance were over, they would perform a ceremony before Baal, asking for blessing, fertility, and wealth. She must have this blessing!

Then the feasts would go on for over a week. Various groups would be entertained each night until her father had looped every person of importance into the ceremony. Her father's charismatic ways would have each group or family feeling like they were the king's best friend. If only she could recall how her father had handled things when she arrived in Jerusalem, she would be better equipped to cope with any crisis or situation.

The feast would be filled with music, dancing, acting performances, and exotic foods. Each feast would honor the people who were present. For the feast that the Israeli delegates would attend, they would feast on their favorite foods, including Sidonian delicacies and desserts. The entertainment would include skits and plays that reflected life.

But best of all, Jezebel would get to have a shopping spree in the souks downtown. She knew exactly which one she wanted to go to. Her dad would pay for the best tailor and designer, once she picked out the fabrics. She liked the finest Tyrian purple silks that would be bedecked with jewelry and gems from the finest Sidonian master artisans. She had this image in her mind of what it would look like as it clung to her body, showing every curve and detail. It would be provocative just enough to have Ahab drooling, wanting to up the date. A Hebrew servant in the kitchen had told her that Jewish betrothals were a minimum of 12 months long. She could not wait 12 months; he might change his mind. She was going to have to spend more time on this topic and research ways around it—note to self, she wrote on her pad—she began adding to her betrothal to-do list.

CHAPTER TWO:
The Marriage Negotiations

Whenever two families from separate countries decide to marry off their children, there will be considerable compromise, with both sides feeling the stress. Each country had its own wedding traditions. It was no different for Ahab and Jezebel. The wedding ceremonies of the two countries differed, making written marriage contracts essential. It was a law in both countries, but these laws applied to royal families. They could not afford to get anything wrong or leave out any crucial points—their entire countries. However, the focus of these contracts differed due to religious preferences.

Jezebel was familiar with her country's customs and her father's shrewd negotiator skills. She could not help herself this morning. She had a dream last night that was tormenting her so much his morning--she wrote down the key components, ensuring she would not forget to check anything. Then she would create a "betrothal and wedding checklist" and allow her to double-check her father's agreement.

Jezebel instructed her servant, "Mona, please try to keep everyone away from my room today, even Momma. I need to concentrate on making out my checklists so I don't forget anything that Father needs to include in my marriage contract with the Jewish King, Ahab. I also need a favor from you. I need you to find me all the scrolls you can that deal with our laws of marriage and betrothal feast."

Bewildered, Mona replied, "Your Royal Highness, you know that I cannot read. How am I to find scrolls for you?"

Jezebel laughed, "Oh, my silly girl! You do not have to read to find them. Just go down to the library on the third floor and see if Jared is in there. Ask him. He can read. He will pull the scrolls for you. Once you have brought me those scrolls, please go to the Temple of Baal, located down the street, and ask for Jael. When he comes out to meet with you, ask him if he can create a list of the events that will occur in the order they should happen for the betrothal ceremony. He will write it down and hand it back to you. I will work on the betrothal today. We can work on the wedding ceremony tomorrow. Hurry, now; I need that first scroll from the library as soon as possible."

Like lightning, Mona was out the door. She was in such a hurry that she forgot to curtsy and back out the door as per custom. Normally, Jezebel would have hollered, scolding her and then issuing some punishment to the servant. But today she was too happy. She had too much to do to get Mona's mind in a twist. She needed her servant functioning at her best!

Twenty minutes later, Mona returned with three scrolls from the Palace Library. Then headed right back out the door to go to the Temple of Baal. Jezebel wrapped her robe around her and grabbed her glass of fresh-squeezed mango juice, and sat down to begin reading.

The Phoenician Betrothal and Wedding

The Phoenicians were named after a Greek word meaning "purple." So, they became known as the purple people. Not because their skin had a bruised or purplish tint to it, but because the people in the area from Thyatira to Tyre and Sidon were known for the purple dye that they were able to produce from their natural resources. As a result, the Phoenicians became closely linked with the Mediterranean Sea, the coastal lands (now known as modern-day Lebanon), and their ports, which provided them with a means to sell their goods as far as North Africa, the Iberian Peninsula, and beyond with ease. They had a significant advantage over land-bound empires like Mesopotamia and Egypt due to their maritime trade options.

Considering the history of the people of Tyre and Sidon, Jezebel needed to ensure that the finest silks from Egypt were brought to her as soon as possible, so that they could be dyed purple and gold. The Phoenicians were also expert craftsmen. She would ensure that her ceremony featured the finest cedarwood tables and accessories. The metalworks in Tyre would provide the gold-overlayed candle arbors, and the cedarwood stools would be covered in gold and purple silk. Only the best would do for a royal ceremony!

She quickly added to the list a note that would remind her to ask her father to have Timotheus at the Tyre Metalworks to prepare a tabletop-sized statue of Baal, overlayed with gold, placed on a piece of cedarwood, and purple silk wrapped around the base of the statue to use as the centerpiece for the bride's table at the betrothal ceremony. She must ensure that Baal would give her children—she must have this blessing, so she would be able to secure her position in Israel.

The table that her father (King Esthbaal) and Ahab's father (King Omri) would sit at would need a table top statue of the Canaanite god El, who was the supreme deity. He was a god held in high esteem and worshipped as the deity who deeply intertwined the daily lives of individuals with public affairs. It was like the god El was the Deity that managed the others, keeping them in line. El was responsible for social influences and prosperity. It was only appropriate for him to be on the "King's table."

Jezebel immediately added to her "to-do" list several line items that she would need for the betrothal (*shiddukh* in related Semitic languages) ceremony:

1) Have Haggin (her father's treasurer) give her a budget
2) Have Mona get the seamstress and tailor to the palace to begin working on her two wedding dresses, four dresses for the receptions, and two dresses for the betrothal ceremonies here and for the one in Israel; she might have to purchase them there in Jerusalem.
3) Hair accessories, scarves, jewelry, shoes, and other accessories would be needed for all of these events.
4) Locate the best rug and tapestry maker locally. Meet with them and have them design rugs to use as the backdrops behind her and Ahab's chairs. This would provide a beautiful backdrop that was colorful to go behind their chairs. She would need to order them to include the colors of Israel's flag, as well as the purple and gold of her father's flag.
5) She had no idea what she would have to decorate with in Israel; she needed to talk with one of the servants for the delegation.
6) Ask the Kitchen Manager about the silver and gold serves that they would use for a royal wedding.
7) Have Dad find out from King Omri if they have these gold trays and services. If not, we will need to take this to Jerusalem as well.

Jezebel knew that for most Phoenicians, marriage was primarily a contractual arrangement, often accompanied by a betrothal celebration ceremony. The wedding was more private because most citizens of Tyre and Sidon did not possess the wealth of the King or the Merchants. The majority of marriages in the area were often merely business deals to expand the father's vast network of trade or a union between two families of trade workers aimed at controlling the competition. But Jezebel wanted her union with Ahab to be more than this—she could feel it—it was going to be something supernatural that was going to happen when she married Ahab!

Once a groom or bride was selected, the next item on the agenda for a Phoenician family was the written contract of marriage. The father of the bride would require a dowry. Most went for a dowry of money that was put up to care for the daughter later if the husband died, and the daughter returned to her parents' home with a bunch of children that had to be supported. If the two families could afford it, then the bride's family would ask for moveable goods, property, cattle, and other items of value, such as gold, silver, and bronze items, as well as jewelry. The father of the groom was also responsible for providing housing, servants, and other items as deemed necessary, depending on the financial status or social position of the parents. The length of time between the betrothal and the actual wedding day was flexible according to the scroll she was reading. This was good news. She continued to read, making sure she was familiar with the exceptions, especially those related to marriages performed outside of Tyre and Sidon.

The one thing she found alarming in these scrolls, which she was not aware was practiced anymore, was the "limiting of interactions between the bride and groom, to only contact with a chaperon from the time of betrothal until the wedding ceremony. Maybe the peasants and the poor practiced this, but royals always had exceptions. In Jezebel's mind, the most important part was the public declaration with the signing of the contracts, exchange of money and the party that followed. Oh my, she was in for a surprise when she met with her father and the Israeli delegation.

For the Phoenicians, the wedding ceremony was a simple procession of the wedding party from the bride's house to the groom's home his father had prepared for them. The bride would wear her finest attire and jewelry and be presented to the groom at the door. They would consummate the marriage, then return to the party or feast that would be going on with the two family members. The presence of friends, relatives, and community leaders completed the public commitment clause. For families who could afford it, it was recommended that there be religious observances, including prayers and sacrifices to the deities of Baal, El, and Astarte, with minimal offerings to ensure prosperity, a harmonious union, fertility, and blessings for their offspring. Typically, one of the temple priests would perform these rituals. This scroll emphasized the fact that simply an offering to Baal or Astarte would be ok if the family was poor.

Jezebel knew that she was not poor, but she was looking for a loophole for the Israel ceremony. They could go all out with the religious component here in Sidon, but she might have to agree to only a prayer to Baal in Israel and no sacrifice if the Jews did not allow sacrifices to other gods. This was good—she felt like she had found her option to present to Ahab if they refused the Phoenician-style wedding.

The second scroll outlined how the cultural exchange of customs from foreigners who married a Phoenician was permitted. This scroll gave examples of marriages between traders and colonizers from different countries. So, Jezebel felt that she was armed with the legal proof she needed to compromise with Ahab and his family. Another example was provided, where elements of Greek or Egyptian marriage rites were incorporated into the Phoenician ceremony. This scroll stated that these exceptions were allowed to facilitate a balanced cultural exchange—to promote tolerance—so that there would be unity between all gods and people.

Jezebel also knew that the court of King Ethbaal of Sidon, like any significant monarch in the ancient Near East, presented a specific image to the world, which included a nexus of power, ritual, and intricate social maneuvering. Within its walls, the customs surrounding royal marriages would have been a particularly elaborate affair, reflecting not only the personal union of individuals but also the consolidation of political alliances, the display of immense wealth, and the reinforcement of dynastic legitimacy. The grandeur expected of such an occasion would have been amplified by Sidon's status as a preeminent Phoenician city-state, a hub of maritime trade and cultural exchange. King

Ethbaal would have to keep up political appearances. These appearances could present an impasse with the Israeli delegation if her father did not tread softly.

The third scroll covered the agreement process. The sealing of the agreement was always accompanied by a banquet for the esteemed guests, during which toasts were made to the longevity of the alliance and the prosperity of the future offspring. The gifts exchanged would have been of considerable value – perhaps intricately carved ivory caskets filled with precious stones for the bride, and exquisitely crafted daggers or royal seals for the groom. These were not mere tokens but statements of intent and symbols of the wealth and power that the union represented. The period between betrothal and marriage could be extensive, allowing for further diplomatic exchanges and the meticulous planning of the wedding festivities. During this time, the bride-to-be may be educated in the customs and responsibilities of her future role, while the groom's court prepares for her arrival and the integration of her entourage. At this point, Jezebel's head was swimming with all of this legal ease. When was she going to get to the ceremony? Just as she was about to take a food break, Mona walked in with five scrolls in a bag and a letter with an official seal on it in her other hand. Yep, break time—the five scrolls would have to wait!

Her Wedding Attire:

Jezebel had not considered that there would be any question of how she would dress. She was King Ethbaal's daughter; her dress would be elegant, despite her limited means. So, why had the priest sent a scroll labeled 'wedding attire'? She put this scroll to the side and was going to check out the next scroll when she noticed the letter with the seal on it. She stopped and opened it. The priest had given her instructions on which scrolls to read and the order in which they should be read. The scroll about attire was the first one to read. His note stated that this was critical because he did not know if the King of Israel would allow any part of this process, as the bride was wrapped from head to toe. No one saw what she looked like until after the marriage was consummated. With that, Jezebel went on cursing the moon and the stars. No way was she being wrapped up so that people couldn't see her!

<u>Jezebel picked up the scroll and began to read the expectations of the bride, the ceremony, and the rituals required:</u>

The scroll read: The attire of a royal Phoenician bride is a visual manifestation of the wealth and prestige of the royal family.   Every detail must be carefully curated into an ensemble designed to captivate and impress. There were sketches and drawings for inspiration. The finest materials are to be used, and the silks are to be imported from the East and dyed the legendary Tyrian purple (a deeply saturated crimson derived from murex shellfish is the favorite color). The bride's adornment would have been completed with an abundance of jewelry, including gold and silver, as well as expertly crafted, intricate necklaces, bracelets, earrings, and headpieces that would shine, illuminating her. Precious stones, such as lapis lazuli, carnelian, and perhaps even pearls, would be incorporated into these ornaments, further enhancing her splendor. The bride's hair, often elaborately styled and perfumed, would be adorned with golden pins and delicate fillets. While a veil might have been worn during specific parts of the ceremony, especially in more sacred or private moments, the overall emphasis was on the magnificent display of her beauty and the material wealth that underscored her eligibility and the importance of the union.

The religious ceremony expectations were:

The religious dimension of the Phoenician wedding was integral to its solemnity and its perceived success. The gods, patrons of fertility, prosperity, and familial bonds, were invoked to bless the new union and ensure its fruitfulness. Astarte, in particular, was revered as a goddess of love, fertility, and beauty, making her an obvious choice to seek favor from for a new marriage. The ceremony typically involved prayers and offerings at a local shrine or temple, or sometimes even within the groom's household if it had its own sacred space. The act of sacrifice, often involving a chosen animal such as a lamb or a bull, was performed by a priest or a senior family member as a solemn ritual intended to appease the deities and secure their benevolent attention. Libations, pouring of wine or oil, would also be offered as a gesture of reverence and supplication. The invocation of divine favor was not a mere formality but a deeply held belief that the gods' blessing was essential for a marriage to thrive, to produce offspring, and to ensure the continuation of the family line and the prosperity of the community. The marriage was seen as a microcosm of the larger cosmic order, and its sanctity was affirmed through these acts of piety.

The Social Expectations were:

The social expectations placed upon a Phoenician bride were as significant as the outward displays of wealth and religious observance. While the exact societal roles varied depending on her background, certain overarching principles likely applied, particularly for women of the elite. A bride was expected to be virtuous, to possess domestic skills, and to be capable of managing a household. Her primary duty after marriage would be to bear children, particularly sons, to continue the family lineage and ensure the transmission of property and status. This expectation of fertility was a crucial aspect of marriage across the ancient Near East, and Phoenician society was no exception. The bride was also expected to be loyal to her husband and to contribute to the social standing and economic well-being of his family.

In merchant families, this could involve actively participating in business management, overseeing trade ventures, or engaging in social networking, all of which were vital to commercial success. For women of royal or noble families, their role would extend to upholding the prestige of their new household, engaging in diplomatic courtesies, and setting an example of proper conduct and grace.

While Phoenician society, as evidenced by figures like Jezebel, did not necessarily confine women to purely domestic spheres, the fundamental expectation was that they would be pillars of their households, contributing to their stability, prosperity, and continuity. The transition from her natal family to her husband's was a profound shift, requiring adaptability and a willingness to take on new responsibilities. Her education and upbringing would have prepared her for this, instilling in her the values and skills deemed necessary for a successful marital life. This preparation would likely have included lessons in household management, perhaps including accounting for trade goods, and an understanding of social etiquette, all of which were crucial for navigating her new environment.

The Betrothal:

The period of betrothal, leading up to the wedding, was also a significant time for the bride. It was a phase during which her character and suitability were further assessed, and the final arrangements for the marriage were solidified. During this time, the bride might spend more time with her future mother-in-law, learning the intricacies of her new home and its customs. It was also a period where gifts might continue to be exchanged, solidifying the bond between the two families. The bride's personal preparations would also be intensive. She would likely be secluded for periods, focusing on her personal grooming, selecting her trousseau, and the ritualistic cleansing that might precede the wedding.

According to the scrolls, these steps were designed to prepare the bride, both physically and spiritually, for the transformative event that awaited her. The anticipation of the wedding would be a time of mixed emotions – excitement for the new chapter, perhaps apprehension about the unknown, and a deep awareness of the responsibilities that lay ahead. Jezebel knew that she would likely create numerous lists before this ceremony took place in Sidon, and even more lists that would probably change daily once she arrived in Israel. The people at the docks had always described the Israelites as a backward group of people who were nomads and not civilized. She was wondering what she was getting herself into.

Other things needed for these ceremonies:

Plenty of lamps and torches to light the home or building where the ceremony would be, and the place where the feast would occur. In addition, there would need to be lights that could be carried to light in various forms as the wedding procession moved down the road or path to the groom's house. Gifts, items for the bride's trousseau, figurines of the gods, pregnant women, voluptuous women, and jewelry would need to be present to the bride and groom. These things were not required if the family could not afford them.

Food of all types for the two couples, if they were from different areas of countries, would need to be there in abundance. Housing arrangements for the guest of honor were considered a thoughtful gesture, along with places for the elderly to relax, rest, or nap if necessary to last through the all-day and late evening events.

Special preparations for the marriage bed included soft sheets, accessories for cleaning up afterwards, fertility symbols, and idol lines in the room. Special fragrances and perfumes were used to counteract any odors caused by the heat. Artist renderings of the couple with a fertility god were present in the room in extremely wealthy families. Flowers would be placed throughout the room, accompanied by ample lighting that the couple could adjust or dim as desired. Plenty of fruits and water would be on a tray for consumption after they consummated the marriage.

Jezebel had been reading all day. She fell asleep on the lounger beside her window before she finished the third scroll from the temple. Mona came to check on her around midnight, when she noticed that all the lamps in her room were still burning. The servant put the lamps out and put a throw over the princess. Then laid four more scrolls on the Princess's bed. These were the scrolls her father had sent up, saying that the Israeli delegate had brought them translated into Greek and Aramaic, since they did not know which language the princess would be more fluently in.

Mona whispered to one of the lawn servants who was entering the main foyer as she passed by the door. "The poor princess is going to be so exhausted by the time this marriage contract is agreed upon that she will not even be able to sign that she agrees!" The lawn servant looked at her like she was crazy for even worrying for one moment about something so trivial!

The next morning, Jezebel wakes up to more scrolls and more reading. She decided to go down to the main dining room to eat this morning. She had to have fuel to tackle this pile of scrolls. She ordered Mona to bring all of the scrolls and place them on the deck off the library hallway. The one that overlooked the sea was her favorite deck to lounge on and read. After eating her morning meal, she began to devour the Jewish wedding customs.

While Israelite marriage customs also sought divine favor, the emphasis was often placed on Yahweh, the singular God of Israel, and the covenantal relationship between God and his people. The focus was less on harnessing the generative power of a storm god and more on obedience to divine law and the continuation of a lineage within a divinely ordained covenant. The Phoenician approach, with its polytheistic framework and direct appeal to deities such as Baal for earthly fertility and prosperity, reflects a distinct theological orientation and a more immanent understanding of divine power.

This meant that Jezebel had a lot to learn—but she was motivated. She was a woman on a mission from her god,

Baal, and she was not going to fail. She was going to conqueror King Ahab and his God, Yahweh, if it was done with her dying breath!

So prophetically declared!

The Jewish Betrothal and Wedding

The societal structure of ancient Israel, like many ancient cultures, was fundamentally patriarchal. This meant that authority and lineage were traced through the male line, and men held primary social, economic, and legal power within the family and the wider community. This patriarchal framework directly influenced the understanding and practice of marriage, positioning it as a union of two individuals, plus as a significant contract and agreement between the families. The father of the bride and the groom are the two arbiters.

Within this system, the father was not only the head of the household but also the legal and social guardian of his daughters until they were married. His consent, and often his active participation in negotiations, was indispensable for a legitimate marriage to take place. This control extended to any property, assets, or dowry (savings) that the bride had or had received. The groom's family always paid a *mohar* (bride price) in the form of a dowry that could be property, gifts, money, etc., to the bride's father for the bride when the marriage contract (*ketubah*) was signed. In some wealthy families, the bride's father would allow the husband (groom) to assume responsibility for the bride's assets. However, the father retains the "dowry or mohar" to keep it safe in the event he needed to care for his daughter and any children from this marriage in the future, or in the event of the groom's death.

Marriage in ancient Israel, like that in Tyre and Sidon, was thus understood as a contract—a legal and social agreement with clearly defined rights and obligations for all parties involved. A single, formal document did not symbolize this contractual nature as we might understand it today, but rather through a series of established customs, agreements, and exchanges that carried legal weight. The core of this contract revolved around the transfer of a woman from her father's authority and household to that of her husband. These exchanges were not merely economic transactions; they formalized a legal covenant, signifying the establishment of a new family unit under the husband's headship and the continuation of the lineage.

This contractual framework provided stability and clarity to marital relationships, defining the responsibilities of both spouses and their respective families. It ensured that the union was recognized not just socially but also legally, with provisions for breaches of contract, infidelity, and other marital disputes that could be addressed through established legal or societal mechanisms. The emphasis on the father's role and the contractual nature of the union laid the essential legal groundwork upon which the practices of betrothal and marriage were built. The legal and social underpinnings of marriage in ancient Israel were deeply rooted in the patriarchal social structure of the time. The father, as the primary authority figure, held significant power and responsibility regarding his children's futures, especially his daughters.

Upon reaching marriageable age, a daughter was a valuable asset, not in a purely commercial sense, but in terms of the alliances her marriage could forge and the continuation of the family lineage. The father was thus responsible for ensuring her welfare, her chastity, and her suitability for a husband, all of which contributed to the honor and standing of his own family. This paternal control meant that the process of finding a spouse for a daughter was often initiated and managed by the father, sometimes with the assistance of male elders or trusted family members. While romantic love might have played a role, it was secondary to the practical considerations of securing a suitable match that would benefit both families. Such considerations included economic stability, social standing, the potential for a fertile union, and the continuation of the family name and property.

The father's decision about who she would marry was final, and his negotiations with the groom's family were crucial in establishing the terms of the marriage. This paternal authority also extended to the property and assets that a daughter brought into the marriage, often in the form of a dowry. While the dowry was intended to provide for the bride and establish her new household, the husband usually managed it, and the father's initial agreements could influence its legal disposition. The father's role was therefore not just that of a facilitator but of a legal guarantor, ensuring that the union met the prescribed social and economic standards and that his daughter's future was secured.

The concept of marriage as a contractual arrangement was central to these legal and social structures. Unlike modern notions of marriage as primarily a personal and emotional bond, ancient Israelite marriage was fundamentally a legal and social agreement—a covenant between two families, facilitated by the union of a man and a woman. This contractual understanding was manifested in various practices and expectations, all of which had legal implications. The primary purpose of this contract was the transfer of a woman from the legal authority and household of her father to that of her husband. This transfer was not a simple handover but a formal process that established new legal relationships and obligations. Through all this reading, Jezebel was learning a great deal about Jewish culture.

These scrolls, while not presenting a codified marriage law in the modern sense, allude to these contractual elements through descriptions of the acquisition of wives, the exchange of bride-price and dowry, and the consequences of marital infidelity or broken betrothals. The *mohar* could take various forms, including money, livestock, or other valuable possessions, and its amount was subject to negotiation between the families. This payment was legally binding and served as a tangible symbol of the groom's commitment. Failure to pay the *mohar* could result in the dissolution of the betrothal and potentially lead to legal repercussions for the groom's family. The existence of the *mohar* underscores the transactional nature of marriage, where the groom's family essentially acquired the bride.

Complementary to the *mohar* was the dowry, or **nedunyah**, provided by the bride's family. The dowry was intended to equip the new couple and give a measure of financial security for the bride, especially in the event of her husband's death or divorce. It could include movable property, livestock, or even land. The dowry was intended to remain under the bride's control or, at the very least, be available for her support, although its ultimate management often fell to the husband. The presence of a dowry reinforced the idea of marriage as a partnership, albeit one in which the husband held primary legal and economic authority. The legal status of the dowry was important, as it could potentially be reclaimed by the bride or her heirs under certain circumstances, offering a degree of protection to the woman.

The interplay between the *mohar* and the dowry created a reciprocal exchange that formalized the union and established the economic basis of the new family unit. These exchanges were not merely financial; they were imbued with legal significance, marking the transition of the woman from her father's ownership to her husband's. The laws regarding divorce and inheritance also reflect this contractual understanding, outlining the rights and responsibilities that arose from the marriage agreement. For example, if a man divorced his wife, he was typically required to provide her with a bill of divorce, formally severing their legal and contractual ties. This highlights that the termination of a marriage, like its formation, was a legally regulated process.

The concept of kinship and lineage further shaped the legal framework of marriage. Marriage was seen as a means of consolidating and expanding family ties, forging alliances between different clans and lineages. The emphasis on procreation within marriage was crucial for the continuation of these lineages and the preservation of family property. A barren wife, or one who failed to produce male heirs, could face significant social and legal consequences, including the possibility of divorce or the husband taking a second wife.

The institution of marriage in ancient Israel was deeply intertwined with religious and cultural practices, all of which contributed to its legal and social standing. While the specific rituals and ceremonies might have varied across different periods and regions, the underlying principles of paternal authority, contractual agreement, and familial alliance remained consistent. The legal framework established by these customs provided a robust structure for marital unions, ensuring order, stability, and the perpetuation of society.

These foundational principles of Israelite marriage law, rooted in patriarchal structures and contractual understandings, set the stage for the subsequent development of more specific legal stipulations and social expectations surrounding betrothal and marriage, forming the bedrock of familial relationships in ancient Israel. The following sections will explore how these foundational principles were manifested in the concrete practices of betrothal and the formal marriage contract.

Jezebel's head was reeling from all of these legal requirements. She had no idea that the Israelites were so organized with such a profound legal structure. She had always considered them just a group of nomads who drifted to Canaan from Mesopotamia, probably as refugees from exile. Her heart swelled with pride at the thought of joining this sect of people. After a break for the noon-time meal, Jezebel was ready to tackle the next scroll. These scrolls were much longer than the scrolls Mona had brought her back from the Temple of Baal.

The Second Israeli Scroll:

Refreshed, Jezebel settled down on her room lounger bed by the window to start reading. She was shocked at the emphasis on securing a wife from within one's own kinship that this second scroll implied. Other acceptable groups or closely allied communities were listed, along with the countries from which the Israelites were not to select wives. Abraham had said no to the Canaanite women because of idolatry. She did not see Tyre, Sidon, Greece, or Phoenician women listed on the "no" list. So, she breathed a sigh of relief, only to have a pang hit her heart as she suddenly realized—oh no, **Idolatry**—there was that word—the phase or rule she was afraid she was going to see in these scrolls.

She began to worry. Could this delegation deny her a contract of marriage if she mentioned that she wanted an idol of Baal at the wedding? She would have to think this through before making suggestions to them. She jumped up, grabbed one of the pieces of Egyptian papyrus from off her desk and the ink well. She had to start a new list. "Things to investigate before talking with the delegation." The thing that bothered her most, if she hid this until after the wedding was the clause that said, "The violation of these obligations, including involvement with familiar spirits and idolatry, or failure to meet the contracted requirements of this ketubah could lead to legal consequences, including the possibility of divorce and the return of the dowry paid by the grooms' family to the bride's family." She knew her dad would be stricken if she did something that caused him to have to return the money the King of Israel would have paid to him (*mohar*).

The legal standing of children born within marriage was secure, granting them rights to inheritance and lineage. Conversely, children born outside of a recognized marriage often faced social stigma and legal disadvantages, further reinforcing the importance of adhering to the established marriage contract. The concept of honour (honor), *kavod* in Hebrew, played a significant role in the legal and social fabric of marriage. A woman's chastity before marriage and her fidelity within it were directly linked to the honor of her father's and her husband's families. Any transgression in this regard could result in shame, disgrace, and severe legal repercussions. This emphasis on honor contributed to the strict social controls placed upon women and the stringent penalties for sexual misconduct. The legal framework provided mechanisms for addressing breaches of marital vows, particularly adultery, which was considered a serious offense with potentially capital punishment for both parties involved, although historical enforcement varied.

The protection of a wife's honor and the husband's right to possess her exclusively were key components of the marriage contract, and their violation had serious legal and social ramifications. The legal system of ancient Israel, as reflected in the early biblical laws, aimed to maintain social order and protect family structures. These principles governed the formation of unions, dictating the rights and obligations of all parties involved, and laid the essential groundwork for the intricate customs and contractual agreements that characterized the betrothal and marriage process. The ensuing sections will explore the practical manifestations of these principles, detailing how they were enacted through the formal stages of betrothal and marriage.

The period preceding the formal marriage ceremony was not a passive waiting period but a dynamic and legally binding phase known as **betrothal, or *erusin*** in Hebrew, which translates to "sanctification" or "setting apart" in the Phoenician language and Greek. Betrothal was not merely an engagement in the modern sense; it was a legally and socially binding commitment, virtually as significant as the marriage itself, and its dissolution carried the same legal weight as a divorce. This initial covenant established the woman as set apart for her future husband, preventing her from entering into any other marital contract or engaging in intimate relations with any other man.

The breaking of this betrothal required a formal act of divorce, just as the termination of a marriage did. So, once she agreed to and her father signed the ketubah, it was a done deal, which alarmed Jezebel. What if she did not like Ahab or living there with him after she arrived? She had never been made to go or do anything she did not want to do, so how on earth was she going to handle a marriage that she could not tolerate? Lots to think about. She had to do some soul searching and decide if the mission she felt so strongly about for Baal was worth it.

Scroll Three:

The duration of the betrothal period could vary, from several months to a year or more, depending on the families' arrangements and the time needed to prepare for the wedding festivities and establish the new household. During this time, the couple was recognized as husband and wife in the eyes of the law and society, though they did not yet live together as such. This period allowed for the building of anticipation and for the final preparations to be made, reinforcing the significance of the eventual union. But did not afford the couple the rights to consummation or sexual interaction.

The betrothal, or *mo'ar,* was, therefore, far more than a mere promise; it was the initiation of a legal covenant that fundamentally altered the status of the individuals involved. The exchange of the *mohar*, the bride-price, served as the tangible and legally binding act that solidified this covenant.

This third scroll mentioned "holy scripture" and referred to something Jezebel did not understand. Still, it was listed: For example, in the holy scroll of Exodus (In the Bible this is Exodus 22:16-17), the *mohar* is described: "If a man seduces a virgin who is not pledged to be married and sleeps with her, he shall pay the bride-price for her and marry her. Suppose her father absolutely refuses to let him marry her. In that case, he must still pay the bride-price for a virgin." This scroll went on to explain that this "holy scripture" clearly indicated that the *mohar* was a prerequisite for marriage and a form of restitution for seduction if the marriage is not to proceed. This legal stipulation underscores that the *mohar* was not optional but a legally mandated payment that established the groom's right to the bride.

If the bride died without giving the groom children, it was within the rights of the groom's family to request a refund of the mohar (bride price), severing their legal ties. Similarly, if the groom died before the marriage was consummated, the betrothal still conferred certain rights and obligations upon the betrothed. The woman was considered a widow and might be entitled to a share of her deceased fiancé's estate or receive a specified provision from his family. The *mohar* paid would typically be returned to the groom's family, or its use determined by the specific agreements and legal precedents. This highlights that the *mohar* was not merely a gift but a component of a legally recognized contractual arrangement that had lasting implications even in the event of premature termination.

The Ketubah—The legal contract:

The **ketubah** was typically drawn up and signed during the betrothal period, before the final marriage ceremony and the establishment of the shared household. This legal instrument was not a one-size-fits-all document; its contents could be tailored to the specific circumstances of the families involved, the social standing of the bride and groom, and the negotiated amounts of the *mohar* (bride-price) and the *nedunyah* (dowry). The very existence and detail of the *ketubah* highlight a society that valued legal clarity and sought to ensure that unions were entered into with a clear understanding of all parties' commitments.

A central component of the **ketubah** was the provision for the bride's financial security, often referred to as the *tosefet ketubah* or "addition to the *ketubah*." This was an additional sum that the groom pledged to pay to his wife in the event of divorce or his death, in addition to the return of her dowry. It was a form of financial protection, ensuring that the wife would have a means of sustenance should the marriage dissolve. The amount of this additional sum was a critical point of negotiation between the families. It reflected the groom's capacity to provide and his commitment to his wife's long-term welfare. The higher the agreed-upon **tosefet ketubah,** the greater the groom's incentive to maintain the marriage and the more secure the bride's financial future. This provision demonstrated a societal recognition of the woman's potential vulnerability within the patriarchal structure and a legal mechanism to mitigate that vulnerability.

Furthermore, the *ketubah* would meticulously record the **nedunyah,** the dowry that was paid. The *ketubah* would itemize the dowry's contents, ensuring that it was clearly documented and could be accounted for. In the event of divorce, the dowry was typically returned to the bride's family. The *ketubah* also stipulated the groom's obligations regarding his wife's maintenance and support during the marriage. This included providing her with food, clothing, and shelter, according to his means and social standing. The contract made it clear that the husband was legally bound to care for his wife's basic needs. This provision was crucial, as it legally obliged the husband to provide for his wife's livelihood, regardless of her own ability to contribute financially.

The *ketubah* also addressed the rights of the wife in the event of the husband's death. As mentioned previously, it would specify the amount of the *tosefet ketubah* that she would receive. Moreover, in cases where the husband died without a will, the *ketubah* provided a legal basis for the wife to claim her rightful inheritance from his estate, in addition to her dowry and the *tosefet ketubah*. This ensured that the widow was not disinherited and had the means to support herself and any children from the marriage. The legal precedence established by the *ketubah* provided a degree of security and continuity for the surviving spouse, preventing undue hardship.

The wording and specific clauses of the *ketubah* could vary, but certain elements were considered standard. These typically included: the names of the bride and groom, the names of their fathers, the date and place of the betrothal and marriage contract, the amount of the *mohar*, the particulars of the dowry, the amount of the *tosefet ketubah*, the groom's obligations for maintenance, and the conditions for divorce.

The contract needed to be witnessed by at least two qualified individuals, whose signatures or marks would validate the agreement. This requirement for witnesses underscored the public and legally binding nature of the document, ensuring its authenticity and enforceability. Most families had two witnesses for the groom and two witnesses for the bride, in addition to the fathers of the bride and the groom. In essence, the *ketubah* was more than just a marriage certificate; it was a comprehensive legal and financial agreement that governed the marital relationship from its inception.

The period between the formal betrothal, the *mo'ar*, and the final wedding ceremony, often referred to as the **nissuin,** was far from a passive interlude. It was a crucial phase, imbued with specific customs and expectations, that served to solidify the impending union and prepare both families for the new relationship. This interval, which could vary in length but was generally significant, was a time of active preparation and a carefully managed period of anticipation, ensuring that the eventual consummation of the marriage was met with readiness and reverence.

During this waiting period, the bride's focus shifted towards her personal and domestic preparation for married life. This involved intensive instruction and practical training from her mother and other female family elders. The aim was to equip her with the skills necessary to manage a household, oversee servants (if the family's status warranted it), and fulfill her wifely duties. The bride's education encompassed a wide range of competencies, from culinary arts and textile production—such as spinning wool, weaving cloth, and sewing garments—to the meticulous management of household supplies and finances. The successful running of a home was a mark of a woman's capability and a reflection of her family's upbringing. Thus, considerable effort was invested in ensuring the bride was well-prepared.

Beyond domestic skills, she would also be instructed in the social proprieties expected of a married woman, understanding her role within the broader community and her husband's family. This preparation was not merely about acquiring skills; it was also about instilling a sense of responsibility and readiness for the new life she was about to enter. The acquisition of these practical skills was often seen as a tangible demonstration of the dowry's value, as the bride would bring not only material goods but also the ability to manage and utilize them effectively.

Simultaneously, the groom also undertook specific preparations, which often centered on demonstrating his capacity to fulfill his obligations as a husband. While the bride was being schooled in domestic management, the groom was typically involved in solidifying his financial standing and ensuring that he had the resources to support his future wife and family.

For the groom, this could include continuing his apprenticeship in a trade, working diligently in his father's business, or managing his own burgeoning enterprises. The successful completion of his own training or the establishment of his livelihood was a critical component of his readiness for marriage. The groom was expected to demonstrate his understanding of his legal and financial commitments as outlined in the *ketubah*. This involved ensuring that the agreed-upon *mohar* (bride-price) and any other financial arrangements were in order, ready to be formally transferred or secured as the marriage approached.

This period enabled him to solidify his economic independence and demonstrate his ability to provide for his household, a crucial factor in the societal evaluation of a suitable husband. The groom's readiness was thus measured by his industry and his preparedness to meet the financial responsibilities of marriage. The interval also provided an opportunity for the families themselves to further solidify their relationship and prepare for the integration of their households. There were often exchanges of visits and continued consultations regarding the practical arrangements for the wedding ceremony and the establishment of the new home.

This could involve discussions about where the couple would reside, whether they would live with the groom's family or establish their own independent household, and the finalization of the contents and logistics of the dowry. These discussions were crucial for ensuring a smooth transition and minimizing potential friction between the families as they became more closely intertwined. The ongoing dialogue fostered a sense of shared purpose and mutual respect, reinforcing the alliance that the marriage represented. The families, having made the initial commitment, now engaged in the detailed planning required to bring the union to fruition, ensuring that all practical aspects were addressed in advance.

The social implications of this waiting period were also significant. It served to maintain a high degree of anticipation and reverence for the marriage itself. The delay between betrothal and consummation allowed the commitment to be deeply felt and publicly acknowledged, while the eventual union retained its celebratory and culminating character.

The groom's responsibilities during this period also included the preparation of his own household or a suitable dwelling for his future wife. This might involve ensuring that the marital home was ready, furnished, and provisioned. If the couple were to live with his parents, then the familial home needed to be prepared to accommodate the new bride and any eventual children. This practical aspect of setting up a house was a tangible manifestation of the groom's commitment and his ability to establish a new family unit. It was a visible sign of his readiness to transition from an unmarried son to a husband and potential father, fulfilling his societal role. The preparation of the dwelling was often a communal effort, involving the groom's family and contributing to the collective anticipation and support for the new couple.

The Fourth Scroll:

The bride, meanwhile, would often be involved in preparing items for her new home. This included weaving and sewing linens, garments, and other textiles. These handcrafted items were not only practical necessities but also represented the bride's personal contribution and skill, adding a layer of personal significance to the shared life they were building. These preparations were often displayed during the wedding festivities, showcasing the bride's diligence and the generosity of her family. The act of preparing these items was a tangible expression of her commitment and active participation in creating their shared future, a prelude to her role as manager and nurturer of the household.

In addition to the practical preparations, there were also legal and ritualistic aspects that could take place during this interim. While the major legal framework was established during the betrothal and formalized in the ketubah, further discussions or confirmations of details may be necessary to finalize the arrangements. For instance, the specific date and timing of the wedding ceremony are often finalized, usually in consultation with religious authorities or elders. The arrangements for the wedding feast, a significant communal event, would also be made, involving extensive planning for food, drink, and entertainment. These preparations underscored the communal aspect of marriage, highlighting its importance not just to the couple but to the entire community.

The period of waiting also provided an opportunity for the couple to become more familiar with each other, within the bounds of societal norms. While direct, unsupervised interaction might have been limited, there could be opportunities for them to see each other at family gatherings or during specific supervised occasions. This allowed for a gradual acclimatization to each other's presence and personalities, further preparing them for the intimacy of married life. The families also played a role in facilitating these interactions, ensuring that they were conducted in a manner that preserved the decorum and anticipation of the union. This controlled introduction aimed to build a foundation of mutual understanding without diminishing the eventual joy and wonder of the wedding night.

In essence, the period between betrothal and the wedding was a multifaceted phase characterized by diligent preparation, sustained anticipation, and communal awareness. It was a time when the bride's education in domestic management and the groom's efforts to secure his financial standing, coupled with the families' collaborative planning, ensured that the union commenced on a solid foundation.

With the discussion of all of these new roles that Jezebel had never heard of, her head was swimming with questions, and her eyes burned from so much reading. But the weight of all of this made her think she was going to faint when she stood up to walk over to her desk and get another glass of water. Looking at her servant, Jezebel remarked, "Mona, I feel faint. Can you get me a cool cloth and go to the kitchen to get me something to drink that has sugar in it?"

"Your Royal Highness, you have not eaten your afternoon snack. You should probably eat the pomegranate that I brought you. Do you want me to peel it for you? Then I can go get a new pitcher of cool water, some mango juice for us, and a piece of meat—maybe there is something left over from lunch in the kitchen." With that last comment, Mona was extracting the seeds from the pomegranate before Jezebel even had a chance to answer her. Once she handed the princess the plate, she flew out the door and down the stairs to the kitchen.

Jezebel waited until Mona returned with the mango juice, a grilled piece of beef, and a piece of chicken with potatoes on a stick. She loved the simple way Mona always said, "My highness, here is some meat on a stick for you!" It made Jezebel feel like a girl on an adventure!

She read on for over four hours as she completed the scroll; the only thing she was sure of was the fact that the Israeli delegation that King Ahab had sent was a "selection" from the community, intended to garner support for the marriage or to recommend against it. Now, she was fully aware that impressing this delegation was more critical than impressing the king himself. She would have years to bring him around, but if the first impressions of this delegation were not good, then the Israeli citizens would not be accepting. She could control one man more easily than a nation. So, she grabbed her papyrus again and made a list of things she would need to tell King Ahab to impress him about her ability to be queen. Of course, I must remember to tell them I am willing to do whatever they suggest or recommend to help lighten the load for King Ahab!

She sat down on the corner of her bed and proofread her notes to herself. Her heart swelled with pride. Oh, she had to admit to herself that she was really clever. She was the best of both her mother and father. She actually thought she was not devious than her dad's sister, whom he called cunning and evil all the time. She had this—El, the chief deity, obviously blessed her!

Jezebel got up to stretch her legs and give her eyes a break. She walked over to the windows on the west side of her room, where she could see all the way to the fish market that was on the other end of the "downtown" docks. While she was watching the scurry of people rushing around to pick up what they needed for the evening meal before it got dark, she heard the sound of camels long before her eyes focused on the caravan. It was the Israelite envoy. They were moving fast. They were packed entirely with large loads. Where were they going? What was up with this? Her heart skipped a few beats as she closed her eyes and said, "Oh, for the love of Baal, I pray Dad has not made them mad and they are leaving before I even get a chance to learn about them!"

Jezebel observed the Israelite envoys, noting their earnestness, their adherence to their own distinct customs. It is evident in everything they did, including packing the camels. What interested people, with such a fantastic work ethic, was Jezebel looking at Mona, who had just joined her at the large triple window in her room, which had double glass doors to the right of the windows.

"You know, Mona, I wish that our slaves and servants were like you and those Israelites—so bound to their work with a work ethic that is directly connected to their hearts. Those Israelis are like you; they work so hard. Most of the servants in the palace appear to be unenthusiastic about their work on most days. I wish I could motivate them to have a purpose like this, Israelites!"

I was in the library with the door open the day they arrived here, and they were talking to Dad in the foyer. They were extremely respectful, showing great reverence in their actions.

Merging Marriage Agreements

At the evening meal, Jezebel began going over the four lists she had made out based on the scrolls that she had been given to read. She assumed that her dad had given them to her so she could decide what she wanted in the Ketubah. What she did not know was that he had already read those scrolls weeks ago. He had his list made out with an alternate 'compromise" list so that he could secure Israel as one of his trade ports and control the market. He wanted Jezebel to be able to continue to worship her gods, but if he had to say that she would not worship them to get the contract, he would.

King Esthbaal had lied before to secure a contract; this was no different. He knew his daughter. When it came to getting things she wanted, she was just like her mother—a master con artist! "Pumpkin, you know that I love you and I want you to have everything in this marriage that you want. But the most crucial part is the trade agreement for us here in Tyre and Sidon. I read those scrolls weeks ago. I just sent them up to you so you could see what you are going to be up against. But you do not have to worry. I agreed to everything that the Israelites wanted about their God, Yahweh, but I did not compromise where it mattered. After we eat, we can go out on the veranda, and I will review everything with you."

Catching his breath, the king continued, "However, please make sure to read the five scrolls I sent up by Mona. You may need to read them two or three times. You have to know what is expected of you, so you can find a way around it after the marriage is consummated. Do not try anything diabolical before the consummation. To help you navigate all of these political minefields, they have agreed for your servant, Mona, and your mother to accompany you to Jerusalem. They will stay with you for the betrothal period. After the last day of the wedding feast, your mother and I will return to Sidon.

Mona will stay with you if she wants to. She has agreed to the year-long betrothal. She will come back with us to visit her parents, say goodbye to them, and then return to Jerusalem to be with you indefinitely. If she does not like Jerusalem, we will provide you with another servant." King Esthbaal took a few sips of his wine, cleared his throat, and continued.

"My only request is that you do not get forced into accepting an Israeli servant. They will report your idol worship, and you will be stoned to death. That fifth scroll covers their religious practices. Study it diligently. Your knowledge of their laws and compliance is essential for me to set up the ports and trade routes. Once I am 'in,' and everyone is comfortable working with me, you can begin a gentle shift to what you want, but not before! Do you understand me?" he coarsely pipped.

"Yes, Abba, I understand. It may not be fair to me, but I know it is for the sake of our home, family, and country. So, yes, I will sacrifice. But there better be something wonderful in this Ketubah if you expect me to give up my heart and soul for a while."

"Honey, you do not have to worry. Mona will ensure you have the necessary items to continue worshiping Baal. She will put them up and hide them each day. She will be your protector in this matter, so you can pray and worship Baal each day without anyone knowing. As for the other gods, they will have to understand. It is too risky to have those larger idols. Ibrahim, the master silver craftsman out at the docks, is making you a statue of Baal that will easily fit into one of those carry bags that you have with a shoulder strap on it. It will have a lock on it. I am having a necklace made that will hold the key to that case. Your Baal idol will be safely stored in that carry bag. No one will be the wiser. Having carry bags and a chest for your items when you travel is normal. Trust me, honey. Your mom and I have been planning for months already for this marriage, hoping that the gods would shower us with blessings, favor, and honor on this mission."

Jezebel looked to the other end of the table to where her mother sat. Her mother, Athena, was nodding her head in agreement with her dad. "Jezebel, honey, you have got to know that we want the best for you and us. I will be there through this year of transition to help you navigate the pitfalls." Athena interjected.

"Why does it have to be a year? If you had negotiated for less time, then I would be safer and quicker. Once the marriage is consummated and I know that I am with child, I can do what I want, and he cannot throw me out."

"That is just what your dad said that you would say. But honey, you are wrong. You need the maximum amount of time to learn all the rules. There are always hidden rules that they forget to cover or do not realize are significant, because they worship this God. If you are already married, you will be in the King's chamber. I will not have access to you to train you or guide you through the political minefield without getting blown up!"

Then Athena took a couple of sips of wine and continued. "Jezebel, you are so young. It is hard for a 16-year-old to know how to do all of this. You will turn 18 three months after your wedding. This is going to be a crammed-packed year. I think we really need 18 months, but I didn't want to suggest that, because they might think we were taking advantage of them for the gifts and free access to their palace. They cannot sense anything that we are doing. They recommended that the 12 months of purification start the week after we arrive. Once that is complete, they will announce the wedding ceremony, and a feast will be held throughout the kingdom. They have asked for 90 days to pull all of that together."

"However, the feast that they have the first week of the New Year, according to their calendar, begins the third week in August on our calendar," Athena continued. "They cannot do a wedding feast the week before, the week of, or the week after a major holiday with feasts. Plus, it is unbelievably hot at that time of year. So, they want to wait till after the Barley harvest in Av (October here in Sidon). The event will be a week-long feast, whereas ours is normally three days; their wedding feast lasts seven days. You will be required as queen to participate in Shabbat (Sabbath-Holy Day of the week celebration). It is going to take a year to learn all of this, trust me!"

Athena continued, "The first thing I have to do is make those priests of Yahweh my best friends. Then I can find out what they expect—that way I can design a counterfeit routine for you that will deceive them. They cannot get any warning that you are even thinking about Baal, the mightiest still worshiping him. You will never be able to do this by yourself at your age. They will not trust you. However, as the mother of the queen to be, they will relish the opportunity to convert me from Baal worship to the worship of Yahweh. This is how I will get access to what I need to train you. Do you understand, dear?"

"Yes, Mother. I feel relieved to know that I do not have to do this alone. Those scrolls were overwhelming." Jezebel whimpered.

Athena sighed, then smiled at her daughter and said, "I know. I felt that way, my dear, when I read them for the first time. I have read each scroll now seven times. I will re-read them on the boat when we leave for Jerusalem. I will obtain more scrolls with additional details from the priest and the king's secretary upon our arrival. Remember, Jezebel, knowledge is power. Power is needed to control!"

You do not have to worry. Your dad and I have made sure this marriage contract is the best one in history. Never has a father been so persistent. We got everything we wanted, plus some extra gifts and gold they threw in—we just had to compromise on the Baal worship, so they think.

Signing of the Agreement:

On the morning before the day of the royal departure from Sidon, King Ethbaal, along with Jezebel and the Israeli delegation, would need to engage in a brief but extremely important signing ceremony. It was scheduled to take place at the Palace Rose Garden and would have numerous witnesses. King Esthbaal and his officials signed and agreed to the specific terms according to Sidonian law. Now that this was complete, the Royal Entrouge would go to Samaria. There would be another signing of this agreement in Samaria to secure the signature of King Ahab of Israel in the Jewish ceremony of "signing the Ketubah."

So, finally, the agreements were signed and sealed. The gifts had been exchanged. The entire city of Sidon was aware at the reception last night that this was an official marriage agreement. Now, in private this morning with witnesses, the contracts had been signed. Now it was time for the goodbyes. This resulted in tears from Jezebel as she bid her friends farewell. Athena and Jezebel were placed into the double carriage that eight servants carried. Walking steady and slowly, they proceeded toward the downtown area from the Palace. Once downtown, Jezebel looked out toward the Mediterranean Sea, took a deep breath, and closed her eyes.

CHAPTER THREE:
The Travel to Samaria and the Betrothal

Jezebel and Mona were up early, getting the final items packed into the trunks for the trip to Jerusalem, when Athena knocked on the door. "Good morning, girls. Are you ready to head to the docks? Our boat going to Samaria is waiting for us?" "Samaria? Why Samaria, not Jerusalem?" questioned Jezebel.

Her mother replied, "King Omri moved the capital of Israel from Jerusalem to a hill in the country, or area known as Samaria (where Samaritans lived). He built a city and a palace on this hilltop and called it Samaria. So, that is now the capital of Israel. It is Samaria, Samaria." (Much like New York, New York).

"I thought those scrolls said Jerusalem and mentioned that the King's wedding had always to be officiated in Jerusalem. So those scrolls were wrong?" defended Jezebel.

"Sweetheart, the scrolls had not been updated, but they told us when we were given the scrolls. It is that your father and I forgot to pass that information on to you when he sent the scrolls up to your room by Mona. Sorry for the confusion," Athena explained.

"I forgot about this transition until I just heard you tell Mona what you needed to go to the shop and get as soon as we got to Jerusalem. It is going to be Samaria. Since we do not know anything about that city, it will be best to let one of the servants from King Ahab's staff go for you. At least we will arrive at the docks in Samaria a day sooner. The journey inland to the Palace will be about 30 miles. So, it will take us a day and a half by caravan. I will go ahead and tell you, because I know you are going to ask. Jerusalem is 35 miles northwest of Jerusalem. If you go there later with King Ahab, it will be another two-day journey." Athena shrugged her shoulders in a "I do not know" maneuver, then walked away to meet with her husband, the king.

The procession took two hours to reach the dock and board the ship. It appeared to Jezebel that her father was sending everything in the palace with them. After getting on the ship, to walked to the rail so she could see what hall he was sending—camels, horses, camel saddles, camel carriages, hand carriages, and trunks. She knew that she had packed 10 trunks herself. But over 50 trunks were being loaded.

"Mother, what are all of those trunks for. I packed 10, and I am sure that 10-15 are yours, but what about the 30 or so remaining? Who do they belong to? "

"Those trunks have the gifts you will need to give out, the clothes and accessories for the various types of meetings anticipated during this betrothal period. I am sure I have left something off the list. Your father will need to bring or send us the necessary items for the year. I really need to get to Samaria and make a list depending upon what we will need and the weather." Athena added.

For Jezebel, the most exciting part of maritime travel was the moment just before the ship left port. Jezebel was charged with a profound sense of transition, a physical and spiritual crossing of thresholds. The sea, her lifelong companion, the very source of her kingdom's wealth and identity, was now the pathway to a new, unknown world. The farewell was a grand affair, a carefully orchestrated display of Phoenician royal power and prestige, yet beneath the outward show of celebration, there was an undeniable current of melancholy. She was sure that her father had arranged all of this to impress the Israeli delegation.

She stood on the quayside of the ship, a figure of regal bearing even in her sorrow, surrounded by her family, her retinue, and the most esteemed members of the Sidonian court. The air was thick with the scent of salt and the lingering fragrance of cedar, the familiar symphony of her homeland now tinged with the poignant notes of goodbye. The weight of her royal robes, intricately embroidered with symbols of her lineage and her gods, felt both a comfort and a burden, a tangible representation of the kingdom she was leaving.

Her mother, Queen Athena, her face etched with a mixture of pride and deep affection, held her close, whispering words of encouragement and love. "Remember who you are, my daughter," she murmured, her voice thick with emotion. "Carry the strength of Asherah in your heart, the courage of Baal in your spirit. The gods will be with you." Her father, King Ethbaal, his arm around her shoulder, offered a more stoic, yet equally heartfelt, farewell. He spoke of the importance of her mission and the strategic alliances she represented, but his gaze held a father's concern —a quiet acknowledgment of the vast distance she was about to traverse, both geographically and culturally.

The fleet of ships, adorned with colorful banners and the proud emblems of Phoenicia, bobbed gently in the harbor. Among them was the royal vessel that would carry Jezebel, a marvel of Sidonian shipbuilding, its sails emblazoned with the symbols of her house. The weight of the moment settled upon her, the immensity of the journey ahead, the separation from all that was familiar and beloved.

She looked back at the city, its white stone buildings gleaming under the relentless sun, the familiar silhouette of the temples dedicated to Baal and Asherah reaching towards the sky. These were the sacred spaces of her childhood, the places where she had learned to commune with the divine, where her faith had been forged. The thought of leaving them, of being so far from their hallowed presence, brought a pang of genuine sadness. She whispered a silent prayer, a plea for her gods to watch over her, to guide her steps in the new land.

As the ships pulled away from the shore, the distance between Jezebel and her homeland began to grow, the coastline of Sidon receding until it was no more than a hazy line against the horizon. The vast expanse of the Mediterranean, once a source of comfort and familiarity, now felt like an immense barrier, a shimmering expanse separating her from everything she had ever known. The rhythmic creak of the ship, the gentle swell of the waves, and the constant rush of wind through the sails—these were the new sounds of her journey, a stark contrast to the bustling life she had left.

Jezebel clutched a small, intricately carved ivory amulet, a gift from her father, depicting the goddess Asherah. It was a last-minute gift he had placed in her hand, and he was hugging her goodbye on the gangway. The smooth, cool stone felt reassuring in her palm, a tangible link to the divine protection she had always known. Asherah, the mother goddess, the benevolent nurturer, was a constant presence in the religious landscape of Phoenicia. To leave her worship and her imagery would be akin to severing a vital artery. Yet, her father had assured her that her faith and heritage would be a source of strength, not a weakness, in the new kingdom.

The sails, now fully unfurled, caught the wind, propelling the galley forward with a steady, determined momentum. The city of Sidon, once a vibrant panorama of life, began to shrink, its grandeur slowly dissolving into the hazy distance. The sounds of the harbor, the calls of the merchants, the laughter of children, the rhythmic pounding of hammers from the shipyards, all faded into a gentle hum, eventually lost to the growing expanse of water.

As the ship sailed further from the coast, the faces on the shore became indistinguishable, mere smudges of color against the verdant backdrop of the land. The sea, stretching endlessly in every direction, was a vast canvas upon which the sky painted its moods – at times a brilliant azure, reflecting the clear intentions of her father's political maneuvers, and at other times a deeper, more contemplative blue, mirroring the introspection that was beginning to stir within her.

As she stood on the deck, her gaze fixed on the receding shore, her mind was a whirlwind of emotions. There was the sorrow of leaving, the ache of separation, but also a burgeoning sense of anticipation, an eagerness to discover what lay ahead. This was not a journey undertaken lightly, nor was it merely a political assignment. It was a momentous transition, a stepping onto a path that had been subtly laid out for her, a path that would lead her to a new kingdom, a new people, and a destiny that would irrevocably shape the course of history. The farewell to the sea was not just an ending; it was the profound, and perhaps irreversible, beginning of her extraordinary, and ultimately tragic, story.

The wind picked up, filling the sails with a renewed vigor. The ship surged forward, its prow cutting through the waves with a clean, decisive motion. Jezebel stood tall, her gaze fixed on the horizon, her heart filled with a complex mixture of sorrow and anticipation. She was leaving behind the familiar comfort of her homeland, the reassuring presence of her gods, and the loving embrace of her family. But she was also embracing a future that beckoned with the promise of power, of influence, and of a destiny far grander than she could have ever imagined on the shores of Sidon.

The sea, her lifelong companion, was now her path, carrying her toward the unknown heart of Israel, toward the city of Samaria, and toward the role she was destined to play. This was not just a voyage; it was a crossing of thresholds, a passage from one life to another, a farewell to the sea and a greeting to a destiny waiting to unfold. The iridescent shimmer of the water, the vast, unbroken sky above, and the steady onward push of the galley were all testament to the profound change that was now underway. Her journey had begun, and the world of Sidon, as she knew it, was already becoming a memory painted in shades of sunlight and sea spray.

Two days late, Jezebel thought about the last time she had been on the royal ship with her father, which had been so long. That too was a two-day journey.

By noon on the second day, the rough sea winds that had beaten the ship so badly for the last 12 hours had driven it off course somewhat. Now the captain was saying that it would be another day at sea to make up for the time lost rowing into the wind and the corrections needed to get back on course. Jezebel quickly tired of miles and miles of water, although she loved the salty sea breeze. She was thrilled to hear Mona say that the captain had just announced they would be arriving at the port in a few hours.

"Mona, let us get everything packed up and ready for the servants to unload at Caesarea. Your father gave his business manager instructions on which inn to take us to for the night. We will get up in the morning early and start our journey via camels to Samaria," Athena instructed.

They dock at the port of Caesarea:

The journey across the azure expanse had been long, a rhythmic passage marked by the ceaseless play of sun and sea. Now, the horizon began to assert itself not as an unbroken line of blue, but as a jagged silhouette against the sky. As the royal galley approached the shores of Caesarea, a palpable shift occurred within Jezebel, a subtle tremor of anticipation mingled with a burgeoning unease. The air, once thick with the salty tang of the Mediterranean, began to carry a different scent – dry, earthy, with an undertone of something wild and untamed. This was the scent of the land she had only known through maps and whispered tales, the land that would soon be her home. "Now that I can see the shore, I am getting nervous. I think I am going to throw up. Momma, what is happening to me?"

"Nerves, just nerves, honey! You will be fine. Here suck on this ginger and honey concoction that I have……" Their ship has finally anchored and been tied off to the dock there at the port of Caesarea. This port was located in the city of Caesarea, in northern Israel, near the region of Samaria.

As the galley anchored and the ramp lowered, Jezebel stepped onto foreign soil. The sand beneath her sandals was coarser than the fine, powdery grains of Sidon's beaches. The sounds that greeted her were not the cheerful clamor of a thriving port, but a more muted hum, punctuated by the bleating of sheep and the distant, guttural calls of men tending to their flocks. The people who had gathered to greet her were different, too. Their attire was simpler, less ostentatious, favoring rough-spun wools in muted earth tones rather than the vibrant silks and embroidered linens of her own people. Their faces, tanned and weathered by the sun, held an expression that was harder to decipher than the open curiosity she was accustomed to. There was a gravity to them, a solemnity that seemed to permeate the very atmosphere.

She observed them with the keen eye of a diplomat and a princess, cataloging every detail with precision. The men wore simple tunics and cloaks, their hair often tied back or cropped short. The women, too, favored modest dresses, their heads often covered by veils or headscarves. There was a palpable lack of adornment, a stark absence of glittering jewelry, elaborate hairstyles, and richly dyed fabrics that were the lifeblood of Phoenician fashion. This austerity was not just a matter of taste; it felt like a deliberate statement, a rejection of the very things that defined the splendor and sophisticated artistry of her homeland.

The air of Samaria, she quickly discovered, was not merely dry; it was infused with a different kind of spirit. It was as if the very air was holding its breath, waiting. Waiting for what, she could not yet fathom, but the anticipation was a palpable entity. The architecture, too, offered a stark departure. The buildings of Sidon were a testament to skilled craftsmanship, featuring intricate carvings, polished columns, and grand facades. Here, in Samaria, the dwellings were more functional, built from sun-dried brick or rough-hewn stone, with flat roofs and small windows. There were certainly signs of burgeoning development, but it lacked the innate sophistication, the aesthetic refinement that she associated with civilization. It was a kingdom still in its formative stages, a rough diamond yet to be polished.

As she was escorted from the ship towards the waiting entourage, Jezebel could not help but notice the subtle ways in which the people reacted to her. Their gazes, while not overtly hostile, were filled with a mixture of awe and apprehension. They whispered amongst themselves as she passed, their voices low and reverent, but also tinged with something akin to suspicion. She was a foreigner, a woman of a different faith, and the weight of that difference settled upon her shoulders like a physical cloak.

The religious landscape was perhaps the most alien aspect of this new world. In Phoenicia, the gods were everywhere – in the soaring temples, in the intricate amulets worn by every citizen, in the songs and stories that filled their lives. The very air thrummed with the presence of Baal, the powerful storm god; of Asherah, the benevolent mother goddess; of Astarte, the goddess of love and war. Their images were woven into the fabric of daily existence, their worship a vibrant, communal act. Here, however, the presence of their God, Yahweh, was a different matter entirely.

The tales she had heard of Yahweh were unsettling. He was a singular deity, a jealous God who demanded absolute devotion and brooked no rivals. The concept of an invisible God, a God without form or idol, was difficult for her to grasp. Her own faith was rich with imagery, with tangible representations of the divine that allowed for a more immediate connection. The idea of worshiping an unseen force, a force that explicitly forbade the creation of any likeness, felt sterile, even barren, in comparison to the colorful, sensual, and vibrant religious expression of her homeland.

She saw no grand temples dedicated to Yahweh in the immediate vicinity of her arrival. Instead, she glimpsed simple structures, perhaps places of assembly, but nothing that approached the architectural majesty of the temples of Sidon. The people's devotion seemed to be a more internal affair, a matter of adherence to laws and commandments rather than outward displays of grandeur. This inward focus, this singular, unwavering devotion, was a concept that would require significant adjustment.

Land Travel:

As the royal entourage was led away from the harbor, towards the heart of Samaria, Jezebel found herself scanning the faces of those who accompanied her, and those who merely observed from a distance. There was a strength in their bearing, a determination etched into their features that spoke of a people who had forged their identity through hardship and struggle. Yet, beneath this strength, she perceived a certain rigidity, a lack of the easy camaraderie and the sophisticated social graces that came naturally to her.

The very language, though related to her own tongue in its Semitic roots, sounded different – harsher, more guttural, lacking the melodic cadence she was accustomed to. Even the way they moved and interacted seemed to possess a gravity that was both admirable and, at times, a little daunting. It was as if she had stepped into a world where the very rhythms of life were set to a different, more austere beat.

She remembered her father's words, his emphasis on the strategic importance of this union. He had spoken of alliances, of trade, of a unified front against common enemies. But he had also spoken of her own role, of her being an ambassador of Phoenician culture, a beacon of its sophisticated civilization. The task, she now realized, was far more daunting than simply marrying a foreign prince. It was about navigating a cultural chasm, about bridging a spiritual divide, and about introducing the richness of her own heritage into a land that seemed to actively resist it.

The dust of Samaria settled on her fine Phoenician sandals, a tangible reminder of her displacement. The sun beat down with an intensity unlike the warm, embracing heat of Sidon. It was a harsh, unforgiving sun, one that bleached the colors from the landscape and seemed to bake the very essence of the land into its dry earth. She felt a pang of longing for the cool shade of cedar forests, for the vibrant hues of Tyrian purple, for the presence of Asherah's familiar symbols.

Yet, as the entourage moved onward, and the nascent city of Samaria began to reveal itself more fully – a collection of dwellings clinging to the hillsides, a central citadel rising above – Jezebel's initial unease began to mingle with a growing sense of... purpose. This was not a land of soft comforts and established traditions. This was a land that was still being shaped, a people still finding their definitive voice. And she, the Phoenician Princess, was about to become a significant part of that shaping.

The contrast, the starkness, the very unfamiliarity of it all, presented not an insurmountable barrier, but a canvas upon which she could begin to paint. The first impressions were of a land that was parched and austere, but also of a people that possessed a deep-seated strength. It was a land that demanded respect, and a people that would undoubtedly challenge her in ways she could not yet fully comprehend. The journey from the familiar shores of Sidon had ended, and the true voyage, the one that would redefine her and the kingdom of Israel, had just begun. Her first impression of Samaria was one of profound difference. This difference would prove to be both a challenge and an opportunity, a stark awakening from the vibrant dreams of her homeland in Phoenicia.

Athena was up before dawn. She was strategizing and praying to the travel idol of Baal that they had made for Jezebel to use in Israel. She pleaded with Baal for traveling mercy. She had been on caravans before, but this was going to be a first for Jezebel. She and her father had always used horses on their travels. However, the use of camels to transport all the things she would need in her new home was an absolute necessity.

At the last minute, King Esthbaal decided to send a few pieces of furniture that were Jezebel's favorite. He had the servants load them onto the things that he called "sleds." They just looked like two pieces of wood nailed together with an air space between them, and some long boards going in the opposite direction to help the wood slide. There were ropes attached to it on both sides.

When Athena questioned her husband about this funny-looking contraption, he remarked, "Oh, that is the new sleds I was telling you about. You can load them up, and the ropes connect them to two horses or two camels, and they pull whatever you load on them. I am going to have the servants put the furniture on the sleds. The camels will pull it. You will see, honey, this is the latest. Do not worry. I have got you and Jezebel your favorite chairs and loungers."

Athena knew that this would mean extra loading time for today. Before Jezebel woke, she decided to find the king's servant whom he had appointed to oversee the matter. She needed to get them working on loading everything up early. She did not want to leave at midday. Two days on a camel was enough.

Athena and Jezebel were about to be in for a surprise. Besides the stress, they were about to experience dust, filth, tanned, blistered skin, and matted hair! The journey across the Great Sea was long and arduous. When, at last, the shores of the Promised Land hove into view, Jezebel felt a strange mixture of relief and apprehension. The landscape that unfolded before her was starkly different from the verdant, sea-kissed coast of Phoenicia. The land was drier, the hills more rugged, the air carrying a distinct scent – one of dust and sunbaked earth, rather than the pervasive aroma of salt and cedar.

Last day of travel to the Palace in the city of Samaria:

It has been six days since they left Sidon. Everyone is tired and irritable. The Israeli delegation has been complaining all morning that they have to hurry. Something about "Shabbat is coming. We have to be unloaded and through before sundown."

"Momma," Jezebel cries, "What on earth is Shabbat? These crazy men are ranting about this and are upset. I hear one of them swearing at his servant because he was not moving fast enough. What do we need to know about this event or whatever it is?"

Athena replied, "Oh, Shabbat, you did not read about that in the scrolls? Maybe it was in the scroll I read yesterday. I do not think you have made it to that one. It is what they call the beginning of their holy day each week. They work six days, and on the seventh day, they rest, dedicating the entire day to Yahweh and their families. I think it is great that they have a countrywide day of rest. We should do something similar in Sidon. Anyway, at sundown on the 6th day of the week, they start their day of Thanksgiving with prayer and a meal. They do no further work after that meal. They do not cook or clean. They eat the food left over from the Shabbat meal the next day. At sundown on the 7th day, Shabbat is over. Everyone can cook and clean and be ready to start back to work on the first day of the week."

"Oh, by the way, I forgot to tell you on the morning of the seventh day, they go to the Temple they have built for Yahweh. They read scriptures and offer a sacrifice to Yahweh there. You will be expected to attend this service. I have not reached the part where you should participate, or if you will have to do anything. I am still reading. Maybe we can finish it today on the camel ride!"

Arrival at the Palace in Samaria:

The initial view of Samaria was a stark contrast to the bustling, sun-drenched grandeur of Sidon. Where her Phoenician city sprawled along the coast, a vibrant tapestry of white stone, red-tiled roofs, and towering temples dedicated to a pantheon of gods, the approaching Israeli landscape appeared more subdued, more weathered. The hills rose in shades of ochre and brown, sparsely dotted with olive groves and clusters of what appeared to be rudimentary dwellings.

There was a ruggedness to the terrain, an ancient, unvarnished quality that spoke of resilience rather than opulence. The air, she noted, was thinner, hotter, and carried a pervasive dust that seemed to cling to everything. It was a land that felt as if it had been sculpted by the very hands of the elements, rather than refined by human artistry.

Her arrival in Samaria, the newly established capital of the Israelite kingdom, was met with a mixture of awe and guarded curiosity. The city, though a center of royal power, lacked the ancient grandeur of Sidon. Its buildings were less ornate, its streets less bustling with the cacophony of a centuries-old trading hub. The people were different. Their customs, attire, and the very cadence of their speech all spoke of a distinct heritage, a people shaped by a different history and, most strikingly, a different relationship with the divine.

It is about four hours before sundown when the caravan pulls through the palace gate and heads toward the main house. The property is lit up like the trees that they decorate in the Temple of Moloch. They put candles on the branches of the tree, lighting the path to the altar.

"Moma, it looks like someone has travelled to Sidon to the Temple of Moloch and used the tree lights to light this garden. I love it. They are already moving in the direction I need them to go! I am so excited for this welcome and lights!" Jezebel squealed out like an excited five-year-old.

At the palace entrance, the servants are lined on both sides of the walk. King Ahab is at the top of the steps for the entrance into the Palace. He is so tall and handsome. She was not expecting this specimen of beauty. With all that her father kept adding to the contract, she began to worry if he was marrying her off to a physically and mentally deranged specimen of a man, who was not a young man. It would not be the first time in history that a king had done something so cruel to one of his daughters for the sake of money.

Quick introductions were made, and apologies were offered that Shabbat was about to start and that they would have to meet tomorrow after the temple service to discuss further. King Ahab informed the princess and her mother, "After the temple service tomorrow, you can rest, and we will begin our talks at the evening meal that will start at sundown. After Shabbat has ended, I can have the servants finish unpacking for you. Tonight, focus on what you need for tomorrow and leave the rest for another day. I know this may sound strange to you, especially if you haven't read the scroll about Shabbat that I sent to you on the journey. I promise it will be clear soon. I was planning for you to be here two days ago. I thought we were going to have plenty of time to talk about these customs before you got thrown into them."

With that word and a few curtsies and handshakes and the king was whisked away by one of his guards to the unknown parts of the palace. Jezebel did not get a chance to talk to him, only to shake his hand. She did not see him again until the evening meal the next day. He was not present in the dining room where they ate tonight or at the temple the next day. She thought this was strange, but let it go.

Jezebel meets the Priest and Leaders of Israel:

It is the Shabbat service at the Temple there in Samaria. Athena and Jezebel had been led by palace guards and instructed where to sit. They are both paralyzed with fear and discomfort as they wait for the king or a familiar face to appear. But no one shows. Jezebel is trying so hard to understand what they are doing. But everyone was speaking Hebrew, and she had no idea what they were saying. Apparently, they are praising their God, Yahweh.

Jezebel, accustomed to the vibrant public displays of faith in Phoenicia, found the religious landscape of Israel to be remarkably austere. The worship of Yahweh, as she had heard, was centered not on grand temples filled with images and incense, but on an internalized devotion—a reverence for an unseen God whose presence was felt in the hearts of His people and in the pronouncements of His prophets. The stark contrast to her own deeply ingrained faith, where the divine was palpable in the natural world, in the sacred groves and the imposing temples dedicated to Baal and Asherah, was striking.

She observed the Samaritans with a critical, yet keenly observant, eye. She noted their earnestness, their deep-seated piety, and the seemingly unwavering conviction in their singular God. There was a certain resilience about them, a spirit forged in hardship and in the establishment of their own kingdom. However, there was also, to her Phoenician sensibilities, a certain lack of worldly sophistication, a focus on spiritual matters that seemed to eclipse the more practical concerns of earthly power and prosperity, which were so central to her own worldview.

Her royal retinue, a colorful and opulent contingent from Sidon, drew stares and whispers. Their fine linens, their exquisite jewelry, the very air of exotic grandeur they carried with them, served as a stark reminder of the cultural divide that separated them from the people of Israel. Jezebel, though aware of the attention, carried herself with an innate regality; her Phoenician pride served as a shield against any perceived slight or misunderstanding. She was a princess of Sidon, a daughter of a powerful and ancient lineage, and she would not easily be diminished.

Jezebel noticed that when the priest came to greet them after the ceremony, several of the people from the Israel delegation joined them. They spoke in Aramaic instead of Hebrew to Athena and Jezebel. As they talked, both recognized that everyone spoke with reverence of their king, of his growing kingdom, and of the God they served. Jezebel listened, her sharp mind absorbing every detail, her curiosity piqued by their descriptions of a land so different from her own. Here in Israel, worship of Baal and Asherah was unknown, replaced by fervent devotion to a singular, unseen deity. This divergence, this profound spiritual difference, was not a deterrent to her; it was, in a way, an added layer of fascination, a challenge that ignited her innate desire to understand and, perhaps, to influence.

Her father, King Ethbaal, would often speak with her privately, his voice a mixture of paternal pride and regal counsel. He emphasized the importance of her role, the weight of the responsibility she would soon bear. "You will be more than a queen, my daughter," he would say, his eyes, keen and assessing, meeting hers. "You will be an ambassador of our people, a bridge between two worlds. Carry the strength of Sidon within you, the wisdom of our gods. Let your voice be heard; you will be known." Her father often spoke of the strategic alliances and the benefits to their kingdom, while noticing a fire in her eyes that mirrored his own.

The elders of Sidon had offered their blessings and prayers over her before she left to come to Israel. They recognized the significance of this moment, the intertwining of royal bloodlines, and the expansion of Phoenician influence. There were also whispers of concern, of the potential challenges she might face in a foreign land with unfamiliar customs and a drastically different religious framework. But these concerns were largely overshadowed by the prevailing sense of opportunity and the deep-seated pride in their princess, a daughter of Sidon destined for a throne in a land of growing prominence.

Back at the Palace:

The royal palace, though undoubtedly the seat of power, felt different from the palaces of her homeland. It was functional, a symbol of a kingdom still in its formative years, rather than the ancient, sprawling structures steeped in generations of history and tradition that she was accustomed to. The court itself was a complex web of loyalties and ambitions, with advisors and officials who spoke of Yahweh with a fervent devotion that was both intriguing and, to Jezebel, somewhat unsettling.

She began to learn about the traditions and laws of Israel, absorbing them with the same sharp intellect that had served her so well in Sidon. She studied their history, their covenant with Yahweh, their struggles and triumphs. But as she learned, she also began to form her own judgments, comparing and contrasting the ways of Israel with those of her own people. The monotheistic fervor of the Israelites seemed, to her, a limiting factor, a denial of the rich diversity of divine power that she believed governed the universe.

CHAPTER FOUR:
Meeting the King

The air within the royal reception hall of King Ahab's palace at Samaria was thick with the unspoken. Sunlight, filtered through intricately carved alabaster panels that were perhaps the closest Samaria possessed to the grandeur of Sidon's artistry, cast a diffused, golden glow. It illuminated the faces of the assembled courtiers—men and women whose attire, while respectable, lacked the vibrant dyes and intricate embroidery Jezebel was accustomed to. Their faces, a study in solemnity and expectant curiosity, turned as one towards the grand entrance. This was the moment. Her arrival, the culmination of a journey across sea and land, was now to be consummated in the presence of King Ahab himself.

Jezebel, a vision sculpted by generations of Phoenician refinement, entered not with hurried steps, but with a deliberate, measured grace. Her gown, a creation of the finest Tyrian purple silk, cascaded around her, the rich hue a stark, almost defiant contrast to the muted tones of the Samarian court. The fabric shimmered with every subtle movement, catching the light and drawing every eye to it. Around her neck rested a collar of finely wrought gold, inset with lapis lazuli and pearls, each gem seeming to hold a fragment of the sea from which her people drew their wealth and their gods. Her dark hair, intricately braided and adorned

87

with delicate gold filigree, framed a face that was both regal and undeniably captivating. There was a firmness to her chin, a keen intelligence in her deep-set eyes, and a subtle curve to her lips that hinted at a spirit not easily subdued.

Behind her, a procession of her own attendants, a carefully curated collection of women from Sidon, followed with similar poise. They carried her personal belongings, not in rough bundles, but in polished cedar chests inlaid with ivory. One woman bore a gilded stool, another a silver basin and ewer, small but significant indicators of her accustomed standard of living. The scent of exotic perfumes, jasmine and myrrh, clung to them, a fragrant whisper of a world far removed from the dry, earthy air of Samaria. This was not a mere display; it was a statement, a quiet declaration of her identity and the civilization she represented.

As she advanced further into the hall, her gaze swept across the assembly, registering the curious mixture of awe and apprehension in their expressions. They had undoubtedly heard tales of the Phoenician princess, of her beauty, her lineage, and the wealth of her dowry. Yet, seeing her in person, witnessing the sheer radiance of her presence, seemed to have an effect that transcended mere rumor. There was a tangible shift in the atmosphere, a collective intake of breath. And then, her eyes met his. This had not happened when they came into the palace from the ship two nights ago.

King Ahab had scanned across the crowd, focused his eyes on the delegation leaders with a puckered brow that indicated his mind was full of questions. One was immediately answered because the royal entourage was present, so King Esthbaal had obviously agreed. But what had it cost him? By the looks of this crowd, she brought with her, he was in for the shock of his life with a Princess Diva that was spoiled. He did not dare let his gaze fall on any of the females. He did not know which one it was. There was a middle-aged lady in royal attire, as well as a younger one. "Oh, God, please do not let it be the older battle ax with the hideous makeup, please, God, now." Ahab prayed under his breath. He was afraid to ask anything or say anything except that they would all meet the following evening for dinner. He had shaken the hands of the two ladies that his servant pointed to, but he did not make eye-to-eye contact.

Standing there, he realized it was the younger one, and the older one was apparently the mother or someone, whom he did not see at the moment, which allowed him to catch his breath. "Thank you, God," he muttered to himself!

King Ahab stood a short distance away, a figure of commanding presence, though in a manner that was distinctly different from the princes of Sidon. His frame was broad, his shoulders powerful, suggesting a man accustomed to both the weight of a crown and the rigors of a kingdom that, by all accounts, was still building itself. His hair and beard were dark, neatly trimmed, and his eyes, a piercing blue that seemed to absorb the light, fixed upon her with an intensity that was both unnerving and strangely compelling. He wore robes of fine linen, embroidered with simple geometric patterns, and a diadem of hammered gold adorned his brow. There was a certain ruggedness to him, a sense of raw power that had not been polished smooth by centuries of courtly artifice.

He did not rush forward. Instead, he waited, allowing her to approach him, a subtle display of respect for her station and the gravity of the occasion. Jezebel, in turn, paused a few paces from him, her posture erect, her gaze unwavering. The silence stretched, not an awkward silence, but one filled with the unspoken language of introductions and assessments. This was not merely a meeting between a king and his new bride; it was the convergence of two distinct worlds, two powerful wills, and perhaps, two souls destined to intertwine in ways neither could fully anticipate.

She offered a small, regal inclination of her head. "King Ahab," her voice was clear and melodious, carrying the refined accent of Phoenician speech. It was a voice that had been trained in the courts, accustomed to conveying both diplomacy and charm. "I am Jezebel, daughter of Ethbaal, King of the Sidonians."

Ahab inclined his head in return, a gesture that, while courteous, held a certain kingly reserve. "Princess Jezebel," his voice was deeper, resonant, with a timbre that spoke of authority. "Welcome to Samaria. Your journey was, I trust, not without comfort."

There was a subtle probing in his question, a quiet assessment of her fortitude. Jezebel met his gaze without flinching. "The seas were generous, Your Majesty," she replied, a hint of a smile playing on her lips. "And the sun of the Almighty guided my passage. Though the shores of Israel are indeed... different from those of my homeland."

Her understated observation was a masterstroke, acknowledging the contrast without directly criticizing. It was a subtle dance of words, a delicate probing of his perception. Ahab's lips curved into a slight smile, a rare softening of his stern features. "We are a people of the land, Princess. Our strength is not in the adornments of the sea, but in the soil beneath our feet, and the God who has led us through trials."

His words were a quiet counterpoint to her own, a gentle assertion of his kingdom's identity. Jezebel felt a flicker of intrigue. He was not the effete prince she might have feared, nor a barbarian. He was a king, a leader, and his words carried a conviction that resonated. She had been prepared for a more primitive court, a less sophisticated ruler. Ahab, in his own way, possessed a gravity that was undeniably kingly.

The air between them began to hum with an invisible current. It was the potent magnetism of two rulers, each accustomed to command, now finding themselves on the precipice of an intimate union. Ahab's eyes, as they continued to regard her, seemed to hold a mixture of admiration for her undeniable beauty and a profound curiosity about the woman who embodied the distant, opulent culture of Phoenicia. He was a king who had, by all accounts, ascended to the throne through his own strength and prowess in battle. He was not a man easily impressed, yet Jezebel felt a distinct sense of having captured his attention.

She, in turn, found herself observing him with a keen, appraising eye. He was not the idealized prince of her youthful dreams, but there was a compelling virility and grounded power that was far more potent. His hands, as he gestured subtly towards a more private seating area, were strong and calloused, the hands of a warrior and a ruler who was not afraid of exertion. The simple, yet rich, fabric of his robes spoke of a king who was more pragmatic than ostentatious, a contrast to the silks and gold worn by the king of Sidon.

"Come, Princess," Ahab motioned for her to precede him towards a more intimate alcove, furnished with low, cushioned seats. "You must be weary. Allow me to offer you the hospitality of my house."

Jezebel inclined her head once more, her gaze meeting his for a fleeting moment. In that shared glance, a silent understanding passed between them. The negotiations, the political alliances, the grand pronouncements – all of that would come. But in this quiet moment, before the assembled court, it was simply a king and his future queen, their destinies now irrevocably bound. The weight of her heritage and the responsibility of her people still lay upon her, but as she walked towards the king, a new, more personal anticipation began to stir within her. This was not just a political alliance; it was the beginning of something else entirely, something that promised to be as challenging as it was potentially exhilarating. The arrival was complete, but the reign had only just begun.

As Jezebel settled onto the cushioned seat, the rough-hewn texture of the fabric beneath the finer woven cover was a subtle reminder of the land's nature. Ahab sat opposite her, his posture relaxed but alert. The courtiers maintained a respectful distance, their whispers muted, their gazes now more speculative than purely apprehensive. They were witnessing the first moments of their new queen's assimilation, the initial unfolding of a union that would undoubtedly reshape the kingdom.

Ahab, with a gesture, signaled for a servant to bring refreshment. A chalice of wine, richer and darker than any Jezebel had tasted, was presented. She accepted it gracefully, her fingers brushing against his as the chalice was passed. It was a brief, almost accidental contact, yet it sent a surprising jolt through her. His skin was warm, his grip firm. She brought the chalice to her lips, the taste of the wine bold and earthy, lacking the delicate sweetness of the vintages from the Phoenician coast. It was a flavor as unpretentious and potent as the man who offered it.

"You bring with you the grace of Sidon, Princess," Ahab remarked, his eyes tracing the line of her throat as she drank. "A grace we have, perhaps, only glimpsed in our tales."

Jezebel lowered the chalice, her gaze meeting his directly. "Grace is a cultivated thing, Your Majesty," she replied, her voice retaining its practiced poise. "But substance is innate. And I sense your kingdom, and its king, are not lacking in substance."

Her words were a compliment, but also a subtle challenge, a recognition of the strengths she observed beneath the surface austerity. Ahab responded with a nod, a slight deepening of the smile that had appeared earlier. "We build our substance on the foundation our God has laid for us. It is a foundation that has withstood much."

The mention of God, of this singular deity Yahweh, always brought a subtle shift in Jezebel's perception. To worship an unseen entity, a God who demanded singular devotion and forbade the very idols that gave form to the divine, felt like an alien concept. Yet, the unwavering conviction in Ahab's voice, the quiet strength that seemed to emanate from him, spoke of a faith that, however different, was clearly a powerful force within him.

"My father, King Ethbaal, speaks often of the gods of our land," Jezebel ventured, testing the waters of conversation. "Baal, whose might commands the storm; Asherah, whose bounty nourishes the earth; Astarte, whose beauty inspires love and courage. They are the lifeblood of our people, their presence felt in every aspect of our lives."

Ahab listened intently, his expression thoughtful. When she finished, he remained silent for a moment, perhaps contemplating the vast chasm of religious belief that separated them. "Our God," he said, his voice low and deliberate, "is one. He is the creator of all, the sustainer of all. His presence is not to be found in carved images, but in His commandments, in His covenant with our people."

There was no judgment in his tone, only a quiet assertion of his deeply held beliefs. Jezebel felt a strange mix of respect and a nascent sense of something akin to pity. To have a faith so devoid of visual splendor, so reliant on abstract adherence, seemed a barren prospect. Yet, she could not deny the sincerity in Ahab's demeanor.

"A singular god," Jezebel mused, swirling the wine in her chalice. "It is a concept that requires... understanding. In Sidon, our worship is a celebration, a vibrant expression of gratitude and devotion. We revel in the presence of the divine, their forms etched into our very souls."

"And perhaps," Ahab countered gently, "our God requires not revelry, but obedience. Not artistic representation, but pure devotion. It is a path that demands a different kind of strength." He leaned forward slightly, his gaze intent. "You are a woman of great spirit, Princess. I have heard the tales. You are not one to shrink from a challenge."

Jezebel met his gaze, a slow smile spreading across her lips. "Indeed, Your Majesty. A challenge is merely an invitation to demonstrate one's mettle. And I am certain that you, as king, will provide ample opportunity for us to both shine!"

The conversation, though brief, had laid bare the fundamental differences in their worlds, not just in terms of culture and custom, but in the very core of their spiritual understanding. Yet, paradoxically, it had also revealed a shared current of strength, a mutual recognition of leadership and conviction. Ahab saw in Jezebel a formidable presence, a queen who would not merely be a figurehead, but a force in her own right. And Jezebel saw in Ahab a man of substance, a king who, despite the unfamiliarity of his ways, possessed a powerful and unwavering spirit.

The air in the reception hall, though still carrying the faint, lingering scent of exotic perfumes that marked Jezebel's arrival, now vibrated with a different kind of energy. It was the quiet hum of mutual observation, a palpable current that flowed between King Ahab and the new future Queen of Israel. The initial awe of the assembled court, the whispers of speculation, seemed to recede, becoming a muted backdrop to the unfolding drama between their rulers. Jezebel, having navigated the intricate dance of her introduction with the practiced grace of her upbringing, found her gaze drawn back to Ahab, and his attention was fixed upon her, unwavering.

He was not simply looking at a foreign princess, a political acquisition. His eyes, startling and piercing dark brown, held a different kind of appraisal. It was the look of a man who recognized a kindred spirit, a force that mirrored his own ambitions, albeit clad in the shimmering silks of Phoenician sophistication. Jezebel felt an answering spark, a recognition that transcended the political imperatives of her marriage. Here was a man who commanded respect, a ruler whose presence exuded a raw, unvarnished power that was both unsettling and undeniably attractive. The whispers of his victories, the tales of his reign, had painted him as a warrior, a king forged in the crucible of a young kingdom. Now, in his gaze, she saw not just the king, but the man, a man whose own spirit seemed to recognize the magnitude of hers.

"You speak of substance, Princess," Ahab said, his voice cutting through the lingering quiet. He leaned forward slightly, the gesture drawing her attention more fully. "And I see it in you. Not the grace of the sea, but a strength that runs deep, like the roots of the ancient cedars of your homeland."

His words were more than a compliment; they were an acknowledgment, a validation of the persona she had carefully cultivated, the image of a queen as capable and determined as any king. Jezebel met his gaze, a slow smile spreading across her lips, a smile that was both genuine and strategically subtle. "And I, Your Majesty, see in you a foundation that is as solid as the very mountains of this land. A king who is not merely a figurehead, but the heart and sinew of his kingdom."

The exchange was a delicate dance, a subtle mirroring of strengths. Each recognized in the other a reflection of their own desires, their own drive to lead, to shape. But beyond the political, there was a fascination with her very being – her foreignness, her confidence, the aura of an ancient civilization that clung to her like the rich dyes of her gown. He was a builder, a consolidator of power, and here was a woman who, he sensed, possessed the vision and the will to be a partner in that grand endeavor.

Jezebel, for her part, saw in Ahab not just the throne of Israel but also the opportunity to wield influence and imprint her own vision upon this land. His position, his authority, was the very leverage she craved. Yet, it was not merely the abstract concept of power that drew her. It was the man himself, his directness, the unpretentious strength that radiated from him, a stark contrast to the sometimes-excessive opulence and political machinations of her own court.

"My father, King Ethbaal," Jezebel began, her tone shifting, becoming more intimate, more personal, "always emphasized the importance of understanding the heart of one's dominion. He taught me that a ruler must not only command, but must also understand the people they lead, their needs, their aspirations." She paused, her eyes holding Ahab's. "Tell me, Your Majesty, what is the heart of Israel?"

The question, seemingly innocent, was a deliberate probe —an attempt to gauge his depth and his understanding of his own kingdom. Ahab's expression remained thoughtful, his gaze never wavering from hers. "Israel's heart," he replied, "is its covenant with Yahweh. It is the unwavering faith that has guided us through the wilderness, the promise of a land flowing with milk and honey, a land that we, under His watchful eye, are making strong." He gestured subtly towards the latticed windows, beyond which lay the burgeoning city. "It is the sweat of our brow, the strength of our arms, and the unwavering belief that we are His chosen people."

His answer was fervent, deeply rooted in the nation's religious identity. Jezebel listened, absorbing not just the words but the passion behind them. Here, it seemed, faith was an all-consuming force, a singular, absolute devotion. It was alien, perhaps even severe, compared to the vibrant pantheon of her homeland, yet she could not deny the power it lent him, the unwavering certainty it instilled.

She looked back at Ahab, a glint of challenge in her eyes. "How does one venerate a God unseen, a God without form or image?" Ahab met her gaze, his expression earnest.

"Our God demands not images, but obedience. Not outward spectacle, but inner devotion. His presence is felt in the very fabric of our laws, in the justice we mete out, in the faithfulness we show to one another. It is a different kind of strength, Princess, one that requires a deep well of conviction." Ahab saw in Jezebel not just the dazzling Phoenician princess, but a woman of formidable intellect and will, a potential partner who could match his own ambitions. Her exoticism and sophistication were captivating, but it was the underlying strength—the unwavering core of her being— that truly drew him. He was a king who had built his kingdom through force of arms and keen diplomacy; he recognized that same fire in her.

Jezebel, in turn, felt an undeniable pull towards Ahab. He was not the idealized prince of her youthful fantasies, but a man grounded in his reality, his faith, his kingdom. His directness and lack of pretense were refreshing. The sheer power of his conviction, his unwavering belief in his God and his destiny, was compelling. He was a man who had, by all accounts, earned his crown, and there was an inherent respect in that. She saw in him a vessel for her own grander visions, a king whose kingdom could, under her influence, become something even more magnificent.

As the initial formalities of the reception faded, and the courtiers began to withdraw discreetly, leaving the king and his future queen to their private audience, the intensity of their connection deepened. Ahab rose, extending a hand towards her. It was a simple gesture, yet it held an unspoken invitation, a silent declaration of his desire to draw her closer. Jezebel, without hesitation, placed her hand in his. His grip was firm, warm, and in that touch, a current of unspoken promise passed between them.

"You are a woman of great spirit, Princess," Ahab said, his voice low, his dark eyes fixed on hers. "I have heard the tales. You are not one to be easily contained." Jezebel's smile widened, a genuine, unvarnished expression of her pleasure. "And you, Your Majesty, are a king who commands not just loyalty, but admiration. I do not doubt that this kingdom will provide ample opportunity for both of us."

The palpable chemistry between them was undeniable, a powerful undercurrent that belied the political significance of their union. It was the intoxicating allure of two powerful souls recognizing each other, drawn together by the magnetic force of ambition, strength, and a burgeoning, undeniable passion. He led her from the reception hall, not towards the chambers prepared for a visiting dignitary, but towards his own private quarters, a subtle indication of his intentions. The courtiers, observing their king and future queen depart together, sensed the shift—an understanding had replaced the initial apprehension. This was intended to be a political marriage, uniting strong, focused dreamers who promised to reshape the kingdom.

As they walked, their shoulders occasionally brushing, a silent acknowledgement of the physical proximity, Jezebel felt a growing sense of anticipation. The air between them thrummed with unspoken desires, a potent cocktail of power, attraction, and the promise of a future that would be as turbulent as it was glorious. The king's desire was clear, and in its reflection, Jezebel found her own passions ignited.

The path they took was not one of ostentatious display, but of quiet purpose. Ahab's hand, still warm within hers, was a steady anchor, a reminder of the man she had come to know in these brief, intense hours. He spoke little, his focus seemingly on her, on absorbing her presence into the very essence of his world. "You find our palace... austere?" Ahab asked, his gaze flicking towards her as they ascended a flight of stairs.

Jezebel's smile was genuine. "I find it honest, Your Majesty. It speaks of purpose, of building, of a strength rooted in the land itself. My homeland is rich with the artistry of generations, with embellishments that speak of wealth accumulated over centuries. Your kingdom," she met his eyes again, her voice soft but firm, "speaks of a future yet to be fully realized, a future you are actively shaping." His eyes met and held Jezebel's gaze. "We are building, Princess, and perhaps," he squeezed her hand gently, "we will build or finish it together." Jezebel's heart quickened. This was more than she had dared to hope for. She had been prepared for a life of duty, of political maneuvering, but this... this felt different. This felt like the beginning of something truly extraordinary. The magnetic pull between them was not merely that of a king and his queen, but of two souls who recognized in each other a shared destiny.

As they entered Ahab's private chambers, the atmosphere shifted again. The subtle opulence here – rich woven tapestries depicting scenes of harvest and battle, a finely crafted cedar bed, polished bronze vessels – spoke of a king's comfort, but not of excessive indulgence. It was a space that felt lived-in, functional, yet imbued with a quiet regality. Ahab released her hand, turning to face her fully. The remaining courtiers, who had followed at a respectful distance, discreetly withdrew, leaving the king and his future queen in the intimate solitude of their shared space. But Jezebel froze as a paralyzing thought crossed her mind. "Wait a minute. I am definitely attracted to you, which is much more than I had hoped for. I thought this would be a political marriage and I would have my wifely duties, but I never thought I would feel this way about you. Is that the same feeling you have?"

With a raspy voice, Ahab murmured more than spoke, "Yes." The silence that fell between them was charged, thick with unspoken emotions. Jezebel broke the silence as she saw those blue eyes go black, the pupil dilating with a passion.

"I thought that the marriage agreement that I signed said that there would be a one-year betrothal and that we could only have chaperoned visits during this year as we learned about each other. After the year, there would be a wedding ceremony, followed by consummation. Are you trying to trick me into making the ketubah null and void?"

"No, God, no! This is not a trap. There is something about you that is electric. I cannot help myself. I cannot wait. A year of you in this palace will drive me insane. I do not think that I can wait even one night! There is something about you that is intoxicating."

Athena had warned Jezebel, while on the ship, not to allow anyone in Israel or Samaria to trick her into breaking any of the points of the covenant. So, she pulled away from his hands and with eyes filled with the same longing she saw in his, she says softly, "This is our first time to talk. It is our first meeting. I am not saying that I will have you wait a year, but we will have to wait until the wedding feast. I signed my life to that document. I cannot disappoint my father. If you are not pleased with me in the morning, you could send me back to Sidon disgraced and my father financially devastated."

"You are everything the tales promised, and more, Jezebel," Ahab said, his voice a low rumble that resonated with sincerity. He reached out, his calloused fingertips gently tracing the curve of her cheekbone. The touch was both reverent and possessive, a declaration of his claim. "Your beauty is that of the dawn, your spirit a flame that I have never before encountered." Jezebel leaned into his touch, a shiver of pleasure coursing through her. His admiration was a potent elixir, feeding her own burgeoning feelings. She saw in his eyes a reflection of her own ambition, her own desire to be recognized, to be powerful. His strength was not just physical, but an inner fortitude that drew her in.

"And you, Your Majesty," she replied, her voice barely a whisper, "are a king who is forging a new destiny. I see in you a leader, a warrior, and... a man whose strength is as captivating as any god's embrace." She dared to lift her hand, her fingers brushing against the strong line of his jaw. "My father believed that a wise ruler must know the strengths of their allies. I believe a wise queen must understand the heart of her king."

Ahab's smile was slow, genuine. He covered her hand with his, holding it against his skin. The contrast of her smooth, delicate fingers against his rougher, stronger hand was a tangible symbol of their union, their differences, and their shared purpose. "And what do you find, Jezebel, as you seek to understand the heart of this king?"

Her gaze met his, unwavering. "I find a man of purpose—a man who believes in his cause, his God, his people. And I find a man who, I believe, can understand the depth of my own convictions. We are… alike, Your Majesty, in ways that surprise even myself."

The admission, spoken with such candor, hung in the air between them. It was a recognition of a shared spirit, a mutual understanding that transcended mere political expediency. The passion that had been simmering beneath the surface, sparked by their initial meeting, now flared into a more undeniable flame. Ahab's gaze darkened, a primal instinct taking hold. He was a king, a man of desires, and in Jezebel, he saw the embodiment of everything he sought – beauty, intelligence, power, and a shared vision for the future.

He drew her closer, his arms encircling her waist, pulling her flush against his broad chest. Jezebel melted into his embrace, her own arms winding around his neck. The rich fabrics of their clothing rustled as they pressed together, the scent of his skin, clean and earthy, mingling with the lingering exotic notes of her own perfume. It was a moment of exquisite intimacy, a silent confirmation of the powerful connection that had been forged between them.

"Alike," Ahab murmured, his lips brushing against her temple. "Yes, we are alike. And together, Jezebel, we will build something that will be remembered for generations to come. A kingdom as strong and vibrant as our own desires." His words were a declaration, a promise, and Jezebel returned his embrace with an equal fervor. The political machinations, the grand pronouncements, all of it would come.

"WOW, you have more resolve than I realized. You are truly a remarkable woman. You have just made me want you even more, if you can imagine that. Okay, Princess. As you wish. I will finish touring throughout this area, and we will rejoin our quest downstairs." Ahab growled and murmured something she could not understand, as it was in Hebrew, as he walked away. As they went out the door, the king's personal staff waited and followed them back to the dining hall.

King Ahab, trying to sound like nothing had just happened or been implied, looked at Jezebel and asked about her journey and travels. The two, accompanied by their servants, seemed perfectly normal to the other guests as they returned to the dining hall. As they sat back down, King Ahab leaned over toward the princess and whispered in her ear. "Thank you for that private moment, in the quiet sanctuary of my chambers, where the outside world would not know. In there, it was and will always be just us, our wills entwined, and our hearts beating as one, united by a potent, irresistible magnetic pull. Always remember, in there we can close out the rest of the world!"

However, the future of Israel was about to be shaped by a love that was as fierce and ambitious as the rulers themselves —a passion ignited not just by duty, but by a profound, almost elemental attraction. The king's desire had found its match; a new era was about to begin.

Adjusting to Palace Life in Samaria:

The days that followed the initial, intense meeting between Ahab and Jezebel were a whirlwind of preparation and celebration. The news of the royal wedding rippled through the nascent kingdom of Israel, met with a mixture of anticipation and apprehension. For Ahab, it was the culmination of a significant diplomatic achievement, a pact that promised to weave the young nation into the fabric of established empires. For Jezebel, it was the coronation of her ambition, the moment her carefully laid plans began to bear fruit on the grandest of stages. The union was heralded with a fervor that sought to mask the underlying political calculus.

From Tyre and Sidon, the emissaries arrived, bringing gifts of opulent fabrics, intricately carved ivory, and skilled artisans who would contribute to the grandeur of the occasion. Israel, though growing in strength, still bore the marks of its recent history, its celebrations often marked by a sturdy pragmatism rather than the refined extravagance of its Phoenician neighbor. This wedding, however, would be different. It was designed to be a testament to Ahab's expanding influence, a dazzling display of his ability to forge alliances and attract the finest from the wider world.

The wedding itself was a magnificent spectacle, a deliberate fusion of two distinct cultures, designed to impress and to bind. The ceremonies began according to Israelite custom, in the presence of the elders and the kingdom's religious leaders. Ahab, clad in robes of fine linen embroidered with gold thread, stood before them, his gaze steady, his pronouncements clear. He spoke of the covenant between his people and Yahweh, and of the blessings this union would bring to Israel, a reinforcement of the divine favor that he believed guided his reign. The rites were solemn, imbued with the weight of tradition and the pronouncements of ancient laws. Yet, even within these sacred observances, the influence of Phoenicia was subtly evident. The floral arrangements, cascading in vibrant hues, were of a type rarely seen in Israel's arid lands, brought by skilled hands from the coastal regions. The music, while incorporating the resonant chords of Israelite lyres and shofars, was also laced with the higher, more melodic tones of Phoenician wind instruments, creating a soundscape that was both familiar and enchantingly foreign.

The Royal Wedding Feast:

As Jezebel fanned the flames of passion and she used her powers to gain more and more control over Ahab, it was only a matter of weeks before he was pushing the palace staff and the priest to speed up the wedding. There was no way he could hold out for a year with her living in the same palace. No matter how much space he tried to put between them, there was a pull toward her that he could not explain. She was like a drug. The more he was around her, the more he had to be—she was intoxicating to him!

The wedding feast preparation took over six weeks to complete once all the items required for the feast, as per the ketubah, were in the country. That was a long time for both Jezebel and him, but the Israelites were in shock and talking because it had only been four months since her arrival in Samaria. Now the royal wedding was occurring!

The Phoenician Bride:

Jezebel, radiant in a gown woven with threads of gold and dyed a deep, regal purple — the very color that signaled her Phoenician heritage — stood beside Ahab. Her presence commanded attention, a captivating blend of exotic beauty and regal bearing. She moved with a grace that spoke of generations of courtly training, her expression serene, yet with a knowing glint in her dark eyes. To the Israelite onlookers, she was a figure of profound mystery and immense power, the bride from a land of ancient wonders, now united with their king. The blessing of the priests was sought, the oaths were sworn, and in the eyes of the people, Ahab and Jezebel were officially bound.

But the political symphony was far from over. As the sun dipped below the horizon, casting long shadows across the palace courtyards, the celebrations took on a distinctly Phoenician character. The feasting began, a lavish affair that stretched long into the night. Tables groaned under the weight of delicacies prepared by chefs brought from Sidon – roasted game birds seasoned with exotic spices, platters of fresh figs and dates, and wines of a quality and variety never before witnessed in Jerusalem. The air was alive with the aroma of incense, sweet and heavy, wafting from braziers placed strategically throughout the banquet hall.

Jezebel, now fully embracing her role as future queen, played a central part in this second phase of the celebration. She moved among the guests, her laughter like the chime of silver bells, her conversation flowing with an ease that charmed even the most stoic of Israelite nobles. She spoke of the prosperity of her homeland, of the vast trade networks that connected Tyre and Sidon to distant lands, subtly highlighting the advantages this alliance would bring to Israel. Ahab stood by her side, his hand often resting on her arm, a visible sign of his pride and his intent. He allowed her to lead, to engage, to captivate. It was a deliberate performance, a visual representation of their partnership, and by extension, the new era of prosperity and influence that he envisioned.

Amidst the revelry, however, a keen observer might have noticed the subtle currents of power that were already beginning to flow. Jezebel, despite her outward deference to Ahab as the king, possessed an undeniable magnetism that drew attention. She was not merely a beautiful consort; she was a strategist, a diplomat in her own right, and she understood the weight of her presence. Her interactions with the key figures of Ahab's court were more than mere pleasantries. She engaged them in conversation, asking pointed questions about the kingdom's affairs, offering insightful suggestions that often impressed those accustomed to more traditional forms of counsel.

One such instance involved Shaphan, the royal scribe, a man known for his meticulous record-keeping and his quiet but influential position within the administration. Jezebel approached him, her Phoenician attendants flanking her at a respectful distance, while Ahab was engaged in conversation with a delegation of tribal leaders.

"Master Shaphan," Jezebel began, her voice carrying a polite warmth. "I have been observing the administration of justice within the kingdom. It appears that, although the laws are in place, the process of dissemination and enforcement could benefit from greater clarity. Perhaps a standardized system of public pronouncements, inscribed on durable materials, could ensure that all citizens are aware of their civic duties and rights?"

Shaphan, a man of measured words and observant eyes, paused in his own conversation. He was used to the directness of Ahab, but Jezebel's approach was different. It was couched in respect, yet her suggestion was bold, indicating a keen understanding of governance that went beyond mere social graces. He recognized the underlying pragmatism, the Phoenician emphasis on order and efficient communication.

"Your Majesty speaks with wisdom," Shaphan replied, bowing his head slightly. "Our scribes are diligent, but the reach of our pronouncements can be limited. Your suggestion of durable inscriptions… it is a concept worthy of consideration."

Jezebel offered a small, knowing smile. "It is a practice that has served my homeland well, ensuring that the decrees of the throne are accessible to all, from the bustling port of Sidon to the farthest agricultural settlements. A kingdom thrives when its people are informed and guided."

This brief exchange, seemingly innocuous, was a demonstration of Jezebel's burgeoning influence. She was not content to merely occupy a ceremonial role. She was already identifying areas where her vision could be implemented, subtly guiding the flow of information and the mechanisms of governance. Ahab, observing this interaction from a distance, felt a surge of pride. He had chosen a partner who was not only beautiful and politically valuable, but also intelligent and capable. He saw her suggestions not as an encroachment on his authority, but as a valuable addition to his own considerable strengths.

The journey, the arrival, the initial introductions – all of it had been a preamble. Now, in the quiet heart of the king's own domain, the true beginning was at hand. Ahab's gaze swept over her, from the rich Tyrian purple of her gown to the intricate gold filigree adorning her hair. He saw not just the beautiful Phoenician princess, but the embodiment of a mighty civilization, a woman whose spirit he had already sensed and admired. King Ahab was smitten. He had swallowed the bait, hook, line, and sinker! There was no return, after the consummation of the marriage that would occur after the feast, the spirit that possessed her would now begin to have him gradually and would begin to eat his soul and mind!

The Royal Feast:

The fusion of traditions was not always seamless. Some of the older, more conservative members of the Israelite court exchanged uneasy glances when certain Phoenician deities were invoked in toasts, or when the libations poured were of a type associated with the worship of Baal and Asherah, gods far removed from the singular devotion of Yahweh. Jezebel, however, was acutely aware of the sensitivities. She navigated these potential pitfalls with a deftness that belied her youth. She understood that overt displays of her homeland's religious practices could alienate the very people she intended to rule alongside Ahab. Her approach was more subtle, perhaps more insidious. It was about weaving her influence into the existing fabric of the kingdom, rather than tearing it apart.

The wedding feast continued, a testament to the successful forging of a royal union. It was a political masterstroke, a symbol of the alliance between Israel and Phoenicia that would undoubtedly shape the region's destiny. Yet, beneath the glittering surface of celebration, the true nature of the royal partnership was beginning to reveal itself. Ahab, the strong king of Israel, had found in Jezebel not just a queen, but a formidable ally, a sharp mind, and a will as unyielding as his own. The foundations of their reign were being laid, not just on political expediency, but on a complex interplay of mutual admiration, shared ambition, and the undeniable spark of a passion that promised to set the kingdom ablaze. The king's desire, it seemed, had found its perfect, and perhaps most dangerous, counterpart.

As the night wore on and the celebrations began to wind down, Ahab led Jezebel away from the throng of guests. The murmurs of admiration and speculation followed them, a testament to the impact she had already made. They walked through the moonlit courtyards, the air still thick with the mingled scents of incense and exotic flowers. The solidity of the stone beneath their feet, the familiar silence of the sleeping palace, offered a stark contrast to the boisterous revelry they had left behind.

"You were magnificent, Jezebel," Ahab said, his voice low and filled with a quiet pride. He turned to her, his brown eyes reflecting the moonlight. "You captivated them all!"

Jezebel leaned her head against his shoulder, a rare moment of repose. "It is my duty, Your Majesty, to ensure that our alliance is not just a matter of state, but a source of inspiration for your people." Her hand found his, and she interlaced her fingers with his, her touch conveying a mixture of affection and quiet strength. "But it is your strength, your vision, that truly anchors this kingdom. I am merely here to help it flourish." This was the dance they had begun, the subtle choreography of power and influence. Ahab understood the compliment, but he also recognized the underlying assertion of agency. Jezebel was not content to be a passive spectator.

She was an active participant, eager to shape the future of Israel according to her own designs. And he, in his own way, was anxious to see what they could achieve together. The pragmatic political alliance was solidifying into something more profound, a shared endeavor fueled by mutual respect and a growing, undeniable bond. The king's desire was for a strong Israel, a prosperous Israel, and he believed, with a burgeoning conviction, that Jezebel was the key to unlocking that future. They reached the private chambers that had been prepared for them, a space that blended the regal austerity of Israelite design with subtle touches of Phoenician luxury. The air within was still and expectant. Ahab turned to face Jezebel, his gaze never leaving hers. The political marriage was about to be consummated, and the alliance sealed.

Now, in the quiet intimacy of their private world, a new chapter of their shared destiny was about to unfold. The union of Israel and Phoenicia, embodied in the king and his foreign queen, was more than just a treaty; it was the convergence of two powerful wills, poised to remake the very landscape of the ancient world. The celebratory pomp of the wedding had served its purpose, but it was the quiet strength of their shared ambition, ignited by the king's initial desire, that would truly forge their reign.

As the dawn broke over Jerusalem, painting the sky in hues of rose and gold, a stark contrast to the lingering shadows of the royal chambers. The wedding, a magnificent display of political acumen and nascent passion, had been a success, a testament to Ahab's growing stature. Yet, as the kingdom settled back into the rhythm of everyday life, the actual work—the shaping of a shared destiny—began in the quiet conversations between the king and his Phoenician queen.

Jezebel, with her keen intellect and innate understanding of power, had already grasped the depth of Ahab's ambition. He envisioned an Israel that was not merely a nascent nation struggling for survival, but a beacon of prosperity, a center of influence that would rival the ancient empires of Mesopotamia and Egypt. This was a vision that resonated deeply within her, a kindred spirit recognizing the potential for greatness.

A delicate dance of discovery and exploration marked their early days. Ahab, accustomed to the directness of his military commanders and the reverence of his priests, found himself drawn to Jezebel's astute observations and her pragmatic approach to governance. She spoke of trade routes, infrastructure, the importance of securing Israel's borders with armies, alliances, and economic strength. Her words were not the platitudes of a queen seeking to please; they were the pronouncements of a ruler in her own right, a strategist who understood the intricate mechanics of statecraft.

"Samaria," Ahab mused one afternoon, standing with Jezebel on a balcony overlooking the sprawling city, the foundations of his burgeoning capital spread out below. "It is a place of great promise, but it lacks... the polish of true power. The buildings, while sturdy, speak of practicality, not of majesty. The markets, though bustling, lack the exotic allure that draws merchants from distant lands."

Jezebel turned to him, her dark eyes alight with understanding. "Majesty, Your Majesty, is not merely built of stone, but of perception. Your people need to see in their capital the reflection of your strength, of your vision. They need to witness a kingdom that is not afraid to embrace the world, to learn from its wonders and to offer its own unique gifts in return." She gestured towards the distant, shimmering expanse of the Mediterranean, a subtle reminder of her homeland's maritime prowess. "My father, King Ethbaal, has fostered an empire of trade, built upon the foundations of innovation and a keen understanding of human desire. The ships that leave Tyre carry not just goods, but ideas, craftsmanship, and a certain boldness that inspires awe."

Ahab listened, his gaze fixed on her, absorbing every word. He saw in her eyes a reflection of his own yearning for something grander, something that would lift Israel from its precarious position and elevate it to a place of prominence. "You speak of boldness," he said, a slow smile spreading across his face. "And it is boldness that Israel needs. We have a spiritual heritage that is unmatched, a connection to the Divine that no other nation possesses. But perhaps, in our earnestness to follow Yahweh's path, we have neglected the material world, the tangible signs of prosperity that can also inspire faith and devotion."

"Faith, Your Majesty, is the spirit, but prosperity is the body that gives that spirit form and substance," Jezebel replied. "When your people see a kingdom that thrives, that is admired and envied, they will feel a greater pride in their heritage and a deeper loyalty to their king. They will see that the blessings of Yahweh manifest not just in spiritual triumphs, but in earthly abundance."

Their conversations often turned to the specific challenges and opportunities that lay before them. Jezebel, with her intimate knowledge of Phoenician craftsmanship and engineering, offered practical solutions to problems that had long plagued Ahab. She spoke of sophisticated irrigation techniques that could transform arid lands into fertile plains, of advanced architectural methods that could create structures of breathtaking beauty and enduring strength, and of artistic traditions that could imbue their palaces and temples with a grandeur that would awe all who beheld them.

"The artisans of Sidon," she explained, her voice animated, "can create mosaics that capture the very essence of light and color, murals that tell stories with a vibrancy that will speak to the soul. We can bring them here, to Samaria, to adorn your royal residences, to create temples that are not merely places of worship, but works of art that glorify the Divine in its fullest splendor."

Ahab envisioned it, the white stone of Samaria gleaming with intricate designs, the courtyards alive with the vibrant hues of Phoenician art. He saw his people, not as they were, a hardy but somewhat unrefined populace, but as inheritors of a legacy of beauty and sophistication. "And the trade?" he pressed, his mind already calculating the economic implications. "How do we ensure that our burgeoning prosperity does not become a target for those who would seek to exploit it?"

Jezebel's smile was knowing. "That is where alliances and a strong navy come into play. Phoenicia's strength lies in its control of the seas, in its ability to connect the world. Israel, situated at a crossroads of trade, has the potential to become a vital hub. We can secure our trade routes, establish favorable treaties, and ensure that any who seeks to disrupt our commerce does so at their own peril. It is a matter of projecting strength, Your Majesty, a clear message that Israel is not to be trifled with."

This was the crux of their shared vision: a powerful, prosperous, and influential Israel, a kingdom that commanded respect and admiration from all corners of the known world. Jezebel's initial ambition, rooted in the preservation and advancement of her own people and her own deities, began to intertwine seamlessly with Ahab's aspirations. She saw in Ahab a leader with the raw potential to achieve greatness, a man willing to embrace new ideas and to break from the constraints of tradition if it meant elevating his nation. Her guidance and her resources seemed to align with his path.

"You understand me, Jezebel," Ahab said one evening, as they stood under a canopy of stars so brilliant, "More than anyone has before. You see not just the king, but the man who desires to build something lasting, something that will echo through the ages."

"And you, Your Majesty," she replied, her voice soft, yet carrying an unwavering conviction, "see the queen who can help you build it. My father's legacy is one of expansion, of innovation, of a kingdom that commands the respect of all nations. I believe that Israel, under your leadership, can achieve even greater heights. We can forge a new era, an era of unprecedented prosperity and influence, an era where the name of Israel is spoken with awe and reverence."

Their discussions were not always focused on grand pronouncements and sweeping strategies. Often, they were more intimate, grounded in the everyday realities of ruling. Jezebel would inquire about the welfare of the ordinary people and the challenges faced by farmers and artisans. She would offer suggestions on how to improve their lives, drawing upon her own experiences with the well-organized and prosperous communities of Phoenicia.

"In Tyre," she recounted, "we have established guilds for every craft, ensuring that the quality of work is maintained, and that the workers themselves are protected and fairly compensated. This fosters a sense of pride and loyalty, and it ensures that our reputation for excellence is upheld." Ahab listened intently, recognizing the wisdom in her words.

He understood that the kingdom's strength ultimately rested on the well-being of its people. "We have the Levites, who serve Yahweh, and the priests who guide our spiritual lives," he mused. "But perhaps we need a more formalized structure for the artisans and merchants, a way to recognize their contributions and to ensure their continued dedication."

"Precisely," Jezebel affirmed, her eyes sparkling with the thrill of shared purpose. "It is about building a cohesive society, Your Majesty, where every individual understands their role and value. It is about creating a sense of belonging, a shared identity that binds them to the throne."

This burgeoning partnership was not without its subtle undercurrents. Jezebel's own ambitions, her deep-seated devotion to the gods of her homeland, particularly Baal and Asherah, were not abandoned in this newfound alignment. However, her strategy was one of integration, not imposition. She understood that a direct challenge to Israel's monotheistic faith would be met with fierce resistance. Instead, she sought to weave her own cultural and religious tapestry into the existing fabric of Israel, subtly introducing her gods and their practices in ways that would appear natural, even complementary, to the worship of Yahweh.

She would speak of Baal as the bringer of rain and fertility, a vital element for an agricultural society. She would mention Asherah as the mother goddess, a source of life and abundance, concepts that resonated with the very essence of prosperity Ahab so earnestly desired. These were not overt attempts at conversion, but rather a gradual acclimatization, an introduction of familiar concepts presented in a new light.

"Your people honor Yahweh as the ultimate source of all blessings," she might say to Ahab, her tone respectful and conversational. "And indeed, His power is undeniable. Yet, the bounty of the earth, the life-giving rains that nourish our crops, are also manifestations of divine will. In my homeland, we recognize these forces through the worship of Baal, the mighty bull who commands the heavens, and Asherah, the life-giving mother who nurtures the land. Is it not possible that Yahweh, in His infinite wisdom, allows for other expressions of His creative power?"

Ahab, already predisposed to seeing the positive aspects of alliances and the potential benefits of embracing the wider world, found himself open to these suggestions. He saw no inherent conflict in acknowledging the power of nature as a divine gift, a gift that Phoenicia, through its own traditions, had learned to harness and celebrate. He saw Jezebel's insights not as a threat to his faith but as a way to deepen his understanding of the divine forces that shaped the world.

This convergence of their visions was the engine that would drive their early reign. Ahab's desire for a strong and prosperous Israel found its perfect complement in Jezebel's strategic mind, her vast resources, and her unwavering ambition. They were a formidable duo, united by a shared purpose that promised to transform the nascent kingdom of Israel into something far more magnificent, far more powerful, and ultimately, far more complex than anyone could have imagined. The foundation of their reign was being laid, not on mere political expediency, but on a profound, and perhaps perilous, synthesis of two powerful wills, driven by a king's desire and a queen's boundless ambition.

The king's court, once a place of predictable rituals and established hierarchies, began to hum with a new energy, a subtle shift in the currents of influence. It was not a sudden overthrow, nor a blatant usurpation, but a gradual, almost imperceptible, infiltration of thought and intention. Jezebel— a woman who moved with the grace of a predator and the intellect of a seasoned diplomat—was weaving her subtle web. Her presence alone was a disruption to the established order, a vibrant splash of color and exoticism against the more muted tones of Israelite tradition. But it was her words, carefully chosen and delivered with unshakeable conviction, that truly began to reshape the landscape.

Ahab, still basking in the glow of his successful marriage and the intoxicating promise of a grander Israel, found himself increasingly drawn to his queen's counsel. Where his seasoned advisors, men whose lives had been dedicated to the service of Yahweh and the traditions of their ancestors, spoke of divine providence and the righteous path, Jezebel spoke of tangible results, of strategic advantage, and of the persuasive power of a kingdom that commanded respect through its sheer magnificence. She did not dismiss faith, but she wove it into a tapestry of pragmatic ambition, arguing that prosperity and strength were not antithetical to divine favor, but rather the very evidence of it.

"Your Majesty," she might begin, her voice a silken thread in the boisterous council chambers, her gaze fixed on Ahab, seemingly oblivious to the watchful eyes of the courtiers, "the harvest has been good, thanks be to Yahweh. Yet, imagine if our granaries were not merely filled, but overflowed with grain destined for distant lands, enriching our coffers and securing our borders through the very wealth we create. Imagine if our artisans, their skills honed to perfection, produced not just what is needed, but what is desired by kings and queens across the sea."

Her pronouncements were laced with a tantalizing vision of an Israel that was not just secure, but dominant. She spoke of leveraging Israel's strategic location not merely for defense, but for commerce, transforming it into the fulcrum of regional trade. Her Phoenician perspective, honed by generations of maritime enterprise and cultural exchange, offered a starkly different approach to kingdom building than the predominantly agrarian and spiritual focus of Israel. She presented these ideas not as radical departures, but as logical extensions of Ahab's own burgeoning ambitions.

The courtiers watched, their expressions a mixture of fascination and apprehension. Men like Jehu, a prominent military commander known for his loyalty to Yahweh and his traditionalist views, observed Jezebel's growing sway with unconcealed disquiet. He had seen the king's eyes light up at her suggestions, the subtle nods of agreement that signaled a shift in his thinking. He and others like him were accustomed to a king who sought divine guidance through the prophets and elders. Now, the whispers of a foreign queen seemed to hold an equal, if not greater, sway.

"The queen's counsel is… unconventional," Jehu remarked one evening to a fellow commander, their voices low as they moved through the shadowed colonnades of the royal palace. "She speaks of trade and alliances as if they were as sacred as the ancient laws. And the king… he truly listens."

His companion, a man whose family had served the throne for generations, shifted uncomfortably. "The king is young, and his queen is… captivating. Her words have a certain fire. But is it the fire of Yahweh, or a fire of another kind? One that consumes the old ways?"

Jezebel, meanwhile, was not content to merely offer suggestions in private. She began to subtly influence the very fabric of court life. The meals served in the royal chambers became more elaborate, featuring exotic spices and delicacies previously unknown in Samaria. The music played during feasts incorporated new instruments and melodies, a departure from the traditional strains of Israelite worship. These were not overt acts of defiance, but rather a deliberate infusion of her own culture —a gentle yet persistent introduction of what she considered to be the hallmarks of a civilized and advanced society. She would patronize artisans, commissioning them to create works that reflected Phoenician aesthetics, encouraging them to learn new techniques, and rewarding them generously.

Her charisma was a potent weapon. She possessed an innate ability to engage individuals from all walks of life, from the highest nobles to the humblest servants. She listened to their concerns, offered them words of encouragement, and, when appropriate, subtly guided their perspectives. She understood that actual influence was about commanding obedience, as well as fostering loyalty and shaping desires. When she met with the wives of the leading courtiers, she spoke not of household management or the proper conduct of Israelite women, but of the broader responsibilities of royal consorts and their role in projecting the image of a powerful and prosperous kingdom. She shared tales of the influence wielded by queens in her homeland, of their ability to shape public opinion and to act as patrons of culture.

"A kingdom's strength," she would explain, her voice resonating with passion, "is not measured solely by its armies or its harvests, but by the refinement of its people, by the beauty that surrounds them, and by the intellectual curiosity that drives them forward. As queens, it is our duty to cultivate these aspects, to ensure that our nation is admired not just for its might, but for its grace and its sophistication." Ahab, witnessing this effortless command of social dynamics, found himself increasingly proud of his queen. He saw her not as an outsider, but as an asset, a woman who brought with her a worldliness that could only elevate Israel. He encouraged her endeavors, seeing them as extensions of his own vision for a revitalized Samaria.

However, for some within the court, these changes were deeply unsettling. The prophets, who served as the spiritual conscience of the nation, viewed Jezebel's growing influence with grave concern. They saw in her patronage of foreign arts and her emphasis on material prosperity a subtle erosion of Israel's unique covenant with Yahweh. The veneration of Baal and Asherah, while not yet overt, was a constant undercurrent in their fears. They interpreted Jezebel's every suggestion, her every introduction of Phoenician custom, as a step away from the true worship of the One God.

"The king is enamored with the queen's foreign ways," declared a senior prophet to his brethren, their faces etched with worry. "He sees her wisdom in worldly matters, but he fails to see the spiritual danger. She brings with her the gods of her land, and she seeks to weave them into the very fabric of our worship." His words, though veiled in prophecy and spiritual warning, resonated with the deep-seated anxieties of those who feared the dilution of their faith. They began to speak in hushed tones, their pronouncements of divine displeasure becoming more frequent, though often directed at the king's perceived straying from tradition rather than at Jezebel herself, whom they viewed as the prime instigator.

Jezebel, astute enough to recognize the undercurrent of resistance, did not confront it directly. Instead, she employed a strategy of calculated subtlety. She understood that a direct challenge to the deeply ingrained monotheism of Israel would be met with insurmountable opposition. Her approach was one of gradual integration, of presenting her own deities and traditions in a manner that seemed not to supplant, but to complement, the existing faith. She would speak of Baal as the god of rain and storms, forces vital to an agricultural society. She would mention Asherah as the mother goddess, the source of fertility and abundance. These were concepts that resonated deeply within Israel, concepts that had, in the past, even been associated with Yahweh in His role as provider. She framed her worship not as a replacement, but as an additional layer of understanding, a way to honor the divine forces that governed the world.

"Your people honor Yahweh as the Giver of all," she might say to Ahab, her voice calm and measured, during one of their private discussions. "And rightly so. But the storms that nourish our land, the fertility that blesses our fields – are these not also manifestations of divine power? In my homeland, we recognize these forces through the worship of Baal, the powerful deity who commands the heavens, and Asherah, the benevolent mother who nurtures life. Is it not

116

possible that Yahweh, in His boundless wisdom, allows for these various expressions of His creative energy?"

Ahab, already open to the idea of embracing broader influences and seeing the tangible benefits of his queen's perspectives, found himself drawn to this line of reasoning. He did not see her suggestions as a betrayal of his faith, but rather as an expansion of his understanding of the divine. He was a king who believed in the power of his God, but he was also a pragmatist who recognized the forces that shaped the physical world. If acknowledging these forces, through the traditions of his queen, could bring greater prosperity and stability to his kingdom, then it seemed a reasonable course of action.

Her influence extended beyond religious matters. She began to shape Ahab's foreign policy subtly. While Ahab had inherited a kingdom with ongoing tensions and a precarious relationship with neighboring states, Jezebel brought with her the intricate diplomacy of the Phoenician city-states, a world accustomed to complex trade agreements, shifting alliances, and the constant negotiation of power. She advised Ahab on how to strengthen Israel's position, not just through military might, but through shrewd alliances and crafted treaties.

"The kingdom of Ammon, Your Majesty," she might suggest, "is a potential threat, but also a potential ally. Their control over certain trade routes is significant. Instead of perpetual conflict, perhaps we could forge a pact of mutual benefit, securing our own passage and creating a shared interest that discourages aggression."

Her insights were often couched in terms of economic advantage and mutual security, arguments that appealed directly to Ahab's desire for a powerful and prosperous Israel. She steered him away from the more impulsive and often costly military engagements that had characterized some of his predecessors, advocating instead for a more strategic and measured approach. The court began to notice the subtle shifts. Advisors who had once held Ahab's ear found themselves increasingly competing for his attention with the queen's quiet pronouncements. Decisions that might have once been debated at length among the elders were now often preempted by a conversation between the king and his queen. Some courtiers found themselves adapting, learning to align their own aspirations with Jezebel's vision, while others retreated, their unease growing with each passing day.

Ahab, for his part, felt a new sense of confidence and direction. He saw his kingdom transforming before his eyes, not just in terms of military strength, but in its cultural richness and its growing influence. He attributed this not to any deviation from his faith, but to the enlightened leadership he was now able to provide, a leadership that was amplified by the wisdom and vision of his Phoenician queen. He saw her as his partner, his confidante, and the architect of a brighter future for Israel.

The whispers of influence were growing louder, not yet a roar of defiance, but a persistent hum of change that permeated the very atmosphere of the royal court. Jezebel, with her sharp intellect and her unwavering resolve, was steadily guiding Ahab, shaping his decisions, and subtly transforming the kingdom of Israel into something more akin to her own Phoenician ideals.

The stage was being set for a reign that would be marked by both unprecedented prosperity and profound spiritual upheaval, a testament to the potent, and often dangerous, allure of a king's desire when guided by a queen's formidable will. It was amazing that all of this was done by Jezebel in the four months leading up to the wedding.

Yes, she and Ahab had consummated their wedding after the signing of the Ketubah, not waiting until the wedding feast. They kept their late-night encounters secret, they thought. Two servants assigned to help the future queen's staff were devout servers of Yahweh. They began to pick up on looks, glances, accidental touches, and gestures made with what was just a mere whisper between the two. Also, the way Ahab was incorporating her in court had already had the court officials and business associates of Ahab wondering what hold she had on him—they assumed it was her passionate fire that was already working in the bedroom!

CHAPTER FIVE:
<u>*The Royal Wedding*</u>:
Merging Two Worlds Together

The air within the inner courtyards of the royal palace in Jerusalem was charged with an almost electric vibrancy, a carefully curated symphony of sights, sounds, and scents designed to herald the monumental union. Gone was the dust and weariness of the journey; replaced by an atmosphere of unadulterated grandeur, befitting a king's wedding and a princess's arrival. The chosen venue for the ceremony itself, a sprawling, open-air courtyard adjacent to the main royal hall, had been transformed into a breathtaking testament to both Israelite artistry and the opulent influence of Phoenicia.

Banners and tapestries, woven with threads of gold and silver, cascaded from the colonnades surrounding the courtyard. These were not mere decorations; they were narratives spun in fabric, depicting scenes of divine favor, royal lineage, and the burgeoning alliance between the two kingdoms. Deep Tyrian purple, the color synonymous with wealth and royalty, predominated, interspersed with the vibrant blues of lapis lazuli and the earthy tones of natural dyes. Each pennant and drape seemed to shimmer with an inner light, catching the Jerusalem sun and reflecting it in a dazzling display. The craftsmanship was exquisite, a clear indication of the skilled hands that had been commissioned, both local and undoubtedly those brought with the princess's dowry, to prepare for this day.

At the focal point of the courtyard, where the vows were to be exchanged, a raised dais had been constructed. This platform, draped in the finest linen and adorned with intricately carved wooden panels, was approached by a short flight of steps. The steps themselves were edged with potted plants bearing fragrant blossoms—jasmine, myrtle, and perhaps even exotic spices imported from distant lands—their sweet perfume mingling with the slightly more austere scent of cedarwood, which formed the structural elements of much of the palace's décor. The scent was a sensory choice, designed to evoke an atmosphere of peace, prosperity, and sacredness.

The seating arrangements were a meticulous orchestration of status and influence. On one side, facing the dais, were the honored guests from Phoenicia, their attire a stark contrast to the more subdued, yet still rich, garments of the Israelite nobility. The Phoenicians favored brighter hues and more ostentatious displays of jewelry. Gold, in particular, seemed to be a common element, adorning their necks, wrists, and woven into the intricate braids of their hair. Their presence lent an undeniable air of exoticism and prestige to the proceedings. On the opposite side sat the assembled elders of Jerusalem, the high-ranking officials of the Israelite kingdom, and prominent figures from the various tribes. Here, the emphasis was on traditional Israelite finery – rich woolens, woven linen, and finely crafted leather, often embellished with subtle but expertly worked embroidery.

Beyond the immediate seating for the invited guests, the courtyard was open to a broader, though still select, gathering. The murmuring of the crowd added a constant, low hum to the overall soundscape. This was the sound of anticipation, of hushed conversations, of whispered prayers and excited exclamations. Merchants who had supplied goods for the wedding, artisans whose work adorned the palace, and loyal servants of the crown all occupied spaces with a view of the ceremony.

The auditory landscape was as carefully constructed as the visual. The melodic strains of stringed instruments, perhaps lyres and harps, provided a soft, ambient backdrop. The sounds were not overwhelming, but rather served to enhance the sense of occasion, creating a mood of solemnity mixed with joyful celebration. Periodically, the sound of a trumpet fanfare would cut through the air, announcing the arrival of a particularly distinguished guest or signaling a shift in the proceedings. These blasts were powerful and resonant, echoing off the stone walls and momentarily drawing the attention of every person present. It was a moment when the ancient traditions of Israel met the sophistication of Phoenicia, not in conflict, but in a deliberate act of union. Every element, from the rich fabrics and fragrant flowers to the carefully chosen music and the respectful assembly, was designed to underscore the importance of this marriage.

The air itself seemed to vibrate with the weight of expectation, the hopes of a kingdom, and the undeniable splendor of a royal wedding. The preparations for the wedding ceremony within the royal palace complex were a testament to the meticulous planning and vast resources mobilized for this significant occasion. The specific venue chosen for the core ritual was a large, central courtyard filled with rose bushes and running roses that covered the arbor, trellises, and ran wildly up the stone walls.

The ground of the courtyard was covered with a thick layer of fine, white sand. This traditional practice not only absorbed moisture but also provided a clean, pristine canvas upon which the ceremony would unfold. This sandy expanse was further softened by scattered rose petals and sprigs of myrtle, their delicate fragrance subtly perfuming the air. Along the perimeter of the courtyard, where the stately pillars of the palace's porticoes stood, stood rows of tall, slender cypress trees in large earthenware pots. These evergreen sentinels, with their dark, rich foliage, provided a natural, grounding element amidst the more elaborate decorations, their scent adding a balsamic note to the floral perfumes.

The decorations were a masterful blend of Israelite craftsmanship and Phoenician opulence. Crimson and gold were the dominant colors, reflecting the regal status of both kingdoms. Heavy bolts of dyed fabric, likely the prized Tyrian purple, were draped from the upper levels of the palace, creating a canopy that offered shade and framed the central space. These were interwoven with shimmering gold threads, catching the sunlight and casting a warm, golden glow over the entire courtyard. Woven tapestries depicting scenes from sacred texts and ancient legends of Israel, alongside motifs of maritime prowess and distant lands that spoke of Phoenicia's vast trading network, adorned the walls of the surrounding halls. These were not mere hangings but narrative artworks, each thread carefully placed to convey meaning and impress.

At the focal point of the courtyard, a raised platform, or dais, had been constructed. This was a simple yet elegant structure, its base perhaps of carved stone or a sturdy wooden frame covered in fine white linen. The platform itself was covered with a richly patterned rug, its complex geometric design hinting at skills honed in distant lands. Two ornate chairs, carved from dark, fragrant cedarwood and inlaid with ivory and semi-precious stones, awaited the king and his bride.

The sounds that permeated the courtyard were as carefully orchestrated as the visual elements. A chorus of musicians occupied a raised gallery overlooking the main space. They played a variety of instruments: lyres, whose resonant plucking provided a melodic backbone; harps, whose cascading notes added a touch of ethereal beauty; and flutes, whose clear, high tones lent a sense of joy and celebration. The music was not intrusive but rather formed a continuous, harmonious backdrop, swelling and softening as different parts of the ceremony unfolded. Interspersed with the music were the calls of heralds, their voices clear and strong as they announced the arrival of key figures or proclaimed blessings. The resonant sound of shofars, the ram's horn, would also have been employed, their piercing calls signifying moments of divine presence and solemnity.

The atmosphere was one of heightened anticipation, a palpable blend of reverence and exhilaration. The assembled guests, comprising not only the royal court but also dignitaries from allied cities and prominent religious leaders, were a testament to the significance of this union. Their attire was varied, reflecting their status and origins, but all had clearly made an effort to present themselves in their finest. The air hummed with hushed conversations, the rustle of fine fabrics, and the occasional excited whisper. The scent of exotic perfumes, mixed with the natural fragrances of the flowers and incense burning in strategically placed censers, created an olfactory tapestry that was both intoxicating and evocative.

The visual splendor was undeniable. Sunlight streamed through the openings in the palace's architecture, illuminating dust motes that danced in the air and highlighting the rich textures and vibrant colors of the decorations. The interplay of light and shadow across the adorned courtyard added depth and drama to the scene. The sheer effort and expense invested in transforming this space spoke volumes about the importance of the event, signifying not just a personal union but a strategic alliance. I am running a few minutes late; my previous meeting is running over.

At the heart of the solemnity stood King Ahab, the sovereign of Israel, a figure whose reign was already marked by significant developments and considerable challenges. His attire reflected his royal station, perhaps a more subdued, yet rich, linen garment, likely of fine weave, possibly adorned with subtle embroidery or a clasp of worked gold, signifying his dominion. Soon to join him was the Princess Jezebel, daughter of King Ethbaal I of Sidon.

Her arrival was the focal point of much of the anticipation, and her presence signaled the formalization of the pact between their nations. Her garments were a stark and dazzling contrast to the more earth-toned regalia of the ladies of the Israelite court. Jezebel's gown was made of Egyptian silks dyed Tyrian purple, accented with gold embroidery, and jewelry of exquisite craftsmanship—heavy gold bracelets, ornate necklaces, and earrings that caught the light with her movements. Making her look even more regal.

King Ethbaal, Jezebel's siblings, close family members, and cousins from Sidon were all present. Her father had provided passage on the royal ships to the family and his court officials who desired to attend this royal wedding of the millennia. The Israelite nobility was all present, including close advisors to King Ahab and his extended family from both parents' tribes, the chief ministers of the crown, and key officials who worked in the palace. Seats of honor were designated for all of them. These were the individuals who managed the day-to-day affairs of the kingdom, the architects of its policies, and the enforcers of its laws. Their attendance affirmed their loyalty to Ahab and their acceptance of this new political reality. Each one adorned in their finest apparel, reflecting their individual wealth and status, and their presence served to lend weight and solemnity to the occasion. They were the pillars of the Israelite state, and their visible participation reinforced the legitimacy of the union in the eyes of the populace and the wider region.

Also, from Phoenicia and other surrounding countries were the trade and maritime partners of King Ethbaal had been invited. They were present and sat in the seats directly behind the VIP reserved seating. These individuals all brought with them exquisite gifts for the royal couple. Their presence also brought a cosmopolitan flair, which shook the mindsets of the Israeli royals. Jezebel loved the rift their outfits made as the Israeli citizens gasped as they walked by to be seated. The religious hierarchy of Israel, from the Chief Priest to the Levites who worked in the temple, were all present with their spouses to be the "religious witnesses" of this foreign and non-customary union. It would also have played a crucial role. The High Priest's presence invoked the feeling that there was a divine sanction upon the union. The participation of all the priests transformed this political union into a divinely blessed covenant —a concept deeply ingrained in the Israelite worldview.

Beyond the immediate spheres of royal and religious authority, the ceremony was graced by the presence of distinguished guests from other realms, underscoring the event's broader geopolitical significance. While specific records might be scant, emissaries or representatives from allied or neighboring kingdoms would probably have been invited to witness this union. Such invitations served a dual purpose: to acknowledge the strengthened ties between Israel and Phoenicia formally, and to signal to other regional powers the shifting alliances and power dynamics in the region.

Furthermore, envoys from more distant kingdoms, perhaps even from Egypt or Mesopotamian powers, had arrived. The inclusion of such diverse and high-ranking individuals from across the region transformed the wedding ceremony into a significant diplomatic forum, a stage upon which regional power and influence were subtly but demonstrably displayed. Each foreign dignitary, in their distinct attire and bearing, added another layer of international recognition to the proceedings, elevating their status.

The public ceremony itself commenced with the formal procession of the bride to the groom. In both Israelite and broader ancient Near Eastern customs, the bride was often presented publicly, a significant moment where she was formally handed over from her father's household to that of her husband. Jezebel was escorted by her father, King Ethbaal, making her grand entrance. The path to the ceremonial site was lined with onlookers, eager to witness the union of their king with the foreign princess. The music accompanying her procession was a blend of Israelite and Phoenician traditions, creating a unique auditory landscape for the event.

Upon reaching the designated space, they exchanged covenants and blessings, the heart of any marriage rite. While the exact words are not preserved, we can infer the general structure. The groom would traditionally affirm his acceptance of the bride, and the bride, in turn, would pledge her fidelity. Since sacrifices were an integral part of the marriage ceremony, animals were sacrificed, and their blood, a potent symbol of life and covenant, was utilized according to Levitical Law. The

125

high priest oversaw these sacrifices, ensuring that they were performed according to religious law and that the divine favor was sought for the union.

The prayers and blessings offered during the ceremony were a critical component, a solemn invocation designed to secure divine sanction for the union and its future progeny. For Ahab, as the King of Israel, the primary invocation had been to Yahweh, the God of Israel. The Israelite understanding of marriage was deeply rooted in the covenantal relationship between Yahweh and His people. Therefore, the blessings sought Yahweh's affirmation of this union, a plea for His guidance and protection over the new royal household, and a petition for the continuation of the Davidic dynasty. Priests, led by the high priest, offered prayers that echoed the language of the Psalms and the Deuteronomic blessings, invoking Yahweh to "make you fruitful and multiply you, and fill the earth" (Genesis 28:3)–a blessing with direct relevance to the royal succession and the stability of the kingdom. They prayed for wisdom for Ahab and fertility for Jezebel, recognizing that a strong lineage was paramount for the longevity of the monarchy.

The ceremony incorporated blessings and invocations to Baal and other deities, either explicitly or implicitly, as a way of honoring Jezebel's heritage and acknowledging the multi-religious reality of the union. When these blessings were done, the Priest of Baal did not look at or point to an idol; instead, they pointed to the heavens as if they were talking to God with their blessings, but they were talking to Baal in their native tongue. The main point was to ensure the blessings were said, even if they had to be done undercover, so the Israelites would not recognize what was happening.

The theological implications of invoking different pantheons for the success and fertility of the royal union are profound and speak to the syncretic possibilities of the era. This did not necessarily imply a wholesale abandonment of Israelite faith, but rather a complex negotiation of religious identities. The blessings might have been carefully worded to avoid direct worship of foreign gods by Ahab or his officials.

Jezebel had insisted on the exchange of rings, a practice found in many cultures, which was carried out without most noticing.

While the Deuteronomic Law strictly prohibited the worship of other gods and the adoption of Canaanite religious practices, the reality of royal marriages often necessitated a degree of cultural and religious accommodation. King Solomon, Ahab's predecessor, famously married the daughters of foreign kings. For Ahab, marrying Jezebel, a princess of considerable standing and the daughter of a king, involved acknowledging and respecting her religious heritage. The blessings and prayers had been a crucial arena for this negotiation. Ahab allowed the Phoenician prayers to be said in their native language, so that no one would know they were praying to Baal. At the same time, the ceremony was structured to allow prayers to Yahweh to be a central part of the ceremony, thereby appeasing the people.

The pronouncement of blessings was multifaceted, and the Israelite high priest invoked Yahweh's name, seeking His blessing for the royal couple. These blessings focused on concepts central to Israelite theology: faithfulness, progeny, prosperity, and the continuation of God's covenant. The wording was carefully chosen to affirm the legitimacy of the union within the Israelite religious framework, emphasizing that Yahweh was the ultimate source of authority and blessing.

The blending of these religious elements presents a nuanced picture. It was not necessarily a case of forced assimilation but rather a complex interplay of traditions. The ceremony was a public spectacle, and the inclusion of elements from both cultures was a statement of the union's breadth and the intention to create a cohesive, albeit diverse, royal household. This careful orchestration of religious observances ensured that the union was not merely a political contract but a sacred pact, sanctioned by the heavenly powers recognized by both peoples, thus laying a foundation for a shared future, even amidst inevitable cultural and religious tensions that would later emerge. The very act of blessing the union with prayers to differing divine entities, even if managed with care, foreshadowed the complex religious landscape that Jezebel would introduce into the Israelite court, a landscape that would become a defining feature of Ahab's reign.

The banquet itself was a breathtaking display of opulence. There were long tables richly adorned and groaning under the weight of a lavish spread. The culinary offerings reflected the bounty of both Israel and Phoenicia, a deliberate fusion of tastes and traditions. From the fertile valleys of Israel came succulent, roasted meats — lamb, beef, and fowl — prepared with fragrant herbs and spices.

The coastal regions of Phoenicia, renowned for their maritime prowess, contributed a diverse array of fresh seafood, including plump oysters, delicate fish, and several exotic delicacies, as well as fruits and vegetables ripened under the Mediterranean sun. There were freshly baked breads, some perhaps infused with honey or nuts, alongside fine wines, pressed from grapes grown in both Israelite vineyards and the renowned wine-producing regions of Phoenicia.

The halls where the banquet was held had been decorated with the finest tapestries, woven with intricate designs depicting scenes of historical importance, mythological figures, or symbols of royal authority. Banners hung in the halls with the emblems of the Israelite monarchy and the royal house of Tyre. Torches and oil lamps, their flames casting a warm, flickering glow, illuminated the space, creating an atmosphere of grandeur and festivity. The air was filled with the sounds of music and merriment. Musicians, skilled in both Israelite and Phoenician traditions, provided a rich soundscape. Lyres, harps, and flutes, common in Israelite ensembles, were joined by the resonant tones of Phoenician instruments (string and percussion).

The guest list was a testament to the alliance's reach and importance. Kings and dignitaries from neighboring kingdoms, recognizing the shifting political landscape, were present to pay their respects and solidify their own relationships with the newly strengthened union. High-ranking officials, military leaders, priests from various temples within Israel, and prominent members of the Israelite nobility formed the core of the Israelite attendees.

The toasts given by King Ahab and members of Jezebel's family were pronouncements to reaffirm the bonds of the alliance, the virtues of both royal houses, and express hopes for a long and prosperous future for the united kingdoms. Prayers for fertility, for the continuation of the royal lineage, and for peace and stability echoed the religious sentiments expressed earlier in the day.

King Ahab presented valuable gifts to Jezebel, symbolizing his affection and his commitment to her. Then, Jezebel's family bestowed generous presents upon Ahab and the Israelite court, cementing the diplomatic and familial ties.

The atmosphere of conviviality and shared celebration was crucial in fostering goodwill and solidifying the alliance. The sheer scale and extravagance of this feast sent a clear message to the people of Israel, to the subjects of Tyre, and to the surrounding nations: this union was a powerful one, built on mutual respect, shared prosperity, and divine favor. It was a public declaration that the two worlds, while distinct, were now intertwined, their destinies bound together.

The extended nature of these festivities allowed ample time for informal interactions and the building of personal relationships between key figures from both Israel and Phoenicia. Diplomats engaged in private discussions, solidifying the political and economic agreements underpinning the marriage. Members of the royal courts had opportunities to familiarize themselves with each other, fostering a sense of shared community. This period of celebration and interaction served as a vital bridge-building exercise, smoothing the path for the integration of Phoenician influence into the Israelite court and kingdom.

The celebrations extended beyond the primary banquet, encompassing several days of feasting, entertainment, and public ceremonies. Each day had a different focus, from athletic contests that showcased the strength and prowess of Israelite warriors to musical performances that celebrated the artistic achievements of both cultures. These extended festivities ensured that the message of unity and celebration permeated the kingdom, reaching a wide audience and fostering a sense of shared joy and optimism about the future.

The culmination of these grand festivities marked not just the end of a wedding celebration but the beginning of a new era. The elaborate feast, with its blend of opulence, entertainment, and diplomatic engagement, served as a powerful public endorsement of the marriage between King Ahab and Princess Jezebel. It was a vibrant tapestry woven from the threads of political strategy, cultural exchange. It shared joy, all orchestrated to symbolize the successful union of two worlds, setting the stage for the profound transformations that would soon unfold within the kingdom of Israel. The memory of this grand celebration was etched in the minds of all who witnessed it, a potent symbol of the perceived strength and prosperity that this new, interwoven destiny promised.

CHAPTER SIX:
The Shadow of Baal

Jezebel's devotion was not a mere outward show; it was a genuine desire to appease her husband's people and their God, too. It was a burning ember within her soul, ignited from birth in the sun-drenched lands of Phoenicia, where the crashing waves of the Mediterranean echoed the powerful pronouncements of the god Baal, who was Lord of Storms, and the rustling leaves of the sacred trees whispered the name of Asherah, the Great Mother.

Jezebel's faith was an intrinsic part of her being, as inseparable from her as her royal lineage or her sharp, discerning mind. To understand Jezebel was to understand the profound reverence she held for the deities of her homeland, a reverence that shaped every decision, every ambition, and every interaction within the burgeoning court of Samaria.

Her mornings often began not with the rising sun, but with a private audience with her gods. In a secluded chamber, adorned with rich tapestries depicting scenes of Phoenician maritime glory and lush fertility, she would perform her sacred rites. The air would be thick with the fragrant smoke of exotic incenses – frankincense from Arabia, myrrh from the southern coasts–mingling with the sweet scent of olive oil.

Jezebel would pour the oil with deliberate, graceful movements, her hands steady as she invoked Baal, asking for strength, for victory in battle, and for the prosperity of her kingdom, which she viewed as her personal charge, blessed and guided by his divine hand. Her prayers were not pleas from a subservient supplicant, but affirmations of a covenant, a dialogue between a chosen queen and her powerful patrons.

She saw Baal not merely as a god of storms, but as the embodiment of celestial power, the ultimate authority who governed the very cycles of nature upon which all life depended. His might was the might she aspired to for Israel, a kingdom that would command respect, a kingdom that would flourish under a decisive and divinely favored ruler.

She also held Asherah dear, too. It was not second place in her heart; these two gods were more like on the same level to her. To Jezebel, Asherah was the embodiment of life itself, the source of all creation, the nurturer of both the land and its people. She would often place carved ivory figurines, representing the Mother Goddess, in prominent positions within her private quarters, their serene faces a constant reminder of the generative power she invoked.

Jezebel's prayers to Asherah were for fertility, for abundance, for the continuation of her royal line, and for the well-being of the entire nation. She understood the deep connection between fertility and prosperity, recognizing that a kingdom's strength was rooted in its ability to sustain and grow. This maternal aspect of her faith resonated deeply within her, aligning with her own desire to build and foster growth, not just in the material realm, but also in the cultural and spiritual spheres.

All of these rituals were not performed in isolation. While the grand temples of Baal and Asherah in Phoenicia were magnificent edifices open to the public, Jezebel's personal devotion was a more intimate affair. This direct communion fueled her inner resolve. She sought out the blessings of her gods not through the intermediary of priests who might dilute or misinterpret their will, but through her own fervent prayers and offerings. She believed that as queen, she was a direct conduit for divine favor, and her piety was a crucial element in securing that favor for her people.

The anxieties that might plague any ruler were often assuaged by the certainty she derived from her communion with the divine. This certainty allowed her to face the challenges of governing with an unwavering conviction. To Jezebel, it was not about eliminating Yahweh and replacing him with Baal; it was about recognizing a full spectrum of gods, keeping them all happy so she could enjoy peace and blessings. She was not able to wrap her mind around the concept of one God--no matter how hard she tried!

As the high priest of the Jerusalem temple tried to explain to her many times, she could not agree with him. She would make sacrifices to Yahweh whenever she was told that she and Ahab needed to be present for political purposes. She felt that it would be good always to keep Yahweh happy, so he would not get angry and try to kill her, as she had heard that Yahweh had done to so many in the past. The incident nearest to them had been the killing of King Agag by the Prophet Samuel after Ahab's great-grandfather, Saul, had refused to kill him. She shuddered as she thought of that—how cruel to kill someone because they would not worship the same god!

Anyway, Jezebel was content keeping three gods happy. That was definitely less than the nine she sacrificed monthly in Sidon. What was Jezebel's most deceptive plan was the gradual introduction of her faith into the leadership of the palace, one at a time. Once she had the government officials, palace staff, and other dignitaries convinced that "tolerating" her extra idols would not hurt anything if she kept worshipping Yahweh, then she would roll out her real agenda!

If she played her cards right, they would never see her coming, and they would approve her construction plans long before they realized she would be building a house for Baal and one for Asherah right there in Jerusalem. If she could get it in the same area where the Temple for Yahweh was, then that was even better! Jezebel saw the Israelites' worship of Yahweh as a partial, perhaps even incomplete, understanding of the divine forces at play in the world. She aimed to enrich their spiritual lives, broaden their horizons, and bring them into alignment with the powerful deities who, in her experience, guaranteed success and abundance. She was a mastermind at framing her religious convictions in terms that would resonate with Ahab and his court.

She would walk in her quarters and rehearse the speech she would give to Ahab and the temple priest. They needed to understand that Baal's role was in bringing the life-giving rains, essential for Israel's agrarian economy. She would highlight Asherah's connection to fertility, a concept that was fundamental to any society, especially one reliant on the land. She presented these deities not as foreign intruders, but as powerful allies, capable of bestowing blessings that would benefit all of Israel.

Jezebel had learned from her mother, Athena (history does not give us a name for her, so I selected a common goddess name, considering most wealthy Sidonians were named after famous leaders or gods or goddesses), not to let her subjects know what she was doing ahead of time. A well-laid plan requires careful planning and practice to execute effectively. Athena had taught her daughter well. Athena was a master at initiating and controlling arguments.

Jezebel had learned so well from her mother that she often coached in pragmatic terms, emphasizing the tangible advantages of embracing her faith. "Why would we limit ourselves," she might ask Ahab, her voice laced with gentle persuasion, "when the gods of my people have the power to bestow such immense blessings? To honor Baal is to welcome the rains that fill our cisterns; to honor Asherah is to ensure that our fields yield a bountiful harvest. Is this not wisdom, my love, to embrace all the divine favor that is offered to us?"

It was evident to those closes to her that Jezebel was a beautiful, charismatic, well-educated young woman. She was sincere in her actions. She was a champion for women and education. She showed passion in everything she did—especially in worshipping her gods.

Whenever the conversation shifted to religion or cultural customs, Jezebel's eyes would glow with an inner light, and her voice would deepen with conviction. She never for one second doubted her faith or the power of her gods. She never considered for a moment that her gods were dead, as the Israelites claimed. Her gods were alive, and they responded to her frequently. This sincerity and passion made her a potent force, capable of swaying even the most entrenched skeptics.

Ahab, who was himself predisposed to seeking the most effective means to strengthen his kingdom, found himself increasingly persuaded by her arguments. He saw the tangible benefits that flowed from her patronage of Phoenician arts and crafts, as well as the increased trade and cultural exchange that enriched his court. It was a natural leap, in his mind, to extend this embracing of Phoenician influence to the realm of religion, especially when it was presented as a pathway to greater prosperity and divine favor.

The depth of her personal prayer life also served as a bedrock of her resilience. In moments of crisis or when facing opposition, it was to her gods that she turned for strength and guidance. She would spend hours in prayer and meditation, seeking to understand the divine will and to draw upon the power that sustained her. This inner fortitude, cultivated through her unwavering devotion, enabled her to navigate the often-treacherous currents of court politics and withstand the inevitable criticisms leveled against her. She possessed a spiritual resilience that few could match, a deep-seated belief in the righteousness of her cause that shielded her from doubt and despair. She desired to teach the children of Israel about how to be resilient. Furthermore, her devotion extended to a personal commitment to uphold the sacredness of her gods. She would not tolerate any disrespect or neglect towards Baal or Asherah. When she observed any perceived deviation from the proper forms of worship or any instance where the honor of her gods might be diminished, she would act decisively.

This protective instinct was a testament to the intensity of her faith. She saw herself as a guardian, a protector of the divine presence within her kingdom, and she was prepared to defend that presence with all the authority and influence at her disposal. This unwavering commitment was, in many ways, the very core of her character, the driving force behind her ambitious vision for Israel and her willingness to challenge established norms.

Jezebel's approach was not one of outright conquest, but of a carefully cultivated influence, a gradual immersion that would make the foreign feel familiar, then indispensable. Her first act, a testament to her deeply held beliefs and her conviction in the divine mandate of her marriage, was the construction of a magnificent temple dedicated to Baal. This was no clandestine ritual performed in secret; it was a public declaration, a statement of intent that would be seen and felt throughout Samaria. Jezebel decided that the site she would choose for the Temple to Baal had to be a strategic one. This temple must be the one building that commanded you to look at it as soon as you arrived in town. It was going to be a Phoenician-style building with Greek engravings and columns carved with stylized bulls and celestial symbols, that would rise towards the heavens. The interior was to be a sanctuary of awe, adorned with rich cedarwood brought from the cedars of Lebanon; the very trees whispered to be blessed by Baal himself. Incense, fragrant and exotic, was to fill the air, a stark contrast to the more austere scents that had previously graced Israelite worship. There would be a need for everything glamorous. She wanted all accents in gold. Real gold! A gift that she would give to Israel!

She emphasized how his favor could ensure bountiful harvests, replenishing the granaries and banishing the specter of famine that had historically plagued the region. Her arguments were framed in pragmatic terms, appealing to the tangible needs and aspirations of the people. "Why would we confine ourselves," she might inquire, her voice a silken blend of logic and entreaty, "to a single source of divine power when the very forces that govern our world are so readily accessible? To welcome Baal is to welcome the sky's bounty, to ensure that our land thrives and our people are well-fed. Is this not the wisdom of a strong ruler, to seek the favor of all potent deities who can strengthen our kingdom?"

The construction of the temple was accompanied by the establishment of a dedicated priesthood, drawn from Phoenicia and those within Israel who were willing to adopt the new ways. These priests were not merely to conduct rituals; they were to be the conduits of Baal's power, their pronouncements and ceremonies designed to instill awe and reverence. Jezebel oversaw the selection and training of these priests and temple staff with meticulous care. She wanted the Baal worship to be performed perfectly. She designed elaborate vestments, rich in embroidery and symbolic imagery, to make the elegance of their rituals a spectacle of divine and royal power.

Simultaneously, Jezebel began to cultivate the worship of Asherah, the Great Mother, whose presence was intrinsically linked to Baal's power in Phoenician theology. While a grand temple for Baal was an explicit declaration, the integration of Asherah was often more subtle, appearing in the form of sacred groves and idols placed in prominent positions. These groves, often established on hilltops or near water sources, became places of communal worship, where the fertility of the land and the continuity of life were celebrated. Carved images of Asherah, often depicting a mother goddess nurturing her children or a stately figure adorned with symbols of abundance, were discreetly placed within the palace and in public spaces. Jezebel's personal devotion to Asherah, a practice she had maintained since her youth, now served as a model for her court. She would often be seen in these sacred spaces, her hands raised in prayer, her countenance serene as she invoked the generative powers of the Mother Goddess.

The introduction of these practices was met with a spectrum of reactions. Jezebel continued to add priests that she brought in, providing them with housing and food from the King's table daily, until the number reached 400 for just Baal. Some people accepted the introduction of Baal worship as an expansion of their spiritual, cultural, and financial horizons. While others were suspicious and dismayed that she was turning the majority of the nation away from worshipping Yahweh.

The prophets, in particular, emerged as the most vocal critics. They saw the erection of Baal's temple and the proliferation of Asherah's symbols as a direct affront to the God of Israel, a dangerous deviation from the established path. They preached with fiery conviction, denouncing the new cults as idolatry, a betrayal of the sacred covenant that had guided their ancestors. Their sermons, delivered in marketplaces and public gatherings, were a stark warning, a call to resist the encroaching tide of foreign worship. These prophets saw the appeasement of Baal as a direct challenge to Yahweh's sole dominion, a capitulation to forces that would ultimately lead Israel astray.

Jezebel, however, was not deterred by this opposition. She possessed a keen understanding of political maneuvering and the art of persuasion. She was adept at navigating the complex dynamics of the court, leveraging her influence over Ahab to secure the resources and the authority needed to advance her religious agenda. She understood that outright confrontation with the prophets would likely prove counterproductive, solidifying their opposition and alienating a significant portion of the populace. Instead, her strategy was one of gradual assimilation, subtly weaving the worship of her gods into the existing societal structures.

The royal court itself became a microcosm of this religious transformation. Banquets and feasts, once perhaps focused on traditional Israelite observances, now incorporated elements of Phoenician ritual and symbolism. Music and dance, inspired by the vibrant traditions of her homeland, were introduced, their captivating rhythms and visual splendor serving to normalize and popularize foreign cultural practices, including their religious undertones.

Jezebel ensured that her own children were raised in the familiarity of Phoenician worship, their early years steeped in the prayers and rituals that were integral to her own identity. As Jezebel's gods began to bless her with children, she gained even more control over Ahab. Jezebel and Ahab had three children who succeeded to the throne after Ahab's death. Ahab was king for 22 years. During his reign, his male descendants numbered 70. So, it appeared to the Israelites that Baal was answering Ahab and Jezebel's request. This helped to turn some to idol worship.

The commissioning of Asherah poles, tall wooden pillars often erected in sacred precincts and associated with the goddess's worship, was another visible manifestation of her influence. These poles, carved and sometimes adorned with intricate designs, stood as markers of her devotion and as symbols of fertility and divine presence. While some saw them as merely decorative elements or cultural curiosities, to those who understood their significance, they represented a potent infusion of foreign religious practices into the heart of Israel. The groves associated with Asherah, often established on high places, were also encouraged, drawing upon an existing Israelite tradition of worship at elevated sites, thereby making the new association feel less alien and more like an enhancement of an established practice.

Jezebel's personal piety was a potent tool in her arsenal. Her evident sincerity, her unwavering devotion, and the palpable sense of peace and strength she drew from her communion with Baal and Asherah were undeniable. She did not merely decree; she embodied her faith. When she spoke of her gods, her eyes would gleam with an inner fire, her voice resonating with a conviction that could sway even the most hesitant observer. She would share stories of Baal's victories and Asherah's boundless generosity, weaving a narrative of divine favor and power that was deeply compelling. This charisma, coupled with the visible prosperity that seemed to follow her patronage of Phoenician arts and trade, created an aura of success that many were eager to associate with.

The gradual introduction of Phoenician religious elements was thus a multifaceted strategy, encompassing grand architectural projects, subtle cultural integration, and the potent force of personal example. Jezebel was not simply a foreign queen imposing her will; she was a devout believer, convinced of the righteousness and efficacy of her faith, and determined to share its blessings with her adopted kingdom. Her aim was not necessarily to eradicate Yahwism, but to elevate and expand the spiritual landscape of Israel, to bring it into alignment with what she perceived as the broader, more potent forces that governed the cosmos. The stage was set, and Samaria, whether willingly or by degrees, was beginning to feel the profound and transformative shadow of Baal.

The decree, once whispered in the gilded chambers of the royal palace, had now taken on the weight of law, echoing through the bustling streets of Samaria. Ahab, the King of Israel, had acceded to the heart's deepest desires of his Phoenician queen. The magnificent temple to Baal, with its towering pillars and cedarwood imported from Lebanon, was no longer a mere figment of Jezebel's fervent imagination; it was a burgeoning reality, a testament to her unyielding devotion and her queenly prerogative. Beside it, a house for Asherah, the mother goddess, began to take shape, her presence to be honored with sacred groves and carved idols. The air in Samaria, once thick with the scent of olive oil and burning incense of Yahweh, was slowly becoming perfumed with the exotic fragrances of Phoenician ritual, a subtle yet pervasive shift that spoke volumes about the shifting allegiances within the heart of Israel's leadership.

Ahab's compliance was not a grudging concession, nor was it a calculated political maneuver devoid of personal sentiment. It was, in large part, a profound expression of his infatuation with Jezebel. She was a force of nature, a vibrant supernova against the somber backdrop of Israelite royalty. Her laughter, like the chiming of distant temple bells, could dispel the shadows that often gathered in Ahab's own soul. Her eyes, dark and luminous as the Phoenician night sky, held a depth of passion that drew him in, a captivating allure that eclipsed the counsel of his more staid advisors. He saw in her not just a wife, but a reflection of a world he had only glimpsed from afar – a world of opulence, of vibrant artistry, and of potent, unashamed divine power. To deny her these requests, to stifle the very essence of her being, would be akin to dimming her light, a prospect Ahab found utterly unbearable.

Their union had been a political necessity, but necessity had swiftly blossomed into a love that was as consuming as it was unexpected. Ahab, a man of quiet contemplation and a certain weariness that stemmed from the burdens of his crown. Jezebel challenged him, not with defiance, but with an unwavering confidence that bordered on the divine. Her conviction in the power of Baal and Asherah was not simply a matter of faith; it was a living, breathing testament to a strength he admired. When she spoke of Baal's dominion over the life-giving rains, her voice carried the resonance of thunder, and when she invoked Asherah's blessings, a maternal warmth emanated from her, a profound sense of nurturing that Ahab, as a king responsible for his people's well-being, found deeply resonant.

He saw her religious initiatives as an extension of her very being, an integral part of the woman he adored. To support her temples was to support her; to sanction her gods was to acknowledge and validate the core of her identity. He was, in essence, making a profound declaration of his love, a public affirmation of his commitment to her, and by extension, to the world from which she hailed. The construction of the Baal temple, with its opulent design and the elaborate rituals that would accompany it, was, in his eyes, a fitting tribute to the queen who had brought such brilliance into his life. It was a way of honoring her heritage, of welcoming her into the heart of Israel, not as an outsider to be assimilated, but as a cherished part of it. Still, as a queen to be celebrated, her divine lineage is recognized and respected.

Ahab was not entirely immune to the pragmatic appeals that Jezebel so skillfully employed. Her arguments, woven with the threads of prosperity and divine favor, held a certain persuasive power, especially for a king constantly seeking to secure his kingdom's welfare. She presented Baal not as a rival to Yahweh, but as a potent ally, a celestial force whose favor could ensure bountiful harvests and protect Israel. Ahab, ruling a land dependent on agriculture, could not ignore the allure of such divine guarantees. The historical memory of famines and droughts had haunted every ruler of Israel, and the promise of Baal's life-sustaining rains, as articulated by Jezebel with such compelling eloquence, offered a solution—abundance and security.

He saw the Phoenician influence as a force for progress, a means of enhancing Israel's standing on the international stage. The trade routes that opened with Phoenicia, the influx of skilled artisans, and the cultural exchange that Jezebel fostered were undeniable benefits to the kingdom. To embrace her religious practices was, in his mind, to fully embrace the multifaceted benefits of his alliance with her. It was a package deal: the queen, her culture, her gods, and the ensuing prosperity. He believed that by integrating these elements, he was not only fulfilling his marital obligations but also ushering in an era of unprecedented growth and stability for Israel. He envisioned a kingdom that was both strong in its ancient traditions and open to the influences that could elevate it, a synthesis of the old and the new, guided by his love for his queen.

This willingness to diverge from the established religious norms of Israel, however, was a perilous path to take. The prophets of Yahweh, those stern custodians of the covenant, viewed Ahab's actions not as an act of love or political wisdom, but as a grave betrayal. They saw the grand temple of Baal rising in Samaria, the fragrant incense mingling with the sacred smoke of Yahweh's altar, and the worship of Asherah being woven into the fabric of courtly life as an abomination. Their denunciations, once confined to the hushed whispers of dissent, began to escalate, their voices rising in a chorus of righteous anger. They saw Ahab's infatuation with Jezebel as a blinding force, one that was leading him and, by extension, all of Israel, into spiritual ruin.

The prophets understood that Ahab's compliance was deeply rooted in his personal feelings. They saw how his gaze lingered on Jezebel, how his decisions often deferred to her desires, and how his love for her seemed to eclipse his devotion to the God of his fathers. This, to them, was not mere weakness; it was a fundamental failure of leadership, a capitulation to foreign influence that threatened the very identity of Israel. They preached of the covenant Yahweh and of the dire consequences that awaited those who turned to other gods. Their sermons became increasingly impassioned, filled with apocalyptic pronouncements and stark warnings of divine retribution. They would stand in the marketplaces, their faces etched with grim determination, their voices thundering against the king and his queen, proclaiming that the favor of Baal was a fleeting illusion leading Israel to destruction.

Ahab, though often shielded from the harshest of these pronouncements by his courtiers, was not entirely ignorant of the growing opposition. He heard the murmurs, the disapproving glances, and the pointed silences that followed discussions of his queen's religious initiatives. Yet, the allure of Jezebel's presence, the solace he found in her unwavering affection, and the perceived benefits of her patronage outweighed the counsel of these dissenting voices.

He believed, perhaps naively, that he could maintain a balance, that Israel could incorporate the worship of Baal and Asherah without fundamentally abandoning its heritage. He underestimated the deep-seated conviction of the prophets and the unwavering loyalty of many Israelites to their ancestral God. He was walking a tightrope, his love for Jezebel his guiding hand, but the chasm of religious division was widening beneath him with every step. His compliance, born of adoration and a desire for a prosperous and unified kingdom, inadvertently sowed the seeds of a profound spiritual schism—a conflict that would soon engulf the nation.

The air in Samaria, once resonating with the solemn chants of Yahweh's faithful, now carried the scent of foreign spices and the echo of unfamiliar hymns. The temple dedicated to Baal was built of stone and cedar. It was built to try to "outshine" Solomon's Temple for Yahweh. Jezebel, in her radiant confidence, saw it as a triumph, a testament to her ability to weave her world into the fabric of Israel. Yet, for the prophets of Yahweh, it was a wound, a grievous betrayal that sent tremors of foreboding through their souls. They were the custodians of a covenant, the guardians of a singular truth, and the rise of Baal was an existential threat, a defilement of the sacred bond between Yahweh and His chosen people. Among those prophets was a fearless prophet of Yahweh who had a very unusual anointing on his life!

Elijah, The Fearless Prophet:

Elijah was a towering figure. He was from Tishbe, and he emerged from the rugged hills of Gilead. He was a man whose life was as untamed as the wilderness from which he hailed. Clad in a rough mantle of animal hide, his beard unkempt and his eyes burning with a fierce, unyielding light. Elijah was a stark contrast to the perfumed opulence of Ahab's court. His was a voice that had been silenced by the pervasive influence of Jezebel's pagan fervor, a voice that now felt compelled to rise against the tide of idolatry. He had witnessed the subtle creep of Baal worship, the insidious normalization of foreign gods, and the casual disregard for the laws of Yahweh that had once been the bedrock of Israelite society. He saw Ahab, his king, not as a devoted husband, but as a man ensnared by infatuation, a king who had traded the divine favor of the Most High for the fleeting affections of a foreign queen and the promise of earthly prosperity.

Elijah felt the weight of Yahweh's word upon him, a burning coal in his chest, urging him to speak, to condemn, to remind Israel of their covenant. He knew the dangers, the likely repercussions for openly challenging the king and queen, but the alternative – to remain silent as his people strayed from their spiritual path – was an even greater torment. He saw the seeds of destruction being sown by Jezebel's hands, a harvest of divine wrath that would inevitably fall upon the land. His foreboding was not born of a desire for conflict, but of a profound understanding of the consequences of infidelity to Yahweh. He had seen the prosperity and blessings that came with obedience and righteous living, and he had also witnessed the devastating consequences that followed disobedience.

He began to preach in the hidden places, in the scattered villages and remote pastures, where ancient traditions still held sway. His words were a firestorm, igniting the embers of faith in those who had remained steadfast. He spoke of Baal, not as a benevolent deity, but as a false god, a hollow idol that offered only illusion. He recounted the stories of Yahweh's power, of His deliverance of Israel from Egypt, of His provision in the wilderness, and of His unwavering faithfulness. He painted a stark picture of the future, a future shrouded in drought and famine, a direct consequence of turning away from the God who had made the heavens and the earth. His pronouncements were not mere prophecies; they were pronouncements of cause and effect, rooted in the unalterable laws of the spiritual realm.

Elijah prophecies famine and trouble for Israel:

"The heavens will be shut," he declared to a small gathering of farmers whose faces, weathered by the sun and etched with worry, reflected the precariousness of their existence. "No rain will fall upon this land, not a single drop, until I speak the word, for Yahweh is angered by this turning away, by this embrace of the barren idols of the Phoenicians. Baal promises life, but he is a god of the storm, a capricious force that offers destruction as readily as sustenance. Our true sustenance comes from the God who commanded the waters to part, who brought forth streams from solid rock." His voice, resonant and powerful, carried the conviction of a man who had communed directly with the divine. He saw the anxious glances exchanged between the farmers, the flicker of fear in their eyes, and he knew that his words, though harsh, were planting themselves in fertile ground.

Other prophets, though perhaps less flamboyant than Elijah, shared his grave concerns. Men like Micaiah, son of Imlah, though often confined to the king's dungeons for his unwavering dissent, continued to speak truth to power when given the slightest opportunity. His prophecies were often veiled in riddles and allegories, a testament to his shrewdness in navigating the treacherous currents of court politics. Still, their underlying message was clear: the path Ahab was treading led to ruin. He, too, foresaw a devastating conflict, a divine judgment that would not spare the king or his kingdom if they persisted in their defiance.

There were also the quiet voices, the women of faith who gathered in secret, praying for the repentance of their king and the restoration of Yahweh's favor. They wove prayers into their daily tasks, their whispered supplications rising like the smoke from hidden hearths. They remembered the blessings of the past, the times when Yahweh had intervened so powerfully on behalf of Israel, and they clung to the hope that such intervention was not yet beyond reach. They saw Jezebel's influence as a pervasive sickness, a spiritual plague that was weakening the very core of their nation. Their foreboding was a constant companion, a somber undercurrent to their lives, as they watched the outward manifestations of Baal worship become more brazen and the adherence to Yahweh's laws grow increasingly rare.

The prophets understood that Ahab's devotion to Jezebel was the linchpin of this spiritual apostasy. They saw her as the architect of this religious subversion, a queen who wielded her influence with a strategic brilliance that was both terrifying and effective. Her Phoenician heritage, rather than being a source of enrichment, was, in their eyes, a Trojan horse, carrying with it the seeds of paganism that would ultimately overwhelm Israel's monotheistic faith. They spoke of the covenant as a sacred trust, a solemn vow that could not be broken without dire consequences. They saw Jezebel's efforts to establish the worship of Baal and Asherah not as a matter of personal preference, but as a direct violation of the very foundation of Israel's identity.

Their forebodings were often delivered with a palpable sense of urgency. They understood that the spiritual health of the nation was inextricably linked to its obedience to Yahweh. When a nation turned to false gods, it invited not only divine displeasure but also social and political instability. They saw the inherent danger in the syncretism that Jezebel seemed to promote, the blurring of lines between Yahweh and Baal, as well as between the sacred and the profane. They knew that such a compromise would inevitably lead to a dilution of faith, a weakening of moral fiber, and ultimately, a vulnerability to the spiritual and physical enemies that threatened Israel.

Elijah, in particular, felt the profound sorrow of a shepherd watching his flock stray towards a precipice. He had been raised in the tradition of the prophets, men who had spoken out against kings and princes, who had borne witness to Yahweh's judgment and mercy. He felt the weight of their legacy, the imperative to carry on their work in a time of unprecedented spiritual peril. He knew that his pronouncements would be met with resistance, with ridicule, and perhaps even with violence. The fact that Yahweh's honor was at stake and Israel's existence was being threatened propelled him forward.

He recalled the prophecies of old, the warnings that had been issued when Israel had wavered in its devotion to God. He saw the parallels, the echoes of past transgressions in the current actions of Ahab and Jezebel. The worship of foreign gods had always been a source of contention, a recurring theme of disobedience that had led to periods of hardship and exile. Elijah understood that the scale of Jezebel's ambition, her determination to not only introduce but also actively promote Baal worship throughout the land, was of a magnitude not seen before. This was not a matter of a few individuals straying; this was a royal decree, a state-sponsored attempt to supplant the worship of Yahweh.

His foreboding was a heavy cloak, but beneath it burned the unquenchable fire of faith. He knew that Yahweh was a jealous God, a God who would not share His glory with another. He understood that the covenant was absolute, demanding undivided loyalty. Jezebel's lavish temples and elaborate rituals were an insult to Yahweh, a public declaration that His power was insufficient, His worship outdated. Elijah saw the seductive allure of Baal, the promise of immediate material blessings, as a dangerous deception. He knew that true prosperity, true security, came only from obedience to Yahweh, the God who sustained them through all circumstances, not just when the rains came.

As the construction of the Baal temple neared completion and the worship of Asherah began to permeate the royal court, the prophets' pronouncements grew more urgent and dire. They saw the Israelites swayed by the king's example and the queen's persuasive influence, beginning to falter. This subtle spiritual shift was becoming an upheaval, and the prophets felt the ground tremble beneath their feet. They knew that a confrontation was inevitable, a clash between the unwavering fidelity of Yahweh's servants and the seductive power of a queen who sought to reshape a kingdom in the image of her gods was at hand. They knew the prophecies and that Yahweh would not tolerate Israel worshipping other gods. This was going to be the test to see who had the most power— the Queen or the Prophets!

The polished cedar of the queen's inner chambers did little to soften the sharp edges of her resolve. Jezebel, her silken robes rustling with an almost predatory grace, surveyed the small collection of scrolls laid out before her. They were not sacred texts of Israel, nor decrees from her husband, Ahab, but rather meticulously compiled lists, each name a person who dared speak against Baal or preach against idolatry. Her eyes, dark and luminous like polished obsidian, scanned the parchments, each stroke of her finely manicured finger a punctuation mark on a sentence of condemnation for these righteous men of God—the God they chose, not Baal.

The initial resistance had been predictable. The prophets, those men cloaked in prophecy and righteousness, had voiced their displeasure, their warnings echoing through the marketplaces and private gatherings. They spoke of covenant, of divine jealousy, of wrath to come. Jezebel listened, but their words were like pebbles cast against a fortress wall; they made noise, but they did not breach her defenses. Her faith was not a fragile thing, easily shaken; it was the bedrock of her identity, the very essence of her strength.

What she had not anticipated, however, was the subtle but persistent nature of their opposition. She saw their unwavering adherence to Yahweh as a stubborn refusal to embrace the broader, more vibrant tapestry of gods that illuminated her own world. Baal, the mighty storm god, the life-giver, the sustainer of fertility – he deserved a place of honor in this fertile land. And she would ensure he received it. public pronouncements; it was a quiet withdrawal of support, a refusal to acknowledge the growing influence of Baal in the royal court. Priests who had previously offered their counsel to Ahab now found themselves sidelined, their positions of influence diminished, replaced by those more amenable to the queen's vision. The kingdom, accustomed to a certain deference towards its rulers, began to feel the subtle pressure of exclusion. Those who aligned themselves with the queen found favor, while those who clung to the old ways found doors quietly closing.

This passive resistance began to grate on Jezebel. Her love for Baal was a consuming passion, a divine fire that burned within her. And her love for Ahab was no less fierce, a protective instinct that saw any slight against her gods as an insult to her king, and by extension, to herself. When the prophets continued their murmurings, veiled condemnations, and their difference of opinion, it was an act of rebellion to her. It was a challenge to the authority she wielded.

She recalled a recent encounter, a meeting with a group of elders from one of the northern tribes. They had come to Samaria, ostensibly to pay homage to their king, but their words, though polite, carried an undercurrent of disapproval. They spoke of the importance of honoring Yahweh, of the dangers of embracing foreign deities. One elder, a man with a beard as white as snow and eyes that held the wisdom of seasons, had even dared to suggest that the prosperity of the land was directly tied to its faithfulness to the covenant.

Jezebel had listened, her expression serene, her hands clasped demurely in her lap. She had offered them wine, sweet and spiced, and spoken of the beauty of diversity, of how the gods of her homeland could bring new blessings to Israel. But beneath the veneer of gracious hospitality, a cold resolve had settled within her. These men, bound by their ancient ways, were a hindrance to progress. Their adherence to Yahweh was a stubborn root that needed to be severed for the new growth to flourish.

She had dismissed them with smiles and assurances of royal favor, but as soon as they had departed, her mood had shifted. She had summoned her most trusted attendants, women whose loyalty was as unquestioning as her own. The lists she now pored over were a result of their discreet inquiries, their careful observations of who spoke out, who whispered dissent, who refused to participate in the burgeoning festivals of Baal.

The first instance of her direct intervention had been subtle, almost deniable. A prominent scribe, known for his eloquent defenses of Yahweh's laws, had found himself reassigned to a remote administrative post, far from the centers of power and influence. His writings, once sought after, were now deemed "unsuitable for public dissemination." It was a quiet silencing, a subtle removal from the public discourse. Ahab, perhaps too preoccupied with state affairs or swayed by his queen's persuasive arguments, had readily agreed to the reassignment. To Jezebel, it was a necessary recalibration—a slight adjustment to ensure the smooth progression of her divine mission.

Then there was the matter of the Asherah poles. These sacred symbols, representing the goddess of fertility and motherhood, had always been a part of Phoenician worship. Jezebel was determined to see them erected throughout Israel, not just in private shrines but in public spaces, alongside the altars of Baal. When a contingent of priests from Bethel had voiced their strong objection, their outrage at what they considered a flagrant desecration of their sacred sites, Jezebel had acted swiftly.

She had not engaged in lengthy debates or attempted to reason with them. Instead, she had invoked the king's authority, though it was clear the initiative was her own. The priests were accused of inciting unrest, of undermining royal authority. Their lands were confiscated, their properties seized. They were branded as seditionists; their pious pronouncements reinterpreted as treasonous mutterings.

Some were banished from the kingdom altogether, their families left to fend for themselves. Others disappeared, their fates a grim testament to the queen's intolerance.

This was not the capricious cruelty of a madwoman; it was the calculated ruthlessness of a monarch who believed she was acting in accordance with a higher will. Jezebel saw herself as a shepherdess, guiding her flock towards the true pastures of divine favor. Those who strayed, who resisted her guidance, were not merely misguided; they were a danger to the entire flock. Their stubborn adherence to Yahweh was akin to a disease, a spiritual contagion that threatened to infect the kingdom.

She believed that her love for Ahab, her desire to create a harmonious union between her faith and his kingdom, was paramount. And if that meant removing obstacles and silencing the voices of opposition, then so be it. The prophets, she reasoned, were the primary instigators of this discord. They were the ones who fanned the flames of religious division, who poisoned the minds of the people against the benevolent deities she served.

She began to authorize more systematic removals. Prophets who preached against Baal were no longer merely reassigned; they were actively persecuted. Their teachings were declared heretical, their gatherings outlawed—those who were apprehended faced imprisonment, confiscation of their meager possessions, and public humiliation. The queen's agents, discreet but efficient, moved through the cities and villages, identifying those who still clung to the old ways. Then Jezebel began to hear rumors and whispers in the Palace about a man protecting the Prophet of Yahweh. Who dared protect the men she was trying to rid the country of—this meant war!

Obadiah:

There was a particular incident, recounted in hushed tones by those who had witnessed it, involving a prophet named Obadiah. Obadiah was a man of deep faith, but he also held a position of considerable responsibility within Ahab's household, serving as the overseer of the royal palace. He was a secret admirer of the prophets, a man who, despite his outward loyalty to the king, harbored a profound reverence for Yahweh. He had, in fact, taken it upon himself to hide a hundred of the prophets, providing them with food and shelter in caves, thus saving them from Jezebel's initial purges.

When Jezebel discovered Obadiah's clandestine activities, her reaction was immediate and severe. It was not enough that he had aided the dissenters; his very existence as someone who secretly upheld Yahweh's cause was an affront. Ahab, under Jezebel's relentless pressure, was compelled to act. Obadiah was stripped of his position, and his wealth was confiscated. He was publicly denounced, his reputation tarnished.

While Jezebel, in her thirst for vengeance, might have preferred a harsher punishment, even exile or death, the fact that he was a trusted servant of the king complicated matters. Thus, he was left in disgrace, a stark warning to any others who might harbor similar sympathies. This act, though it spared Obadiah's life, served as a chilling demonstration of Jezebel's reach and her willingness to dispense with even those who had served the crown faithfully if they stood in the way of her divine agenda.

Jezebel's actions were not random acts of cruelty. They were calculated moves, designed to instill fear and obedience. She understood that true power lay not only in decree but in the perception of absolute authority. By targeting the prophets, the spiritual leaders of Israel, she aimed to decapitate the opposition, to remove the voices that could rally the people against her. Her methods were subtle at first, designed to test the waters, to gauge the kingdom's tolerance for her innovations. But as the resistance persisted, her measures grew increasingly draconian.

She saw the construction of the great temple to Baal in Samaria as a monument to her triumph, a testament to her ability to reshape the spiritual landscape of Israel. And alongside it, she was establishing altars and sacred groves dedicated to Asherah, ensuring that her beloved goddess was honored with equal reverence. The queen's fervor was infectious, and many, swayed by her royal position, the lavishness of the pagan festivals, and the perceived favor of the gods of prosperity, began to embrace the new worship. The old ways, the worship of Yahweh, started to seem antiquated, even irrelevant to some.

But for those who remained faithful, the queen's actions were not a sign of divine favor but a terrifying descent into tyranny. They saw the erosion of their sacred traditions, the persecution of their spiritual leaders, and the growing influence of a foreign queen who seemed determined to extinguish the light of Yahweh from their land. The seeds of tyranny, sown in the fertile ground of royal favor and fueled by religious zealotry, were beginning to sprout, casting a long and ominous shadow over the kingdom of Israel. The whispers of discontent were being met not with reasoned discourse but with the iron fist of royal authority, wielded by a queen who believed she was fulfilling a sacred destiny.

CHAPTER SEVEN:
The Cost of Ambition

The jubilant celebrations, a dazzling display of opulence and diplomacy, served as a prelude to the profound and multifaceted integration of Jezebel into the heart of the Israelite kingdom. Her arrival as the newly crowned queen was not merely a personal transition but a pivotal moment that would irrevocably alter the social, religious, and political landscape of Israel. The transition from the grand festivities to the daily realities of royal life in Samaria presented Jezebel with a unique set of challenges and opportunities.

Jezebel's initial days and months in Samaria were a period of delicate adjustment. The immediate aftermath of the wedding feast saw her assuming her new role as queen consort. This was a position of immense influence, but one that was inherently defined by her relationship to King Ahab. Her primary responsibility, as perceived by many in the court and certainly by her own delegation, was to support the king and to contribute to the continuation of the royal lineage.

The practicalities of establishing her household within the royal palace had been a significant undertaking. Jezebel had her a retinue of Phoenician advisors, servants, and perhaps even religious functionaries, who formed her personal court within the larger Israelite royal administration. These individuals were crucial in helping her navigate the intricacies of Israelite court life, but they also represented a distinct

155

foreign element. The introduction of new customs, languages, and potentially even architectural or artistic preferences associated with her Phoenician entourage began to reshape the royal environment subtly. This was not a wholesale replacement of Israelite traditions but rather a gradual infusion of Phoenician elements. This process could be viewed with curiosity, acceptance, or even apprehension by the existing court officials and the broader population.

Her position as queen consort meant that she was now a central figure in royal decision-making, at least in an advisory capacity. King Ahab, by marrying Jezebel, had clearly sought to strengthen political and economic ties with Phoenicia. This alliance provided Israel with access to Phoenician maritime trade routes, advanced naval technology, and limited financial support. Jezebel, as the daughter of King Ethbaal of Sidon, was not just a bride; she was a political asset and an ambassador for Phoenician interests.

The immediate impact of Jezebel's presence on Israelite society was multifaceted. On one hand, the alliance symbolized a period of increased prosperity and international engagement for the kingdom. The influx of Phoenician goods, ideas, and personnel could have stimulated economic growth and introduced new forms of artistry and craftsmanship. This was a period where the horizons of the Israelite kingdom were visibly expanding, drawing upon the resources and expertise of a powerful Mediterranean civilization.

Jezebel's devotion and commitment to the Phoenician pantheon of gods presented a profound challenge to the religious fabric of Israel. Unlike previous foreign queens who might have assimilated or whose religious practices remained confined to their private quarters, Jezebel was a devout worshipper of Baal and Asherah. Her family, the royal house of Tyre, was intrinsically linked to these deities, and their worship was an integral part of Phoenician identity and royal legitimacy. Her intention, and likely her mission, was to establish and promote the worship of her gods within Israel. This prospect ran directly counter to the deeply ingrained monotheistic traditions of the Israelites, which centered on worshiping Yahweh.

The introduction of Baal worship was not a subtle or private affair. Jezebel, supported by King Ahab, actively promoted her religious practices. It involved the construction of temples or shrines dedicated to Baal and Asherah, the appointment of priests and prophets associated with these deities, and the integration of their festivals and rituals into the broader religious life of the kingdom. Many Israelites perceived such actions as a direct assault on their covenant with Yahweh and a betrayal of their ancestral faith. This religious tension became a defining characteristic of Ahab's reign, causing immediate repercussions within Israel.

The Israelite prophets, who served as custodians of the Yahwistic tradition, viewed Jezebel's religious policies with extreme alarm and condemnation. They saw her influence over Ahab as a corrupting force, leading the king and, by extension, the entire nation astray from the path of righteousness. These prophets became the most vocal critics of Jezebel and her religious agenda, often delivering pronouncements of divine judgment against the king and the nation for tolerating, and indeed actively participating in, the worship of foreign gods. The historical accounts, particularly in the book of Kings, portray a stark conflict between Jezebel's religious policies and the prophetic voice of Israel.

Jezebel's personal conduct and her approach to governance would also have contributed to her impact. While the biblical narrative often focuses on her religious activities, she was likely a woman of considerable intelligence and political will. Her actions were not born out of mere capriciousness but were informed by her upbringing in a powerful and sophisticated kingdom, where religious and political authority were closely intertwined. Her efforts to establish the worship of Baal and Asherah can be seen as an attempt to consolidate her influence, to provide a religious framework that supported her authority, and perhaps even to reshape Israelite society in line with Phoenician norms.

The initial establishment of Jezebel's presence in the Israelite court marked the beginning of a complex interplay of cultural exchange, political alliance, and religious contention. Her arrival as queen consort was not simply the addition of a royal wife; it was the introduction of a powerful foreign entity with distinct religious and cultural loyalties. While the alliance offered potential benefits in terms of trade and international standing, Jezebel's fervent promotion of Phoenician deities sowed seeds of deep religious conflict. This initial phase of her integration set the stage for the dramatic events that would unfold, significantly shaping the trajectory of Israelite history and its relationship with the divine. The queen from Tyre, with her strong will and unwavering faith in her own gods, was poised to leave an indelible mark on the kingdom of Israel, initiating a period of profound transformation that ultimately led to considerable upheaval. The delicate balance between embracing foreign influence for political and economic gain and preserving core religious and cultural identity was immediately tested, and the ramifications would resonate for generations to come.

The integration of Jezebel into the Israelite court was a dynamic process, characterized by the subtle and not-so-subtle ways in which her Phoenician heritage began to permeate the royal sphere and, by extension, the kingdom as a whole. Her personal retinue, comprising advisors, servants, and likely skilled artisans and scribes, played a crucial role in this process. These visual changes were not merely aesthetic; they were symbols of the queen's identity and the growing influence of Phoenician culture. The very act of adorning her new home with the art and crafts of her homeland was a statement of her status and commitment to her cultural roots.

Jezebel's role was not that of a passive consort. The historical narratives suggest a woman of strong will and considerable agency, who actively pursued her religious and political agenda. Ahab did not simply dictate her actions; she appears to have been a significant force in her own right, shaping the policies and religious direction of the kingdom. The biblical account, particularly the dramatic confrontations described in the book of Kings, highlights her assertive personality and her willingness to confront opposition.

The initial impact of Jezebel's establishment in the Israelite court can be summarized as a period of rapid and profound transformation. The alliance with Tyre, brokered through her marriage, opened Israel to new economic and cultural opportunities. This integration was accompanied by significant religious tension. Jezebel's unwavering commitment to and active promotion of Baal and Asherah worship directly challenged the core tenets of Israelite monotheism. This religious divergence, coupled with her assertive personality and political influence, created a deep societal cleavage. The stage was set for a prolonged struggle.

One of the most immediate and tangible impacts of this influx was seen in the realm of art and architecture. Phoenician craftsmanship was highly regarded throughout the ancient Near East, known for its exquisite detail, innovative techniques, and the use of precious materials. Jezebel's entourage probably included skilled artisans and craftsmen.

The Levites and Priests saw Jezebel's actions as a direct attempt to usurp Yahweh's rightful place as the sole deity of Israel and to lead the people into idolatry. Their fierce opposition, exemplified by the dramatic confrontations with Jezebel and King Ahab, highlights the intensity of the religious and ideological struggle. This spiritual conflict had significant social and political ramifications, undermining the kingdom's religious unity and fostering deep-seated animosity between opposing groups.

Elijah on Mount Carmel:

For the prophets of Yahweh, worshiping Baal was not just another religious option; it was a direct affront to Yahweh and a violation of the covenantal commandments that strictly forbade worshiping other gods. Figures like Elijah emerged as vocal and uncompromising critics of Jezebel's religious agenda. Elijah's dramatic confrontation with the prophets of Baal on Mount Carmel illustrated the depth of this religious chasm. The narrative presents a direct challenge to Baal's power, with Elijah invoking Yahweh to send fire from heaven to consume his sacrifice, a feat that the prophets of Baal, despite their fervent rituals, were unable to achieve. This event, as portrayed in the biblical text, was not merely a religious debate but a public trial by divine intervention, intended to expose the perceived impotence of Baal and to reassert Yahweh's supremacy. The subsequent execution of the Baal prophets following this event underscores the severity of the conflict and the stakes involved in this religious struggle.

The conflict extended beyond the dramatic pronouncements of prophets like Elijah. On one side stood those who actively promoted and participated in the worship of Baal and Asherah, aligned with the royal court and the perceived prosperity that their cults promised. On the other side were the steadfast adherents of Yahwism, who viewed the spread of Baalism as a spiritual contagion that threatened the very identity and survival of Israel. This division was not confined to theological discourse; it also permeated social and political life.

Those who remained loyal to Yahweh often faced persecution, ostracism, and even violence, as exemplified by the account of Obadiah. This type of persecution was the real danger faced by those who opposed Jezebel and Ahab. The allure of Baal's power and fertility appeared to offer a solution to the challenges of an agrarian society. Still, the prophets argued that true security and prosperity lay in unwavering fidelity to Yahweh, a fidelity that demanded the complete rejection of any foreign gods.

One of the most significant long-term impacts was the deepening of the chasm between those who embraced the Phoenician religious practices and those who remained staunchly devoted to Yahweh. Jezebel's zealous propagation of the cult of Baal, supported by royal decree and resources, created an unprecedented challenge to the worship of Yahweh. This schism was not merely a matter of differing theological viewpoints; it evolved into a deeply ingrained socio-political divide. Families were split, communities were polarized, and the very concept of national identity became contested ground. The religious and political struggles, nonetheless, highlight the profound and lasting impact of religious pluralism, as well as the imposition of a foreign cult.

This religious contestation had direct implications for the monarchy's legitimacy and its relationship with the populace. By actively promoting a foreign deity, Ahab, under Jezebel's influence, alienated a significant portion of his subjects who saw Yahweh as their unique covenant God. The prophetic voice, embodied by figures like Elijah, became increasingly vocal in its opposition, challenging not only the religious innovations but also the political decisions perceived as stemming from this foreign alliance. The dramatic confrontation on Mount Carmel, a pivotal event in the biblical narrative, symbolizes the intense struggle for the soul of Israel. While the immediate outcome may have seen a temporary resurgence of Yahwistic faith, the underlying tensions persisted. The monarchy, by aligning itself so closely with Phoenician religious practices, weakened its traditional claim to divine sanction derived from Yahweh. This created a precedent for future questioning of royal authority when it was perceived to be acting against the perceived will of God. The consequences of this religious alienation would manifest in later periods, contributing to instability and ultimately playing a role in the kingdom's eventual decline and division.

Furthermore, the economic integration that characterized the alliance with Phoenicia, while offering immediate benefits, also contributed to long-term social stratification and potential economic dependency. The increased wealth generated through expanded trade and access to international markets was not evenly distributed.

It is likely that the royal court, merchants, and those directly involved in the Phoenician-influenced economy benefited disproportionately. This could have exacerbated existing social inequalities or created new ones, leading to resentment among those left behind. The biblical texts, though often focusing on religious matters, also contain implicit criticisms of economic injustice and the exploitation of the poor, issues that may have been amplified in an era of increased commercialization and foreign economic influence. The adoption of Phoenician business practices and the influx of foreign capital could have introduced concepts of wealth accumulation and financial power that were at odds with earlier, more agrarian and communal-based Israelite societal norms.

The cultural exchange, beyond religion, also left an indelible mark. Phoenician artistic styles, architectural techniques, and administrative practices likely influenced the development of Israelite society. While this contributed to a more cosmopolitan and sophisticated material culture, it also represented a dilution of distinctively Israelite traditions. The biblical accounts are often silent on the finer points of these cultural exchanges. Still, the evidence of material culture, where available, can suggest the degree of Phoenician influence on craftsmanship, ivory carving, and architectural design. The long-term impact was a society that was increasingly exposed to and influenced by external cultural norms, potentially leading to a gradual erosion of unique Israelite customs and artistic expressions, even as new forms emerged.

The legacy of Phoenician influence, particularly as embodied by Jezebel, also shaped Israel's future theological and historical outlook. The prophetic condemnation of Baal worship and the associated practices became a foundational element of Israelite identity. The struggle against foreign cults and the unwavering commitment to Yahweh were re-emphasized and became central tenets of the Israelite faith. This period served as a stark warning, reinforcing the perceived dangers of syncretism and entanglements with foreign powers. The prophets of later generations would often invoke the memory of this era as a cautionary tale, drawing parallels between the transgressions of Ahab's court and the spiritual backsliding of their own contemporaries. The theological emphasis on divine jealousy and the exclusivity of Yahweh's worship was significantly strengthened by the perceived existential threat posed by Baalism.

Moreover, the history of this period, particularly the dramatic encounters between Elijah and the prophets of Baal, and the eventual purging of Phoenician religious elements, provided a powerful narrative of divine vindication and the triumph of Yahweh. This narrative became a cornerstone of Israelite self-understanding, shaping their historical consciousness and their understanding of their covenant relationship with God. The books of Kings, which record these events, played a crucial role in transmitting this interpretation, ensuring that the religious and political struggles of Ahab's reign were remembered as a pivotal turning point. The enduring impact of these accounts lies in their ability to shape how subsequent generations of Israelites understood their past, their identity, and their religious obligations.

The suppression of Yahwistic worship and the persecution of its prophets by Jezebel were unsuccessful in eradicating faith, even though it had a lasting impact on Israel because of the idolatry she pushed them toward. However, the resilience and unwavering commitment of figures like Elijah, Elisha, and Jehu during Ahab and Jezebel's 22-year reign demonstrated the power of Yahweh over man and any other gods. Resulting in the prophetic movement, forged as a result of this conflict, emerged stronger and more defined. Their role as a conscience of the nation was challenging idolatry and injustice.

The long-term consequences also extend to the political fragmentation of the Israelite kingdom. While the union with Phoenicia brought economic and diplomatic advantages, the internal religious divisions and the alienation of significant segments of the population may have contributed to underlying instability. The eventual Assyrian conquests and the fall of Samaria were the culmination of centuries of internal strife and external pressures. It is plausible that the religious and social divisions exacerbated by the Phoenician influence, including the polarization between pro-Yahwistic and pro-Baal factions, weakened the kingdom's ability to present a united front against external threats. The weakening of the traditional religious foundations of the monarchy might have also eroded its broader legitimacy in the eyes of both its own populace and neighboring powers.

In essence, the reign of Ahab and the influence of Jezebel marked a period of profound transformation for the Northern Kingdom of Israel. The legacy was not one of simple continuation but of radical reorientation, particularly in the religious sphere. The economic and diplomatic ties with Phoenicia provided a catalyst for this change, exposing Israel to new ideas, practices, and cultural influences.

The historical narrative that emerged from this era, heavily influenced by the prophetic tradition, cemented the perception of this period as a critical moment of religious crisis and a foundational chapter in the ongoing relationship between Yahweh and Israel.

Naboth's Vineyard

The king's gaze lingered on the verdant slopes of Naboth's vineyard, a patch of emerald against the parched earth outside Samaria's walls. It was a place of singular beauty, its rows of grapevines heavy with promise, its soil rich and deep, perfect for the cultivation of the finest wines. Ahab, a man whose desires often outstripped his restraint, found himself consumed by a sudden, fervent longing to possess it. The land, though fertile and ample, was no longer enough. He craved *this* specific parcel, this jewel in the landscape that seemed to beckon to him with its sheer loveliness. The adjacent royal property, already vast and meticulously tended, felt incomplete without it. He envisioned expanding his gardens to create an oasis of unparalleled luxury, a testament to his kingly authority and refined taste.

He approached Naboth, a simple man of the soil, a landowner whose family had perhaps cultivated these vines for generations, with an offer. It was a generous offer, he assured himself, a sum that would undoubtedly allow Naboth to acquire even greater tracts of land, perhaps even grander estates elsewhere. But Naboth, his roots as deep as his vines, refused. His response was not born of defiance, nor of greed, but of a profound connection to his inheritance. "The Lord forbid it me, that I should give of the inheritance of my fathers unto thee," he declared, his voice firm, his gaze steady. The law, the sacred laws passed down through generations, protected his ancestral lands, ensuring that patrimony remained within the family, a covenant between the living and the dead, and indeed, between man and his God. He could not, would not, violate this sacred trust, not for gold, not for royal favor, not even for the king himself.

Ahab returned to his palace, his heart a tempest of frustration and wounded pride. The simple refusal of a subject gnawed at him, a persistent irritant that festered into something far more corrosive. He slumped onto his divan, the rich fabrics doing little to soothe his agitated spirit. The vibrant colors of his surroundings seemed to mock his inner gloom. He recounted the encounter to Jezebel, his voice thick with petulance, painting Naboth as a stubborn, ungrateful subject who dared to defy his king's will. He displayed his discontent not with the stoic reserve befitting a monarch, but with the raw, unvarnished disappointment of a child denied a coveted toy. The king's desire, once expressed, had been met with an immovable object, and the resulting collision had left him feeling diminished, his authority questioned in the most personal way.

Jezebel listened, her expression carefully composed, her dark eyes fixed on her husband's face. She saw not the king's petty grievance, but an opportunity. Her devotion to Ahab was absolute, a consuming passion that saw his every wish as a command, his every desire as a sacred trust. If Ahab desired the vineyard, then the vineyard must be his. The obstacles that stood in his way were not to be endured, but to be removed. Naboth's refusal was not merely an inconvenience; it was an affront to Ahab, and therefore, an affront to her, and to the divine order she sought to establish. The ancient laws, the rights of individual citizens, these were secondary to the king's will, especially when that will was, in her eyes, a reflection of divine inclination. Her mind, sharp and incisive, began to weave a tapestry of deceit, a plan so cunning and so cruel that it would not only secure the vineyard for Ahab but also serve as a brutal lesson to any who dared to obstruct the royal prerogative.

She rose, her movements fluid and deliberate, her queenly robes rustling like dry leaves in a sudden gust of wind. She approached Ahab, her voice a low, soothing balm to his wounded ego. She understood him, perhaps better than he understood himself. She knew that his anger stemmed not just from the denial of the vineyard but from the perceived disrespect inherent in Naboth's stand. Her words were carefully chosen, designed to stoke his resentment and to offer a solution that appealed to his sense of power and his inherent, if often unacknowledged, inclination towards injustice when it served his purpose. She spoke of loyalty, of the king's right to command, and subtly, insidiously, of the weakness that such defiance would embolden in others.

"How long shall you remain in this troubled state?" she inquired, her voice laced with a honeyed concern that belied the calculating steel beneath. "Is not the king of Israel, and by extension, his queen, above the petty concerns of a common Israelite? Does the law truly bind the hand of the anointed king when his heart desires what is rightfully within his purview to command?" She paused, allowing her words to sink in, observing the flicker of hope in Ahab's weary eyes. Then, with a subtle shift in her tone, she presented her solution, a chillingly practical application of her unwavering belief in the absolute power of the monarchy. "Go to your rest, my lord. Eat bread. Let your heart be cheerful. I will give you the vineyard of Naboth the Jezreelite."

The sincerity in her declaration was terrifying. She did not frame it as a deception, but as a fulfillment of her duty as queen, as Ahab's devoted wife. She would, she promised, procure the vineyard for him. The method, however, was not a matter of negotiation or exchange, but of manipulation and legal subversion. She summoned scribes, men whose loyalty was to the crown, whose pens could be made to serve any purpose. She dictated letters, sealed with the king's own signet, a potent symbol of royal authority twisted to serve illicit ends. These letters were not addressed to Naboth, but to the elders and nobles of his city, men who held positions of civic responsibility and who, she assumed, would be beholden to the queen's command, or at least intimidated into compliance.

The content of these letters was a masterstroke of wickedness. They were framed as an official inquiry, a call to uphold the sanctity of law and order within the city. Naboth was accused, not of defying the king, but of the gravest possible offense against God and king: blasphemy. The charges were specific and damning, concocted from whispers and imagined slights. It was alleged that Naboth, in a fit of arrogance and contempt for royal authority, had uttered curses against God and the king, a crime punishable by death. The letters instructed the elders to convene, to hear the testimonies of false witnesses, and to condemn Naboth according to the law. The divine law, which Naboth had so staunchly defended when it came to his ancestral land, was now to be perverted and used as a weapon against him.

The speed with which her plan was enacted was breathtaking. The elders, faced with sealed royal decrees and the implicit threat of royal displeasure, dared not question the charges or the process. They gathered, their faces a mixture of unease and reluctant obedience. Witnesses, likely coached and bribed, were brought forth. They spoke with practiced conviction, weaving a tale of Naboth's supposed sacrilege, each word a carefully placed stone in the edifice of his false accusation. Naboth, caught completely unaware, was given no opportunity to defend himself. The process was swift, the verdict predetermined. He was found guilty of blasphemy, his sacred connection to his land rendered irrelevant in the face of manufactured divine wrath.

The sentence was immediate and brutal: death by stoning. The very stones that Naboth might have used to build and nurture his vineyard were now to be his executioners. He was dragged from his home, perhaps still clad in the simple garb of a working man, his face etched with bewilderment and a dawning horror. The townspeople, alerted by the official pronouncements, gathered to witness the grim spectacle. They saw their neighbor, a man known for his quiet piety and his devotion to his family, condemned for a crime none of them truly believed he had committed. Yet, fear kept their voices hushed, their protests unspoken. The power of the crown, amplified by Jezebel's cunning orchestration, had effectively silenced the community.

Jezebel received the news with grim satisfaction. The vineyard was now hers, or rather, Ahab's. She did not attend the execution; her presence was not required. Her will had been done; her objective had been achieved through the subtle manipulation of legal and social structures. The death of Naboth was merely a necessary consequence, an unfortunate but unavoidable step in securing what her husband desired. It was the ultimate demonstration of her power, a testament to her ability to bend even the most sacred laws to her will and to wield the machinery of justice as a tool for personal gratification.

Once Naboth was dead, his possessions, including the coveted vineyard, were declared forfeit to the crown. The elders, having fulfilled their role in the charade, were undoubtedly relieved that their part in the affair was over. Jezebel, with an almost casual air, dispatched messengers to retrieve the vineyard. The land, now cleansed of its original owner through a process of judicial murder, was presented to Ahab as a fait accompli. He entered the vineyard, its vines still heavy with fruit, its soil undisturbed by any agricultural labor of his own. He walked through the rows, touching the leaves, perhaps savoring the sweet air, a triumph of his will made manifest through his wife's ruthless efficiency.

The acquisition of Naboth's vineyard was not merely about acquiring a piece of land. It was a profound statement about the nature of power and justice under Ahab and Jezebel's reign. It revealed a chilling disregard for the lives and rights of ordinary citizens when those rights clashed with the desires of the monarchy. Jezebel, in particular, emerged from this incident as a figure of immense power and terrifying ruthlessness. She was not a queen who ruled by consensus or even by overt force, but by insidious manipulation and the perversion of law. Her love for Ahab was a dangerous force, capable of driving her to commit unspeakable acts in his name, acts that stained the very fabric of justice in Israel and foreshadowed the deeper societal and spiritual turmoil that her influence would bring. The sweet taste of the wine from Naboth's vineyard, when it was eventually pressed, would surely be mingled with the bitter tears of injustice and the blood of an innocent man, a stark reminder of the terrible cost of unbridled ambition and a queen's warped devotion. The kingdom, and indeed the very concept of divine justice, had been irrevocably compromised by this single, calculated act of villainy. Ahab, though he may have reveled in his new acquisition, was now complicit in a crime that would not go unnoticed, a crime that would eventually echo through the annals of Israel's history, a dark testament to the corruption that festered at the heart of his reign.

The silence that descended upon Samaria after Naboth's stoning was not one of peace, but of a chilling, enforced quietude. Jezebel, however, found no solace in it. Her victory, the acquisition of the vineyard, was a tangible testament to her will. Still, it was the lingering echo of Naboth's refusal, the very act of defiance that had necessitated his demise, that fueled her disquiet. It was a crack in the veneer of absolute authority she sought to cultivate, and cracks, she knew, were invitations for further dissent. She required not merely compliance, but a pervasive and unyielding respect born of fear and an understanding of her absolute and unassailable power. Her first move was to consolidate her influence over the judiciary, the very system she had so expertly twisted to her purpose.

The elders who had presided over Naboth's sham trial, their faces still pale with the memory of her decree, were summoned once more. This time, their audience was not one of accusation, but of reinforcement. She did not address them as supplicants, but as instruments of her will. "The King's justice," she began, her voice resonating with an authority that seemed to emanate from the very stones of the palace, "is the bedrock upon which this kingdom stands. It is the sacred trust placed upon us by the divine, a force that shapes the very order of our existence." She let the words hang in the air, a preamble to the true intent of her discourse. "There are those among us," she continued, her gaze sweeping across their anxious faces, "who misunderstand the nature of this justice. They mistake reverence for the past, for the ancestral laws, as a barrier to the needs of the present, to the directives of the throne."

She moved closer, her presence filling the chamber, a palpable force that seemed to dim the very sunlight filtering through the high windows. "Naboth," she stated, the name uttered not with malice, but with a chillingly detached finality, "was a man who clung to the old ways, who saw his own limited inheritance as more sacred than the needs of his sovereign. His refusal to relinquish his land was not merely a matter of property; it was a challenge to the very principle of royal prerogative; a subtle seed of sedition planted in the fertile ground of tradition." She paused, allowing the weight of her words to settle. "And for this transgression," she declared, her voice hardening, "he paid the price mandated by our laws. Laws which, I might add, you yourselves so ably interpreted."

The implication was clear. Their role in Naboth's condemnation, a role they likely felt shadowed by guilt and trepidation, was now to be framed as a testament to their loyalty and their understanding of true justice. She was not merely pardoning their complicity; she was validating it, albeit for her own purposes. "Therefore," she decreed, her voice regaining its smooth, persuasive cadence, "it is imperative that you, the custodians of our legal system, understand the gravity of your responsibilities. You are not to be bound by the petty interpretations of common men, nor swayed by the sentiments of the easily manipulated masses. Your duty is to the crown, to the King, and to the divinely ordained order that we, as his appointed judges, are tasked with upholding."

She unveiled a new decree, a carefully crafted document that would redefine the very nature of legal proceedings within Samaria. This was no mere pronouncement; it was a systematic dismantling of the checks and balances that, however imperfectly, had once existed. "From this day forward," she announced, holding the scroll aloft, its freshly inked script a stark contrast to the worn parchment of older laws, "any accusation of blasphemy against God or the King, when presented under the King's seal and supported by the testimony of witnesses deemed credible by the royal court, shall be considered absolute. The accused shall be brought forth; their guilt shall be presumed until proven otherwise by the evidence presented against them. There shall be no undue delay, no lengthy appeals, and certainly no questioning of the King's authority to initiate such proceedings."

The document was a masterpiece of legal sophistry, designed to grant the crown unfettered power to silence any opposition. It subtly shifted the burden of proof, transforming it from a guarantee of innocence into an almost impossible hurdle for the accused. The phrase "deemed credible by the royal court" was a particularly insidious addition, placing the ultimate authority of judgment squarely in the hands of those most likely to be beholden to Jezebel herself. The elders exchanged uneasy glances. They understood the subtext: their own continued standing, their very livelihoods, depended on their unwavering adherence to this new interpretation of justice.

"Furthermore," Jezebel continued, her eyes sharp and unwavering, "to ensure the integrity of our legal processes, I shall be establishing a special tribunal, composed of individuals whose loyalty is beyond question and whose understanding of the kingdom's needs is paramount. This tribunal will oversee all matters of significant import, ensuring that the King's will is executed with precision and without interference." She did not elaborate on who these individuals would be, but the implication was clear: they would be her loyalists, her confidantes, those who owed their positions and their very lives to her. The established courts, although not abolished, would find their authority severely diminished, relegated to handling minor civil disputes and trivial matters.

At the same time, anything that touched upon the crown's interests, or indeed, Jezebel's desires, would be routed through this new, highly centralized system.

The ramifications of this decree were immediate and profound. The vineyard, now officially and legally belonging to Ahab, was but the first, albeit brutal, demonstration of its potency. Jezebel did not rest on her laurels. The victory, the absolute control, was a heady wine, and she intended to drink deeply from it. She initiated further decrees, each one subtly eroding the nobility's independence and the people's autonomy. Lands that had been in families for generations were suddenly subject to review, their titles scrutinized under the harsh light of royal inquiry. Allegations of financial impropriety, often based on flimsy evidence or outright fabrications, became standard tools for dispossessing those who showed even a hint of independent thought.

One such case involved a wealthy merchant named Elam, whose family had long held a respected position in the merchant guilds. Elam had, on a previous occasion, expressed reservations about Ahab's increasingly lavish spending, hinting at the strain it placed on the kingdom's resources. He had done so in a private discussion, never in public, and certainly never with any intent to incite rebellion. Yet, Jezebel, ever vigilant, had her ears everywhere. A report, likely embellished by a rival merchant eager to seize Elam's assets, found its way to her. The accusation: Elam was hoarding grain, creating artificial shortages to profit from the people's desperation, and in doing so, undermining the kingdom's economic stability and the King's benevolence.

The decree against Elam was swift and devastating. He was summoned before the newly formed royal tribunal, the very body she had envisioned. The proceedings were a mockery of justice. The accusers, anonymous and protected by royal decree, presented their fabricated evidence. Elam, denied the right to confront his accusers, was given a perfunctory opportunity to defend himself, a defense that was met with disdain and outright dismissal. The tribunal, comprised of men whose careers depended on pleasing

Jezebel, found him guilty. His vast estates were confiscated, his wealth absorbed into the royal coffers, and he himself was cast into exile, a stark warning to any who dared to question the economic wisdom of the crown, or by extension, of Jezebel.

The pattern repeated itself across the kingdom. Lands adjacent to royal hunting grounds were declared strategically vital for the King's security and summarily seized, with nominal compensation offered only after protracted and ultimately fruitless legal battles. Families who had held ancient charters and traditional rights found themselves stripped of their privileges through arbitrary reinterpretations of long-standing laws. Jezebel's administration, efficient and ruthless, ensured that these seizures were not only legal but also swift and effective. The scribes worked overtime, drafting new regulations, amending old statutes, and issuing royal edicts that, while appearing to uphold the law, invariably served to expand royal power and consolidate Jezebel's personal authority.

Her control extended even to matters of religious observance. While Ahab, in his often-superficial way, paid lip service to the traditions of Israel, Jezebel's own devotion lay with the gods of her homeland, Baal and Asherah. She saw no conflict in this. The more gods there were, the more avenues of power and influence existed. She began to subtly, and then not so subtly, promote the worship of her own deities. Temples to Baal were erected, funded by the confiscated wealth of those who had opposed her. Priests of Baal were granted positions of influence within the court, their pronouncements often carrying more weight than those of the Levites who served Yahweh.

A decree was issued, ostensibly to foster unity and respect among the diverse religious practices within the kingdom. Still, in reality, it was a subtle mandate for syncretism —a blending of the sacred that bordered on the blasphemous from the perspective of traditionalists. "Let all peoples within this great kingdom," the decree read, its language carefully worded to sound inclusive, "honor the divine in such ways as are pleasing to them, and to the King. For harmony in worship brings strength to the realm, and the King, in his wisdom, encourages all forms of devotion that bring glory to the heavens and prosperity to Israel."

This was followed by a more pointed directive: that the sacred places dedicated to Yahweh should also be open to the worship of other deities, particularly those favored by the crown. This was a direct assault on the established religious order. The High Priest, a venerable man named Ahimelech, dared to voice his concerns. He presented himself before Jezebel, not in the opulent throne room, but in a more private audience chamber, hoping for a more intimate, perhaps even reasonable, discussion.

"Your Majesty," he began, his voice trembling slightly, not with fear but with the weight of his convictions, "the laws of our forefathers, the covenant given to us by the Almighty, are clear. There is but one God, Yahweh, and He alone is to be worshipped. To allow other gods into His sacred spaces is a defilement, a transgression that invites His wrath upon us all."

Jezebel listened, her expression unreadable. She allowed him to finish, and then, with a slow, deliberate smile, she responded. "High Priest Ahimelech," she began, her tone deceptively gentle, "you speak of ancient laws. But the kingdom has evolved. The needs of our people have changed. The King, in his desire for unity and prosperity, has chosen to adopt a broader understanding of the divine. Your loyalty, I trust, is to the King, and therefore, to his decrees."

She then presented him with another document, a royal commission empowering specific individuals, handpicked by her, to oversee the integration of these diverse worship practices. It also stipulated that any refusal to comply would be viewed as an act of disloyalty to the crown, a charge that, under the new legal framework, carried severe penalties.

Ahimelech, a man of deep faith and keen political awareness, understood the trap. To refuse was to invite ruin, not just for himself, but for the very faith he sought to protect. To comply was to compromise his principles and his sacred duty. He bowed his head, a profound sadness settling upon him. "I am a servant of God and of the King," he replied, his voice barely a whisper, the words heavy with unspoken resignation. He knew, with a certainty that chilled him to the bone, that Jezebel's decrees were not about religious tolerance, but about the obliteration of Yahweh's singular authority and the assertion of her own dominance over the spiritual as well as the temporal realm.

The subsequent months saw a systematic erosion of traditional worship. While public displays of devotion to Yahweh were not explicitly forbidden, they were marginalized. Resources were diverted to the support of Baal worship. Priests who clung to the old ways found themselves ostracized, with their offerings refused and their congregations dwindling under subtle but persistent pressure. Jezebel's influence was a pervasive shadow, touching every aspect of life in Samaria, from the grand pronouncements of the royal tribunal to the quiet prayers offered in homes.

The vineyard, a symbol of Ahab's desire, had become the catalyst for a far more insidious conquest: the conquest of the very soul of Israel, orchestrated by a queen whose ambition knew no bounds and whose definition of justice was as fluid and as ruthless as her own will. The decrees were not merely words on parchment; they were chains, forged in the fires of ambition and its darkest consort, absolute power.

Ahab, on this strange morning, woke up remembering his initial proposal to Naboth for his vineyard, the almost casual way Jezebel had presented it, a mere suggestion of acquiring the vineyard. Naboth, she had explained, was an obstinate man, clinging to his ancestral land like a limpet to a rock. Ahab, ever eager to appease his queen, had made his own overtures, couched in the language of royal prerogative and kingdom development. But Naboth's steadfast refusal, his quiet dignity in the face of royal pressure, had pricked something in Ahab. It wasn't outright defiance, but a calm, unwavering adherence to something older, something rooted in heritage and a belief in a right that transcended the King's decree.

And then, the swift, brutal turn of events. Naboth's accusation, the swift trial, the stones. Ahab had not been present for the actual execution, and he clung to that fact with a desperate tenacity. He had been in his palace, wrestling with a gnawing unease, a sense that the proceedings, though sanctioned by royal decree, were a perversion of justice. He had heard the murmurs, the hushed conversations among the courtiers, the subtle shifts in their demeanor that spoke of something more than just legal procedure. They had seen the fear in the elders' eyes, the forced solemnity that masked a more profound complicity.

Jezebel, of course, had been triumphant. She had presented the vineyard to him as a fait accompli, a prize won through her decisive action. "See, my King," she had said, her voice laced with a satisfaction that grated on Ahab's nerves, "how swiftly the will of the crown can be enacted when there is no obstruction. Naboth's stubbornness is no more. And his land, now yours, will yield bountiful harvests for Israel." Her words, meant to be soothing, had landed like stones themselves. He had forced a smile, accepted the gift, but the taste of it was ashes in his mouth.

He knew, with a certainty that chilled him, that Jezebel had orchestrated Naboth's demise. The accusations of blasphemy, the conveniently found witnesses – these were not the spontaneous workings of the legal system, but the calculated machinations of a queen who wielded power with a terrifying precision. And he, Ahab, had allowed it. He had not stopped her. He had not intervened. He had, in his heart, acquiesced. The desire for the vineyard, a foolish, covetous urge, had been a fertile ground for Jezebel's ambition to sow its poisonous seeds. He had wanted what Naboth possessed, and when Naboth refused to yield, Ahab had, in his passive way, paved the path for Jezebel to take it by force.

The internal struggle was a constant, unwelcome companion. He would find himself replaying the events, dissecting his own inaction. Had he been too weak to confront Jezebel? Had his desire to maintain peace within his own household, to avoid the storms of her displeasure, outweighed his sense of right and wrong? Or was it something deeper, a creeping moral decay that had begun the moment he had first coveted Naboth's land? He saw himself as a king, a ruler, yet in this instance, he had been little more than a silent spectator, a willing beneficiary of a monstrous injustice.

He remembered the decree that followed, the one that cemented Jezebel's control over the judiciary, the one that made accusations of blasphemy and treason absolute if supported by "credible" witnesses, with credibility determined by the crown. He had signed it, of course. He had affixed his royal seal. It had been presented to him as a measure to ensure swift justice and royal authority, and he had allowed himself to be convinced. He saw now that it was a tool for silencing dissent, for consolidating Jezebel's power, and by extension, his own, though it was her will that truly dictated its use. Each subsequent seizure of land, each accusation of impropriety that led to confiscation, was a testament to the power he had unwittingly helped to forge, a power wielded with a chilling disregard for the lives and liberties of his people.

The weight of his complicity pressed down on him. It wasn't just about the vineyard anymore. It was about the broader implications of his passivity. He had allowed Jezebel to redefine justice, to twist the very fabric of law to her own ends. He saw the fear in the eyes of his subjects, the unspoken anxieties that now permeated the kingdom. They looked to him, their king, for protection, for a sense of order, and he was failing them. He was allowing their king to be a puppet, a figurehead whose authority was merely a facade behind which Jezebel's ruthless ambition operated unchecked.

There were moments, brief and fleeting, when a flicker of rebellion, a desperate urge to assert his own authority, would stir within him. He would imagine confronting Jezebel, demanding an end to the systematic injustices. But the thought would be quickly extinguished by the sheer force of her personality, by the memory of her chilling pronouncements and the cold, calculating glint in her eyes.

This moral decay was not a sudden collapse but a gradual erosion. It began with small concessions, with the rationalization that a king must sometimes make difficult choices for the good of the realm, even if those choices were not entirely savory. However, the "difficult choices" had become increasingly egregious, with rationalizations that were thinner and more transparent. He had become an accomplice not through active participation in the crimes themselves, but through his conscious decision to look the other way, allowing the transgressions to occur without challenge.

His covetousness had been the initial spark, the chink in his armor that Jezebel had so expertly exploited. He had desired something that was not his, and in that desire, he had surrendered a part of his own integrity. He had allowed his personal wants to cloud his judgment, to mute the voices of his conscience and the laws of his God. The vineyard, a symbol of his initial weakness, had become a constant, agonizing reminder of his complicity —a tangible manifestation of his failure as both a king and a man of principle.

He looked out at the dawn, a new day breaking over Samaria. He knew that Jezebel would already be awake, already strategizing, her mind already on the next target, the following decree, the next victim. And he, Ahab, King of Israel, would follow in her wake, a willing, though increasingly haunted, participant in her ascent to absolute power, his reign increasingly defined not by his own will, but by the shadow of his queen's ambition and the moral compromises he had made to appease her. The cost of his ambition, the ambition to please his queen and his own base desires, was proving to be the very soul of his kingdom.

Elijah's Prophecy of Death:

The air in the royal courtyard crackled with an unseen tension, a palpable precursor to the storm that was about to break. Ahab, still wrestling with the phantom guilt that clung to him like the Samarian dust, found himself standing before

178

a figure who seemed to command the very elements. It was Elijah, the Tishbite, a man forged in the crucible of divine purpose, his presence an undeniable force that dwarfed even the imposing architecture of the palace. His raiment, rough spun and weathered, spoke of a life lived outside the gilded cages of royalty, a life intimately connected to the raw pronouncements of the Almighty. His eyes, piercing and unyielding, fixed upon Ahab, and in their depths, the king saw not mere human judgment, but the blazing intolerance of a celestial power.

"King Ahab," Elijah's voice resonated, clear and resonant, cutting through the hushed murmurs of the gathered courtiers, men who now averted their gaze, sensing the gravity of the encounter. "Thus says the Lord." The pronouncement was delivered with an authority that made Ahab's heart lurch, a primal recognition of a power far greater than his own. "Have you killed, and also taken possession?" The accusation, stark and unvarnished, hung in the air, stripped of any pretense or legalistic obfuscation. It was a direct indictment, aimed at the very core of Ahab's transgressions.

Ahab flinched, the familiar shame washing over him with renewed force. He had tried, in the desolate chambers of his own mind, to distance himself from the deed, to see it as a consequence of Jezebel's decisive action, a regrettable but necessary outcome. But here, before the prophet of God, such self-deception was impossible. The king's labored breath betrayed his inner turmoil, his hands clenching and unclenching at his sides. He could feel the eyes of his guards upon him, the cautious, expectant gaze of his advisors, all waiting to see how their monarch would weather this divine tempest.

"You have shed blood," Elijah continued, his voice rising, each word a hammer blow against the fragile edifice of Ahab's denial. "And now you have taken possession of the inheritance of a man of Israel. Is this the law of the land? Is this how the King of Israel rules?" The rhetorical questions were not seeking an answer; they were pronouncements of guilt, damning pronouncements delivered with the unassailable certainty of divine revelation. The prophet's gaze swept over the courtyard, encompassing not just Ahab but the very foundations of his reign.

Jezebel, who had entered the courtyard with her characteristic imperious stride, her presence radiating an almost tangible aura of power, stopped short upon hearing Elijah's words. Her eyes, sharp and assessing, locked onto the prophet, a flicker of disdain quickly masked by a calculated composure. She had grown accustomed to the reverence, the fear, that preceded her. This man, this unkempt messenger of a vengeful God, dared to confront her, and by extension, her King, with such raw accusation? Her hand instinctively went to the jeweled dagger at her hip, a subtle gesture of defiance.

Elijah's gaze then shifted, meeting Jezebel's directly. There was no fear in his eyes, no wavering uncertainty. Instead, there was a righteous anger, a burning indignation that seemed to emanate from him like heat from a forge. "In the place where the dogs licked up the blood of Naboth, dogs will lick your blood, even yours, O King!" The pronouncement was chilling, a visceral image of retribution that sent a shiver through the assembled crowd. Ahab felt a cold dread grip him; this was not merely a condemnation of his actions, but a prophecy of a bloody end.

"And in the field of Samaria," Elijah's voice continued, unwavering, "dogs will eat Jezebel!" The words hung in the air, a death knell for the queen, a pronouncement of a fate so brutal, so ignominious, that the very air seemed to thicken with the horror of it. Jezebel's carefully constructed composure was shattered. Her face, usually a mask of regal control, contorted with a mixture of shock and incandescent fury. She had faced down armies, orchestrated assassinations. She manipulated the destinies of nations, but she had never before been directly confronted by such a terrifying, unassailable force as the wrath of God channeled through a single, unwavering man.

Ahab, witnessing this exchange, felt a strange duality of emotions. There was the crushing weight of his own guilt, amplified by the prophet's unsparing words. But there was also a nascent spark of something akin to vindication, a desperate hope that perhaps this divine intervention might, in some impossible way, absolve him of his complicity. Yet, the prophecy itself was a terrifying prospect. His lineage, his queen, his very self, condemned to such a gruesome fate. He saw Jezebel beside him, her face pale, her eyes blazing with a hatred that was directed not only at Elijah but, he suspected, at himself as well. Had he allowed this to happen? Had his weakness in the face of her ambition led them to this precipice?

Elijah's pronouncements did not end with the fate of Ahab and Jezebel. His gaze seemed to pierce through the very walls of the palace, encompassing the widespread idolatry that had taken root in Israel under their reign. "You have sold yourselves to do evil in the sight of the Lord," he declared, his voice thundering with divine pronouncements. "You have provoked the Lord God of Israel to anger with your idols." The accusation was broad, encompassing not just the coveting of Naboth's vineyard but the systematic erosion of Israel's covenant with God, the embrace of foreign deities, and the desecration of sacred traditions.

"Therefore, thus says the Lord, I will bring disaster upon you and cut off from Ahab every male, bond or free, in Israel," Elijah declared, his voice chillingly devoid of emotion. "I will make your house like the house of Jeroboam, son of Nebat, and like the house of Baasha, son of Ahijah, because of the provocation with which you have provoked me to anger, and because you have made Israel to sin." The lineage of Ahab, he proclaimed, would be utterly annihilated. Not a single male, from the highest noble to the lowest servant, would escape the coming wrath. The mention of Jeroboam and Baasha, kings known for their wickedness and the subsequent destruction of their dynasties, served as a grim foreshadowing of the magnitude of the impending doom.

The weight of the prophecy settled upon Ahab like a shroud. He felt a profound sense of helplessness, a crushing awareness that he had, through his choices, brought about the ruin of his own house, his own kingdom. He had desired a vineyard, and in seeking it, he had invited divine judgment upon himself and all that he held dear. He had allowed his ambition, fueled by Jezebel's ruthless drive for power and his own covetous desires, to eclipse his responsibility to his God and his people. He had strayed from the path of righteousness, and now, the consequences were upon him, delivered with the unappealable finality of heaven's decree.

As Elijah finished his pronouncements, a profound silence descended upon the courtyard. The courtiers stood frozen, their faces etched with a mixture of terror and disbelief. Even Jezebel, though her rage still simmered, seemed momentarily stunned by the sheer force of the prophet's denunciation. Ahab, however, remained rooted to the spot, his gaze fixed on the prophet, his mind reeling from the pronouncements. He knew, with a certainty that transcended fear, that Elijah's words were not mere threats; they were the pronouncements of an inevitable, divine judgment.

Ahab's reaction, however, was not one of immediate repentance. Instead, a flicker of defiance, born of desperation and a primal instinct for self-preservation, ignited within him. He had been humbled, terrified, but the ingrained habits of kingship, the accustomed exercise of authority, still held sway. He looked at Elijah, this man who dared to pronounce his doom, and a desperate, almost frantic thought took hold. If he could not escape the judgment, perhaps he could at least delay it; maybe he could demonstrate a semblance of remorse, a gesture that might appease the wrath of the Almighty.

"You have found me, O my enemy!" Ahab finally managed to exclaim, his voice hoarse and trembling. It was a confession of sorts, an acknowledgment of the prophet's uncanny knowledge and the undeniable truth of his accusations. But it was also laced with a desperate plea, a king's attempt to negotiate with the divine. "When my enemies have driven me away, will you not kill me?" This was a subtle, yet telling, indication of Ahab's mindset. He was not yet willing to fully embrace his guilt and repent. Instead, he was seeking reassurance, a guarantee that his life would be spared even in the face of divine punishment. He was still, at his core, a king accustomed to bargaining, accustomed to the power to dictate terms, even when facing the ultimate authority.

Elijah's response was immediate and unambiguous, a testament to the unyielding nature of divine justice. "I will not go with you, nor will I return to you this day," he declared, his gaze unwavering. "But I will surely come to you today." There was no room for negotiation, no possibility of deferred confrontation. The judgment was immediate, and the prophet would be its harbinger. The prophet's intention was clear: Ahab's reign, and his life, were irrevocably marked for destruction. The consequences of his ambition, of his complicity in injustice and idolatry, were about to be fully and terrifyingly realized. The divine pronouncement had been issued, and Ahab's terror was merely the prelude to the inevitable unfolding of God's judgment, a judgment that would not only consume him but would also utterly obliterate his lineage, leaving his name a byword for divine wrath and royal corruption.

The sheer weight of Elijah's pronouncements had a profound effect on Ahab, more so than any human opposition ever could. The king, accustomed to the deference of his court, to the subtle manipulations of his queen, found himself utterly disarmed by the unassailable authority of the prophet. He had never before encountered a force that could so directly challenge his power, so fearlessly pronounce his damnation. The words "dogs will lick your blood, even yours" echoed in his mind, a visceral image of his own impending mortality, a fate far more terrifying than any earthly consequence.

He looked at Jezebel, searching for any sign of the unwavering strength that had always defined her, but even she seemed momentarily subdued, the fire in her eyes banked by a palpable fear. Her usual confident posture was subtly altered, a hint of apprehension now betraying her formidable facade. For the first time, perhaps, he saw the true cost of his ambition, the devastating consequences of allowing his desires and Jezebel's ruthlessness to dictate the course of his reign. He had traded righteousness for a vineyard, peace for power, and now, the divine scales were tipping, threatening to crush him and his entire lineage.

The pronouncement of his lineage's destruction was perhaps the most crushing blow. The thought that every male descendant, from his sons to the humblest servant in his employ, would be wiped out was a horror that surpassed personal fear. It was the annihilation of his bloodline, the erasure of his name from the annals of history in a manner most ignominious. This, he realized, was the ultimate price of his ambition, a price far steeper than he had ever imagined.

Elijah, having delivered his pronouncement, did not linger. With the same unhurried, authoritative gait with which he had arrived, he turned and departed, leaving behind a stunned silence and a king grappling with the immensity of his impending doom. The courtiers, still reeling from the prophet's words, began to stir, their hushed whispers a testament to the profound impact of the encounter. Ahab, however, remained immobile, his gaze fixed on the path Elijah had taken, his mind a vortex of terror and despair. He knew that no earthly power could now avert the judgment that had been so clearly foretold.

The seeds of his ambition, sown in covetousness and nurtured by a queen's ruthless pragmatism, had finally bloomed into a harvest of divine wrath, a harvest that would consume him, his queen, and his entire house. The confrontation had been absolute, the judgment delivered, and the inexorable march towards destruction had begun. The taste of Naboth's vineyard, once a symbol of his kingly desire, now tasted of ash and ruin, the bitter prelude to a kingdom's ultimate reckoning. He had dared to challenge the divine order, and now, the divine order would shatter him.

With Elijah gone, vanishing as mysteriously as he had appeared, leaving behind only the lingering scent of ozone and the tremor of divine pronouncements, Jezebel felt a surge of adrenaline. The fear she had momentarily felt was replaced by a burning indignation, not at the righteousness of Elijah's accusations, but at the audacity of his challenge. She saw his divine mandate as her Phoenician gods divinely sanctioned a direct affront to her own power, a power she believed, and which she had painstakingly built through her influence over Ahab. The near-disaster, the chilling prophecy of their demise, had not deterred her; it had merely sharpened her focus. If the God of Israel were so intent on interfering, then she would ensure that His voice was drowned out, His followers silenced, and His worship eradicated, replaced by the glorious altars of Baal and Asherah, which she had so diligently established.

Her initial efforts to establish her foreign gods had been met with a degree of resistance, murmurs of dissent from the more devout Israelites. But now, with Elijah's condemnation ringing in the air, she saw an opportunity to crush that dissent decisively. Ahab, still reeling from the prophet's pronouncements, was easily swayed by her renewed vigor and her insistent arguments. He was a king prone to despair and self-pity, but also susceptible to the allure of unwavering certainty, and Jezebel provided that in abundance. She painted Elijah's words as the desperate cries of a failed prophet, a man clinging to ancient superstitions in the face of a modern, progressive kingdom. Her kingdom, she argued, was being threatened not by divine retribution but by the persistent disruption of a radical zealot.

The Persecution of the Prophets:

The persecution of the prophets of Yahweh intensified, transforming from a subtle suppression into an open, systematic eradication. Jezebel, drawing upon her vast resources and her formidable network of informants, began to hunt down those who dared to speak the name of Yahweh or preach His covenant. These were not merely isolated incidents; they were calculated acts designed to instill widespread terror. Homes were raided, secret meetings disrupted, and individuals known for their piety or their prophetic pronouncements were dragged before tribunals orchestrated by Jezebel's most loyal, and often most ruthless, courtiers. The trials were a sham, the accusations fabricated – sedition, treason, or inciting unrest – and the sentences were predictable and brutal. Public executions became a common sight, serving as grim warnings to anyone who might entertain thoughts of defying the queen's will or adhering to the worship of the God of Israel.

One particularly chilling example of this escalating tyranny was the fate of a group of prophets who had gathered in a secluded cave, seeking refuge and a place to continue their sacred duties. Jezebel's spies, ever vigilant, had tracked them down. The king's guards, under direct orders from the queen, stormed the cave with a ferocity that left no room for mercy. The prophets, unarmed and unprepared for such a brutal assault, were dragged out, their hands bound, their faces etched with a mixture of defiance and profound sorrow. Jezebel herself was said to have overseen the proceedings, her presence a chilling testament to the severity of her intent. She watched, impassive, as the men were led to a desolate hillside outside Samaria, their crime a mere continuation of their faith. Their execution was swift and brutal, a message sent not only to the remaining prophets but to the entire populace of Israel: adherence to Yahweh was now a capital offense.

This systematic silencing of Yahweh's prophets had a profound effect on the spiritual and social fabric of Israel. The prophets had been the conscience of the nation, the voice that reminded the people of their covenant, their history, and their divine calling. Without their guidance, their warnings, and their encouragement, the people of Israel were left adrift, vulnerable to the pervasive influence of Jezebel's foreign cults. The worship of Baal and Asherah, once confined to the royal court and certain select circles, began to permeate every aspect of Israelite life. Idolatrous altars were erected in public squares, temples to the foreign gods were constructed with lavish expense, and elaborate rituals, often involving sensuality and even child sacrifice, became commonplace.

Jezebel's love, or rather her possessive ambition, had metastasized into a destructive force. Her desire to see Ahab powerful, to see his kingdom prosperous and respected on the world stage, had become intertwined with her fierce loyalty to her own gods and her disdain for the God of Israel. She genuinely believed that she was acting in the best interests of the kingdom, that by eradicating the perceived disruptive elements and by embracing the powerful deities of her homeland, she was ushering in an era of unprecedented glory. This self-deception allowed her to justify increasingly barbaric actions, all under the guise of strengthening the monarchy and securing the kingdom's future.

The economic implications of Jezebel's tyranny were also significant. Resources that could have been used for the welfare of the people, for infrastructure development, or for strengthening national defenses were instead diverted to the construction and maintenance of temples to foreign gods. Lavish festivals and sacrifices, often requiring considerable offerings from the populace, became a regular feature of court life. Those who refused to participate or contribute were often met with severe repercussions, including the confiscation of their businesses, ostracism of their families, or worse. The already strained relationship between the monarchy and the ordinary people grew even more fractured, as the visible displays of idolatry and the persecution of their traditional faith bred resentment and a deep sense of alienation.

Ahab, though complicit, was increasingly a figurehead in his own kingdom. His moments of introspection and guilt were quickly overshadowed by Jezebel's unwavering drive and her ability to manipulate his insecurities. He was a man who craved peace and stability, and Jezebel presented herself as the only one capable of providing it, even if it meant resorting to extreme measures. He would often retreat into his palace chambers, seeking solace in his own thoughts, perhaps still haunted by Elijah's pronouncements, but ultimately unable to muster the courage or the conviction to counteract Jezebel's relentless agenda. He had allowed ambition, his own and hers, to lead them down a path from which there seemed no return, a path paved with injustice and the systematic erosion of his people's spiritual heritage.

The social impact was equally devastating. The communal bonds that had once characterized Israelite society began to fray. Neighbors turned against neighbors, informed by Jezebel's spies who encouraged citizens to report any instances of adherence to Yahweh's laws or any criticism of the queen. The sense of shared identity and purpose was replaced by an atmosphere of suspicion and fear. Families were divided, with some members embracing the queen's religious agenda, while others clung to the traditions of their ancestors, leading to internal strife and bitter divisions. The covenant between God and His people, which had been the bedrock of Israelite existence, was being systematically dismantled, replaced by the hollow rituals of foreign gods and the iron fist of a tyrannical queen.

Jezebel's love for Ahab, in its warped manifestation, had become a force of destruction. Her ambition for him, for his kingdom, and for her own gods, had blinded her to the actual cost of her actions. She sought to build a legacy for him, a legacy of strength and prosperity. Still, in doing so, she was inadvertently sowing the seeds of his downfall and the utter devastation of his house, just as Elijah had prophesied.

CHAPTER EIGHT:

Elijah, Elisha, and the Prophets: The Hands of Justice

The air in Samaria, once thick with the scent of sacrifice and the murmur of whispered prayers, now carried the metallic tang of anticipation, a grim prelude to conflict. Though Jezebel's iron will had successfully quelled overt dissent, a disquiet simmered beneath the surface of the kingdom. Ahab, however, seemed remarkably insulated from this unease, or perhaps he had learned to ignore it expertly. The near-disastrous confrontation with Elijah, the chilling pronouncements of doom, had been a fleeting storm that, in Ahab's fractured perception, had ultimately passed. Jezebel, with her potent blend of flattery and manipulation, had skillfully redirected his gaze from the divine pronouncements of Yahweh to the more immediate, tangible threats posed by the encroaching Syrian forces.

The memory of Naboth's vineyard, a brief, sharp sting of guilt, had long since dulled under the weight of Jezebel's relentless ambition and Ahab's own desperate need for reassurance. He had allowed her to weave a tapestry of justifications, each thread meticulously designed to obscure the truth of their transgressions. The prophets of Yahweh, once a mighty chorus of divine guidance, had been systematically silenced, their voices extinguished by Jezebel's decree and Ahab's passive assent. The nation, thus robbed of its spiritual custodians, was adrift, susceptible to the seductive allure of foreign deities and the king's own susceptibility to flattery and fear. It was within this climate of suppressed truth and amplified deception that the seeds of Ahab's final reckoning were sown.

The Syrians, under the formidable leadership of Ben-Hadad, had proven to be a persistent and formidable adversary. Their incursions into Israelite territory had grown bolder, their demands more audacious. Ahab, despite his personal dalliances and his deference to Jezebel's whims, was still a king, and the threat to his kingdom was a matter he could not entirely dismiss. Yet, even in matters of war, the spectral influence of Jezebel's counsel loomed large. The whispers of prophets, those who dared to speak in defiance of her tyranny, were drowned out by her insistent pronouncements. Elijah, though no longer a visible presence, remained a shadow in Ahab's mind, a persistent reminder of divine displeasure.

It was in this atmosphere of burgeoning conflict and lingering divine judgment that Ahab received news of Ben-Hadad's intentions. The Syrian king, emboldened by previous successes and perhaps fueled by a miscalculation of Israel's resilience, was amassing his forces for a decisive assault. Ahab, ever eager to assert his authority and possibly to prove his own mettle, saw an opportunity. He rallied his armies, his heart a complex mixture of kingly duty and personal vanity.

Yet, as he prepared to march, a familiar, unsettling stillness pervaded his thoughts. The memory of Elijah's dire warnings, though suppressed, resurfaced like a persistent phantom. In his hour of need, when the fate of his kingdom hung precariously in the balance, the absent prophet's words echoed with an unnerving clarity. Ahab, in a moment of uncharacteristic introspection, sought out counsel. He did not seek out the silenced prophets of Yahweh, nor did he consult the elders of Israel, whose wisdom might have offered a balanced perspective. Instead, his mind, so accustomed to the soothing balm of Jezebel's pronouncements, gravitated towards a more ominous, yet paradoxically familiar, source of guidance.

He found himself, driven by a complex interplay of fear and a desperate need for divine assurance, seeking out the very source of his kingdom's spiritual turmoil. Whether it was a genuine, albeit misguided, attempt at reconciliation with the divine, or merely a final, desperate grasp at control, remains a subject of historical debate. Ahab, the king who had allowed his kingdom to be swayed by foreign gods and his own desires, found himself drawn to a prophet, an outlier in the very system Jezebel had meticulously dismantled.

The prophet, whose name is lost to the annals of this particular moment, but whose counsel would prove to be Ahab's undoing, stood before the king not as a harbinger of doom, but as an instrument of fate. Ahab, desperate for a sign, for a word of encouragement, presented his intentions, his strategy, the preparedness of his armies, and the righteousness of his cause against the encroaching Syrians. He desired, perhaps more than anything, a divine endorsement, a confirmation that his path was blessed.

The prophet, however, did not offer the comforting words Ahab craved. Instead, he spoke with a somber gravity that chilled the king to the bone. He revealed that the Syrian king, Ben-Hadad, harbored no grand strategic objective; his intentions were more personal, more insidious. He intended to capture Ahab alive, to parade him through the streets of Damascus, a trophy of his victory, a testament to his own power. This revelation, rather than deterring Ahab, ignited a spark of defiance. The thought of such humiliation, of being paraded as a captive, was an unbearable prospect for a king whose ego was as vast as his kingdom.

The prophet continued, his voice devoid of emotion, delivering a message that seemed to carry the weight of centuries of divine covenant. He revealed that Yahweh, the

God of Israel, had granted them victory in a previous engagement, a triumph so complete that it had lulled them into a false sense of security. Now, a new battle was at hand, and the prophet declared that Yahweh would again deliver them into the hands of their enemies. This was not a prophecy of hope, but a pronouncement of impending judgment.

Ahab rejects the Prophet's Warning and goes to Battle:

Ahab, however, was deaf to the prophet's dire warning. The immediate, visceral threat of capture, the ignominy of being paraded as a war trophy, overshadowed any lingering fear of divine retribution. His pride, his kingly honor, felt far more immediate and pressing than the pronouncements of a lone prophet, especially one whose brethren had been so brutally persecuted by his own queen. He dismissed the prophet's words as the lamentations of a prophet from a vanquished lineage, a man clinging to the pronouncements of a God who, in Ahab's jaded view, had long since abandoned Israel to the more potent forces of the world.

Jezebel, ever the shadow advisor, reinforced his defiance. She scoffed at the prophet's words, dismissing them as the superstitious ramblings of a man out of touch with the realities of power and warfare. "Do you truly believe," she might have said, her voice laced with disdain, "that our God would abandon us in our hour of need? Has He not blessed our reign, brought prosperity, and given us strength? This prophet speaks of a past that is no more. We have our own gods now, Ahab, gods of power and victory. Trust in them, and trust in your own strength." Her words, like a potent elixir, dissolved Ahab's nascent doubts and bolstered his resolve. He saw, in her unwavering conviction, the strength he himself lacked. He clung to her assurance, a lifeline in the turbulent waters of his own wavering faith.

And so, against the explicit counsel of the prophet, against the undeniable weight of his kingdom's spiritual heritage, Ahab made his fateful decision. He would not heed the warning. He would not retreat. He would march against the Syrians, confident in his own might and the strategic prowess he believed he possessed. The prophet's dire pronouncement was cast aside, deemed the desperate cry of a forgotten god. Ahab, fueled by pride and Jezebel's persuasive rhetoric, chose to face the enemy, convinced that his earthly kingdom was his own to command, irrespective of any divine mandate.

The ensuing battle was a stark testament to the prophet's foresight. Ben-Hadad's forces, far from being a disorganized rabble, were a well-drilled and determined enemy. Ahab's army, though valiant, found itself outmaneuvered, outfought, and ultimately overwhelmed. The Syrians, their ranks bristling with vengeful fury, pressed their advantage with relentless ferocity. The once-proud Israelite formations began to crumble under the sustained assault, their lines breaking and their courage faltering.

And then, it happened. A stray arrow, loosed from a Syrian bow, found its mark. It was not a shot of strategic brilliance, nor a wound inflicted by a champion warrior. It was a random act of war, a seemingly insignificant event that would, however, seal the fate of the King of Israel. The arrow struck Ahab between the joints of his armor, a vulnerability no king, however powerful, could entirely guard against. The impact was jarring, a sudden, searing pain that brought him to his knees.

King Ahab's Death:

His armor bearers, accustomed to the king's every command, rushed to his aid. They lifted him from his chariot, attempting to shield him from the chaos that raged around them. But the wound was mortal. The blood flowed, a crimson tide that stained the dust of the battlefield and mirrored the unconfessed sins of his reign. He was taken back to the city, the cheers of his victorious enemies ringing in his ears, a chilling counterpoint to the dying groans of his own men.

As he lay on his chariot, his life ebbing away, a peculiar stillness fell upon him. The clamor of battle, the shouts of his men, the war cries of the Syrians – all faded into a distant hum. His mind, however, was far from at peace. The prophet's words, once dismissed, now returned with a terrifying clarity. He saw, with stark, unsparing precision, the full weight of his choices. His dalliance with foreign gods, his acquiescence to Jezebel's ruthless ambition, his disregard for the prophets of Yahweh, and now, his final act of defiance in the face of divine warning – it all converged in this agonizing moment.

He understood, with a clarity that transcended his earthly kingship, that his death was not merely a casualty of war. It was a consequence—a reckoning. The prophet had foretold that he would fall in battle against the Syrians, and so it came to pass. But the true profundity of the prophecy lay not in the where, but the why. He had been warned, given every opportunity to turn back, to repent, to reaffirm his covenant with Yahweh. Instead, he had chosen the path of pride, of self-reliance, of obedience to a queen whose devotion was to other gods.

The blood that stained his armor was not just his own; it was the spilled blood of his people, shed in battles fought for vanity and pride, battles that had cost them dearly in terms of spiritual integrity and divine favor. His kingdom, once a beacon of Yahweh's covenant, had become a monument to idolatry and a testament to a king's fatal susceptibility to the whispers of mortal desires over the pronouncements of the divine.

As the last vestiges of his strength drained away, Ahab's thoughts turned, perhaps with a flicker of regret, to Jezebel. She, the architect of so much of his reign, the driving force behind his spiritual and political compromises, would continue her reign, perhaps unburdened by his presence. Yet, even in this final moment, the echoes of Elijah's prophecy regarding the house of Ahab seemed to resonate, a chilling premonition of a doom that would extend far beyond his own demise. His life, a tapestry woven with threads of ambition, weakness, and misguided devotion, was now drawing to a close, a tragic testament to the dire consequences of a king's infidelity to his God and his people. The battle was lost, but the actual war, the spiritual war for the soul of Israel, had inflicted its deepest wound upon the heart of its king.

The dust of the battlefield, once thick with the desperate cries of dying men, had settled into a grim tableau of Israelite defeat. Ahab, the king who had so readily bowed to the seductive whispers of his Phoenician queen, lay dead, his once proud reign concluded not with a triumphant roar, but a whispered sigh on a foreign field. The arrow that found him between the plates of his armor, a mortal sting delivered by an unseen hand, had been more than just a random act of war; it was the punctuation mark on a prophecy, a divine judgment delivered with chilling precision. And in the silent halls of Samaria, the news struck Jezebel with the force of a physical blow, though she did not let it show.

The immediate aftermath of Ahab's death was a storm of panicked pronouncements and whispered anxieties. Without the mediating presence of her husband, Jezebel's influence, though still formidable, was suddenly more exposed. She was no longer the queen consort, the formidable advisor beside the throne; she was now, by proxy and by sheer force of will, the de facto ruler, guiding her young sons, Ahaziah and then Jehoram, onto a throne that felt increasingly unstable. Yet, her reign, if it could be called that, was not one of triumphant consolidation, but of a desperate clinging to power, a gilded cage built on the foundations of her own ambition and Ahab's fatal weakness. The kingdom, so long adrift in a sea of spiritual compromise, now felt the full, unmitigated weight of divine displeasure. The air itself seemed to hum with an unspoken threat, a palpable tension that seeped into the very stones of Samaria.

Jezebel, however, was not one to be easily cowed. The prophets of Yahweh, those who had survived her relentless purge, now spoke in hushed tones of judgment, their words carrying an even greater gravity in the wake of Ahab's demise. But Jezebel, ensconced in the opulent splendor of her palace, surrounded by her Baalism priests and the lingering scent of foreign incense, remained defiantly unmoved. She saw Ahab's death not as a divine repudiation of their shared path, but as a tragic accident of war, a setback that could be overcome with sheer will and the favor of her own gods. She doubled down on her devotion to Baal and Asherah, believing their power was the faithful bulwark against the encroaching tide of Yahweh's wrath. Her faith, if it could be called such, was a hardened shell of defiance, a refusal to acknowledge the spiritual bankruptcy of her reign.

The kingdom, weary from drought and fractured by the cultic divisions Jezebel had so ruthlessly fostered, now looked to its rulers with a mixture of fear and desperate hope. Ahab's sons, though crowned kings, were largely pawns in their mother's grander designs. Ahaziah, the elder, was a weak and impetuous youth, easily swayed by Jezebel's counsel. He continued his mother's patronage of Baal, further alienating the dwindling faithful of Yahweh. His brief reign was marked by a chilling echo of Ahab's own failings, a testament to the enduring, corrosive influence of Jezebel's legacy. When Ahaziah met his own untimely end, falling through a lattice in his upper chamber, the whispers of divine intervention grew louder. It was a death that seemed to mirror the spiritual brokenness of the house of Ahab.

Then came Jehoram, a king who, perhaps sensing the precariousness of his position, attempted a more moderate approach. He scaled back some of the more overt excesses of Baal worship, a concession that seemed to stem more from political necessity than genuine spiritual conviction. Yet, even this partial retreat did not erase the deep-seated animosity that festered within the kingdom. The cumulative weight of years of idolatry, of the suppression of Yahweh's prophets, and of the queen mother's tyrannical will had left an indelible stain on the nation's soul. Jezebel, now an elder stateswoman of iniquity, remained the true power, her pronouncements carrying the weight of years of ruthless authority. She was a formidable presence; her will as unbending as the cedars of Lebanon, her belief in her own divine right to rule unshaken.

But the land itself seemed to groan under the burden of Jezebel's continued dominion. The memory of Naboth's vineyard, a brutal act of injustice orchestrated by her ambition, remained a festering wound in the national consciousness. The very ground seemed to hold the echo of his blood, a silent testament to the queen's cruelty. The prophets of Yahweh, though scattered and persecuted, found new voices in the escalating troubles. Elisha, the successor to Elijah—a man of formidable spiritual power and unwavering conviction—became a beacon of hope for the faithful. His pronouncements, delivered with the authority of the divine, spoke of a coming reckoning, a purging that would cleanse the land of its defilement.

Jezebel, however, saw Elisha not as a prophet of God, but as another enemy to be crushed —a remnant of a bygone era that dared to challenge her authority. When the Syrians, led by their formidable king Ben-Hadad, once again laid siege to Samaria, Jezebel's confidence in her own gods and her own power remained absolute. She exhorted her sons, urging them to stand firm and trust in the might of Baal. Yet, even as the city starved and its people despaired, Jezebel's defiance did not wane. She remained a figure of terrifying conviction, a queen who believed that her will was paramount, that her gods would ultimately prevail.

The story of Elisha's intervention in the Syrian siege offers a stark contrast to Jezebel's unwavering faith in her own power. While the city walls were closing in, and starvation gnawed at the populace, Elisha, from the safety of his prophetic chambers, declared that by the next day, Samaria would be flooded with an abundance of food. His prophecy, delivered with the authority of Yahweh, was met with skepticism by a commander of the king's guard, who, mirroring the pervasive disbelief, scoffed at the very notion. But Elisha, unmoved by his doubt, declared that the commander would indeed witness the fulfillment of the prophecy, but would not partake of its bounty. And so, it was. The Syrians, inexplicably panicked by sounds in the night, abandoned their camp, leaving behind a vast treasure trove of food and supplies. The city rejoiced; the commander who had doubted Elisha was trampled to death in the stampede of the hungry crowds, a grim fulfillment of the prophet's word.

Jezebel, confronted with this undeniable display of divine power, remained stubbornly resistant to any change of heart. She saw the lifting of the siege not as a sign of Yahweh's intervention, but as a testament to the strategic brilliance of her son, or perhaps even a clever maneuver orchestrated by her own cultic advisors. Her mind, so deeply entrenched in the worship of foreign deities and the self-serving narratives of her own power, was incapable of admitting any other interpretation. She continued to exert her influence, a venomous serpent coiled at the heart of the kingdom, her gaze fixed on maintaining her own authority and the dominance of her gods.

She was a queen who lived by her own rules, who answered to no higher authority than her own will. The deaths of Ahab, Ahaziah, and the subsequent challenges faced by Jehoram were not enough to break her spirit. She remained a potent symbol of defiance, a queen whose story is inextricably linked to the spiritual and political turmoil of her time, a stark reminder of the consequences when mortal ambition overshadows divine mandate. Her isolation grew, the circle of her true allies shrinking with each passing year, yet her resolve, forged in the fires of her Phoenician upbringing and fueled by a deep-seated belief in her own destiny, remained unyielding.

The kingdom of Israel, caught between the remnants of its covenantal past and the intoxicating allure of foreign deities championed by its queen, braced itself for a future that seemed increasingly shrouded in the shadow of divine wrath, a wrath that Jezebel, in her pride, continued to ignore.

The air in the war tents, still thick with the scent of sweat and oiled leather, vibrated with a different kind of tension. It was a nervous energy that simmered beneath the surface of routine, the collective unease of men who knew their king was absent and their leadership was fractured. Jehu, son of Jehoshaphat, grandson of Nimshi, moved among them with an easy authority, a captain whose reputation preceded him in battle. He was a man forged in the crucible of conflict, his eyes sharp, his bearing confident, his loyalty to the crown unquestioned, or so it seemed. His very presence was a calm center in the swirling currents of uncertainty that had gripped the Israelite army.

The prolonged campaign against the Arameans, a grueling test of endurance and resolve, had been punctuated by moments of both triumph and disheartening stalemate. Yet, through it all, Jehu had distinguished himself; his strategic acumen and personal bravery earned him the respect of his men and the notice of the court. He was a man who understood the rhythms of war, the subtle shifts in morale, the precise moment to press an advantage. He spoke little of kings or courts, his focus fixed on the immediate task, the next skirmish, the well-being of his soldiers. This stoic dedication and unpretentious leadership had endeared him to the rank and file, who saw in him a reflection of their own commitment and struggles.

Within the quiet sanctuary of a prophet's dwelling, a different kind of drama was unfolding, a prelude to the thunderclap that would soon shake the foundations of Samaria. Elisha, the successor to the fiery Elijah, a man whose mantle of prophetic power seemed to burn with an unquenchable flame, received a divine summons. The voice of Yahweh, clear and insistent, spoke to him, outlining a destiny, a sacred commission that would irrevocably alter the course of Israel's history. The message was precise, a divine decree delivered with an unyielding finality: Jehu, the celebrated captain of Ahab's army, was to be anointed king. Not king of Judah, the southern kingdom, but king of Israel, the northern ten tribes, the very heartland of the nation's spiritual and political rebellion. This was no casual pronouncement; it was the unfolding of a divine plan, a meticulously orchestrated act of judgment and retribution.

Elisha, accustomed to the directness of divine revelation, did not hesitate. He understood the gravity of the task, the blood that would inevitably flow, the violent upheaval that was to come. Yet, his purpose was not his own; he was a conduit, a vessel for God's will, and that will was, at this moment, focused on the purging of a house steeped in idolatry and drenched in the blood of the innocent.

The prophet, grasping a small vial of fragrant oil, its contents imbued with a sacred purpose, set out with a contingent of his disciples. Their journey was not one of fanfare or public proclamation, but of clandestine urgency. They sought out Jehu, who was engaged with his officers, discussing troop movements and the ongoing strategy against the Aramean forces. The king, Jehoram, was absent, having returned to Samaria to deal with unspecified matters, leaving the army under the command of his trusted generals. It was in this temporary vacuum of royal presence that the divine plan would be enacted. Elisha and his small band approached the assembled officers, their arrival causing a ripple of curiosity. Jehu, ever the dutiful commander, rose to greet the prophet, his expression one of respect, perhaps even deference. He knew of Elisha's reputation, of the miracles attributed to him, and the pronouncements that had so often stirred the hearts of the faithful.

Jehu Anointed King by Elisha:

Elisha, without preamble, fixed his gaze upon Jehu, his eyes burning with an ancient fire. The prophet's words, when they came, were not couched in gentle suggestion or veiled metaphor. They were sharp, direct, and imbued with the unmistakable authority of Heaven. "Thus says Yahweh, the God of Israel: I anoint you king over Yahweh's people, over Israel." The words struck Jehu with the force of a physical blow, echoing in the sudden silence that fell upon the gathered officers. The oil, cool against his skin as Elisha poured it over his head, felt like a brand, a mark of destiny. It was a consecration, a divine commission that shifted the very ground beneath his feet. The prophet continued, his voice resonating with the pronouncements of judgment against the house of Ahab. "You shall strike down the house of Ahab your master, so that I may avenge the blood of my servants the prophets, and the blood of all the servants of Yahweh, at the hand of Jezebel." The mention of Jezebel, the formidable queen mother, a name that evoked fear and revulsion in equal measure among the faithful, sent a shiver through Jehu. He knew of her wickedness, of her ruthless persecution of Yahweh's prophets, of her zealous promotion of Baal worship that had corrupted the very soul of Israel.

The prophet's words then turned to the immediate future, outlining the path of destruction that lay ahead. "And I will strike down all belonging to Ahab, and will cut off from Ahab every male, bond or free, in Israel. And I will make the house of Ahab like the house of Jeroboam the son of Nebat, and like the house of Baasha the son of Ahijah, for the provocation with which they provoked me to anger, and for Israel's sin, which they committed." The references to Jeroboam and Baasha, kings who had also led Israel into idolatry and incurred divine wrath, served as a stark reminder of the cyclical nature of sin and its consequences. The divine mandate was clear: the lineage of Ahab, tainted by Jezebel's influence and their own complicity in widespread apostasy, was to be utterly eradicated. The prophet's final command was a chilling echo of the divine decree: "The dogs shall eat Jezebel in the district of Jezreel, and no one shall bury her." A prophecy of brutal finality, a grim testament to the depth of Yahweh's abhorrence for her wickedness.

As quickly as he had appeared, Elisha departed, leaving Jehu and his officers in stunned silence. The captain, his head still slick with the prophetic oil, his mind reeling from the pronouncements, was a man transformed. The weight of the divine mandate settled upon him, a heavy, yet invigorating, mantle. He was no longer merely a captain; he was the chosen instrument of Yahweh's justice. He looked at his officers, their faces a mixture of bewilderment and dawning realization. They had heard the prophet's words, had witnessed the anointing. They understood the unspoken implication. The divine judgment was at hand. Jehu, his voice steady despite the enormity of his new calling, wasted no time. He emerged from the room where Elisha had spoken, his gaze sharp, his purpose ignited. He turned to the assembled officers, the very men who served under his command, men who had followed him through countless battles. He spoke with the quiet intensity of a man possessed by a singular purpose, his words carrying the weight of a divine commission.

"You know the situation," he declared, his voice cutting through the lingering silence. "You know the state of our kingdom, the corruption that has festered within our leadership, the mockery made of the very God who delivered our fathers from Egypt." He paused, allowing his words to sink in, to resonate with the deep-seated grievances that many of them harbored. The memory of Ahab's reign, marred by his association with Jezebel and her pagan cults, was a bitter one for many of the soldiers, men who still clung to the old ways and the covenantal promises of Yahweh. The idolatry that had permeated the court, the persecution of the prophets, the blatant disregard for the Law – these were not abstract concepts for them; they were the tangible manifestations of a leadership that had strayed so far from the divine path that the land itself seemed to weep.

"King Jehoram is in Jezreel," Jehu continued, his gaze sweeping across the faces of his officers. "He is recovering from his wounds from the Arameans. And his commander, Joash, son of Ahimelech, and his ally, Ahaziah, king of Judah, are also there with him." He laid out the tactical situation, the opportunity that lay before them, an opportunity that had been divinely ordained. The king's absence from the immediate vicinity of the army, coupled with his vulnerability in Jezreel, presented a window of unparalleled significance. This was not a coup born of personal ambition, but a divinely sanctioned overthrow, a purging of a lineage that had become anathema to God.

Jehu's words were not those of a hesitant man, but of a leader who had embraced his destiny with unwavering conviction. He then issued his command, a command that would set in motion a chain of events so bloody and so swift that it would forever etch his name into the annals of Israelite history. "Let no one slip away from this pursuit!" he commanded, his voice ringing with authority. The fervor of his conviction was infectious. The officers, catching the fire of his zeal, the clarity of his purpose, readily pledged their allegiance to this divinely appointed mission. They knew the risks, the sheer audacity of what they were about to undertake, but the prophet's words, the divine mandate, resonated deeply within them. It was a call to arms for the very soul of Israel, a chance to cleanse the land of the pervasive poison of Baal worship and to restore the honor of Yahweh. The loyalty of the troops to Jehu, a commander they respected and trusted, was the final, crucial element. They were ready to follow him, not just as their captain, but as their new king, the agent of God's judgment.

The oil of anointing had transformed a loyal soldier into a righteous avenger, and the army, once a force for the defense of the kingdom, was now poised to become the instrument of its radical reformation. The stage was set for a violent, decisive act, a brutal cleansing that would sweep away the corrupt remnants of Ahab's dynasty and usher in a new, albeit bloody, chapter for the kingdom of Israel. The air itself seemed to hum with anticipation, the unspoken promise of a reckoning long overdue. The days of Jezebel's defiant reign, of the pervasive influence of Baal, were numbered, and Jehu, the zealous captain, was the harbinger of their swift and terrible end. He was the chosen instrument, the righteous sword poised to strike, fulfilling a destiny that had been set in motion from the very foundations of the world.

Jehu's ascent to the throne was not marked by the fanfare of trumpets or the acclamation of a jubilant populace, but by the chilling silence of fear and the swift, inexorable march of vengeance. The divine mandate, delivered through the prophet Elisha, was a baptism of oil and a commission of blood. Armed with the prophet's pronouncements, Jehu turned his keen gaze upon his officers, men forged in the same crucible of war, men who understood the brutal calculus of power and the persuasive force of a decisive act. The words, sharp and unvarnished, ignited a fire in their hearts, a righteous anger that had long smoldered beneath the surface of their obedience to a corrupt monarchy. They knew the rot that had infested the house of Ahab, the insidious spread of Baal worship that had defiled the land and mocked the very covenant of Yahweh. They had witnessed, with growing disquiet, the influence of Jezebel, a queen mother whose devotion to foreign gods had eclipsed her loyalty to her own people and their God.

The king, Jehoram, was not with his army. He was in Jezreel, a city steeped in the history of his mother's pagan rituals, recuperating from wounds sustained in the ongoing conflict with the Arameans. With him were his nephew, Ahaziah, the king of Judah, and his own loyal commander, Joash. This was the moment, the divinely appointed opportunity, to strike at the heart of the apostasy. Jehu, understanding the volatile nature of such a swift and radical change, knew that indecision would be fatal. Hesitation would breed doubt, and doubt would unravel the divinely orchestrated plan before it could be fully realized. He had been anointed, not as a mere figurehead, but as an agent of purification, a shepherd tasked with culling the wolves from the flock.

"Let no one slip away from this pursuit!" Jehu's command was a thunderclap in the war tent, a declaration of intent that resonated with absolute authority. The assembled officers, men who had sworn allegiance to the house of Ahab, now found themselves bound by a higher, divine oath. They looked at Jehu, their captain, their comrade, now their king, and saw not a usurper, but a deliverer. The oil of anointing had transformed him, imbuing him with a zeal that mirrored the ancient prophets. Their loyalty, once tethered to a bloodline, now flowed towards a divine purpose, channeled through the man who had dared to embrace it. The chariot drivers, the captains of fifties, the captains of tens, all understood. The campaign was no longer against the Arameans; it was a purge, a ruthless excision of a dynasty that had become anathema to Yahweh.

The swiftness of Jehu's movement was breathtaking. He mounted his chariot, the very symbol of his military authority, and with a chosen band of loyal followers, sped towards Jezreel. The journey was a calculated dash, a race against time and the potential for resistance. As they approached the city, the news of Jehu's anointing, carried by an eager messenger or perhaps by a disaffected observer, had already begun to spread like wildfire, though perhaps in hushed, fearful whispers. Jehoram, weakened by his wounds and the weight of his mother's influence, was ill-prepared for the tempest that was about to break upon him.

The confrontation, when it came, was stark and brutal. Jehoram, alerted to Jehu's approach, rode out to meet him, accompanied by Ahaziah, the king of Judah. The meeting place was a fateful one, a vineyard that had once belonged to Naboth, a man unjustly murdered at the behest of Jezebel and Ahab to seize his ancestral land. The irony was not lost on Jehu, nor, perhaps, on the very heavens that witnessed this grim tableau. As Jehoram, in his chariot, saw Jehu advancing, a sense of unease must have settled upon him. He knew Jehu, the capable commander, but there was an unsettling intensity in his approach, a fire in his eyes that spoke of more than just military matters.

"Is it peace, Jehu?" Jehoram called out, his voice tinged with apprehension.

Jehu's reply was a chilling indictment; a pronouncement of doom delivered with the cold finality of a judge. "What peace can there be, so long as the whoredoms and sorceries of your mother Jezebel are so many?" The mention of Jezebel, the architect of so much corruption, the idolater who had led Israel astray, immediately signaled the gravity of the situation. It was not a greeting, but an accusation, a declaration of war against the entire lineage she represented.

Jehoram, recognizing the grim implications of Jehu's words, turned his chariot to flee, a desperate attempt to escape the inevitable. But Jehu was not a man to be outmaneuvered. He drew his bow, his aim true and steady, and loosed an arrow that found its mark. The shaft pierced Jehoram's heart, and he fell back into the chariot, his reign and his life extinguished in a single, fatal shot. The blood, hot and visceral, stained the very ground that had witnessed his father's crime.

Ahaziah, the king of Judah, seeing his uncle's demise, panicked. He, too, turned his chariot, attempting to escape the carnage. Jehu, his resolve hardened by the initial act, pursued him. "Strike him also!" he commanded his own drivers. They struck down Ahaziah as he fled towards Megiddo, and he managed to reach Jezreel, where he died. The elimination of Ahaziah was crucial; it severed any potential alliance or support for the house of Ahab from the southern kingdom. Jehu was systematically dismantling the support structure, ensuring that there would be no one to rally against him.

With the kings eliminated, Jehu's focus turned to the palace in Jezreel. Jezebel, the queen mother, was the ultimate target, the serpent whose venom had poisoned the land. Even in her advanced years, Jezebel possessed a formidable spirit, a defiant will that refused to bend. Hearing that Jehu was entering the city, she did not cower. Instead, she adorned herself, painting her eyes with kohl and styling her hair, preparing herself for her final confrontation not as a victim, but as royalty, albeit a queen whose reign had been defined by her unholy alliance with Baal. She stationed herself at a window, a dramatic and defiant gesture as Jehu's chariot approached the palace.

When Jehu entered the palace, he saw Jezebel at the window. His declaration was as scathing as it was absolute: "Have you come to play the king, Zimri, you murderer of your lord?" He invoked the memory of Zimri, a king who had reigned for only seven days before being consumed by fire. This parallel underscored the illegitimacy and doom of Jezebel's influence and the house she represented.

Jezebel's response was not one of fear, but of defiance, a verbal thrust against her assassin. "Is it well with you, my master?" she taunted, her voice laced with the venom of a lifetime of power and corruption. She knew her end was near, but she would meet it with the arrogance that had characterized her reign.

Jehu, however, was unmoved by her provocations. He turned to the eunuchs who stood in the palace, the men who served the royal household, and issued his final, chilling command concerning Jezebel. "Throw her down!" he ordered. And they did. As Jehu's chariot passed beneath the window, the eunuchs pushed Jezebel out. She fell to the ground, her blood splattering against the wall and the horses. The prophecy of Elisha was being fulfilled with horrifying accuracy: "The dogs shall eat Jezebel in the district of Jezreel, and no one shall bury her."

Jehu entered the palace, ate and drank, and then gave further instructions: "Go, see to this cursed woman, and bury her, for she is a king's daughter." But when his servants went to bury her, they found only the skull, the feet, and the hands of her bones. The dogs, as the prophecy foretold, had consumed her flesh. This brutal end, a visceral testament to Yahweh's judgment against her idolatry and her bloodshed, served as a terrifying spectacle for all of Israel, a clear message that the era of Jezebel and her pagan practices was over.

The purge, however, was far from complete. Jehu's divine commission extended to the eradication of the entire house of Ahab. He had already eliminated the kings, but the officials, the prophets of Baal, and the remnants of Ahab's loyalists still held positions of influence and power. Jehu, with ruthless efficiency, began systematically hunting them down. He gathered the princes of Samaria and the elders of the city, men who had been complicit in Ahab's and Jezebel's rule. He presented them with a stark choice: either they would present him with the heads of the seventy sons of Ahab, whom the prominent citizens of Samaria were raising, or he would come and make the city a ruin.

The elders, understandably terrified, complied. They gathered the heads of Ahab's seventy sons and sent them to Jehu in Jezreel. The scene that followed was one of unparalleled horror. Jehu, upon receiving the bloody tribute, had the heads piled in two great heaps at the entrance of the city gate, a gruesome monument to his decisive action. He then proclaimed to the people, "I am a righteous party to

Yahweh this day against the house of Ahab." He declared that he had accomplished the mission that Yahweh had given him.

But Jehu's zeal was not confined to the royal bloodline. His next target was the propagation of Baal worship, the very cult that Jezebel had so fervently promoted. He summoned all the people to Samaria and declared that he would offer a great sacrifice to Baal. This was a masterstroke of cunning and determination. He gathered all the prophets of Baal, all his worshippers, and all his priests from throughout Israel, down to the last one. He instructed them to wear their ritual garments, ensuring that none of Yahweh's worshippers could be mistaken for a Baal worshipper.

Jehu then sent messengers throughout Israel, proclaiming a sacred assembly for Baal. He assured them that this was a great sacrifice to be offered to Baal, so great that no one would be spared. The trap was set. As the crowds of Baal worshippers gathered in the temple of Baal in Samaria, Jehu, with his loyal soldiers armed with swords, positioned himself and his men at the entrances.

When the sacrifice was concluded, Jehu gave the command. His soldiers stormed into the temple, swords flashing, and systematically slaughtered every single worshipper of Baal. The slaughter was so thorough that not a single one escaped. They destroyed the pillars of Baal and broke down the house of Baal, turning it into a refuse heap, a place of impurity and desecration, mirroring the defilement that Baal worship had brought to Israel. The temple, once a center of idolatry, was now a monument to its own destruction.

Jehu's actions were decisive, brutal, and absolute. He had purged the house of Ahab, executing every male member, and had systematically eradicated the worship of Baal from Israel. He had fulfilled the divine commission with a ferocity that shocked his contemporaries and echoed through history. While the prophets lauded his zeal as righteous, the methods he employed were undeniably violent and left a trail of blood and terror. His reign began with a bloody revolution, a violent upheaval that aimed to cleanse the land of its spiritual corruption. Still, it was a cleansing achieved through the sword, a stark reminder of the devastating consequences of prolonged apostasy and the unwavering severity of divine judgment. The consequences of Jezebel's actions, her relentless promotion of paganism and her ruthless persecution of Yahweh's prophets, had finally come home to roost, a legacy of destruction that extended to her entire lineage and all who had followed her wicked ways. The silence that descended upon Samaria after the bloodbath was not one of peace, but of profound, terrified awe.

The dust of battle had barely settled, yet the air in Israel vibrated with a different kind of energy – the hum of divine vindication. For years, the prophets of Yahweh had stood as solitary voices against the encroaching darkness of Baal worship; their pronouncements often met with ridicule, persecution, and even death. They had warned of impending judgment, of the house of Ahab being brought to ruin, and now, they bore witness to the terrifying, yet undeniably righteous, fulfillment of those very prophecies. The oil of anointing had spilled onto Jehu, not as a gentle blessing, but as a potent catalyst, igniting a holy fire that consumed the apostasy Jezebel had so meticulously cultivated.

From the desolate hills and hidden valleys, those who had remained faithful observed the swift, brutal purging. They saw the chariots of Jehu, instruments of earthly power, wielded as extensions of Yahweh's will. The meticulous eradication of Ahab's lineage was not merely a political coup; it was the cosmic recalibration of a covenant fractured by idolatry. The seventy heads, piled high at the gate of Samaria, were a gruesome testament, a visual sermon preached with blood, echoing the prophets' laments over Israel's straying heart. Each severed head represented a silenced voice of corruption, a snapped thread in the tapestry of Baal's pervasive influence. The prophets, who had known the sting of exile and the gnawing fear of persecution, found a profound, albeit somber, satisfaction in this cataclysmic reversal. Their warnings, once dismissed as the ravings of zealots, were now etched in the very fabric of the nation's history, their authority stamped by the divine hand that had guided Jehu's every decisive, bloody act.

The destruction of the temple of Baal was the apex of this terrifying cleansing. For generations, the brazen pillars had stood as affronts to Yahweh, their very presence a constant, taunting reminder of Israel's spiritual infidelity. The prophets had preached against these abominations, their sermons laced with visions of their eventual demolition. To witness their physical dismantling, the shattering of their stones, the tearing down of their very foundations, was to see the tangible manifestation of God's reclaiming of His people. It was a statement, made with force and undeniable finality, that Yahweh alone was sovereign, that His covenant would not be superseded by foreign deities or the seductive whispers of syncretism. The prophets, who had often felt their words dissolve into the indifferent air, now saw those words rebound with the thunderous crash of falling idols.

The spiritual implications of these events reverberated far beyond the immediate bloodshed. Jezebel, the architect of Israel's descent into Baal worship, had sought to eclipse the very memory of Yahweh, to replace Him with the fertility gods of her homeland. She had wielded her royal authority, her wealth, and her considerable influence to foster an environment where paganism was not just tolerated, but actively promoted and enforced. Her relentless persecution of Yahweh's prophets, her orchestrating of their martyrdom, was a direct assault on the divine revelation itself. Jehu's campaign was, therefore, a vindication not just of the prophets' words, but of the very essence of their calling. They were the custodians of a sacred truth, and that truth had proven itself mightier than the machinations of a queen and the allure of a foreign cult.

The prophets saw in Jehu's unwavering resolve a reflection of God's steadfast justice. While the methods were undeniably harsh, a reflection of the deep corruption that had taken root, the outcome was the restoration of divine order. The narrative of divine justice, so often a source of comfort and hope in their own darkest hours, was now being written in the starkest of terms. It was a powerful reminder that God's patience, though vast, was not infinite, and that when sin reached its zenith, the consequences would be equally profound. The prophets understood that this was not merely a change of dynasty, but a spiritual re-consecration of the land, a severing of unholy alliances, and a reaffirmation of the covenant that bound Israel to its God.

The impact on Israel's collective consciousness was immense. The spectacle of Jezebel's end, the dogs consuming her flesh, the annihilation of Ahab's entire male lineage, and the wholesale slaughter of Baal's devotees served as an indelible lesson. The prophets, who had often felt like voices crying in a wilderness of spiritual apathy, now saw the fruits of their labor, albeit through the bloody hand of Jehu. Their warnings were no longer abstract pronouncements; they were fulfilled prophecies, etched in the memory of a nation forever altered by the brutal efficiency of divine judgment. The enduring power and sovereignty of the God of Israel had been on full display, a terrifying, awe-inspiring exhibition that left no room for doubt. The prophets' vindication was complete, their often-painful path validated by the undeniable force of Yahweh's retributive justice. Their faith, tested by fire, had emerged not only intact but demonstrably affirmed.

The spiritual landscape of Israel had been irrevocably reshaped. The idols were cast down, their worshippers decimated, and the lineage that had championed them systematically erased. The prophets who had survived Jezebel's reign, those who had lived in hiding or endured exile, could now look upon the land with a sense of profound, if weary, victory. Their pronouncements, once whispered in secret or proclaimed to a largely indifferent or hostile audience, were now the undeniable truth that had reshaped the kingdom. This was not merely a political victory; it was a spiritual triumph, a testament to the persistent, unyielding nature of divine truth. The narrative of God's faithfulness to His covenant, even in the face of egregious betrayal, was now vividly and violently illustrated. The prophets' vindication was, in essence, the vindication of Yahweh Himself. They had been

His mouthpieces, and their message, though difficult to bear, had ultimately been enacted with celestial authority. The memory of Jezebel, once a symbol of potent, seductive paganism, was now a cautionary tale, a chilling reminder of the ultimate consequences of defying the God of Israel. The prophets, therefore, were not just witnesses to Jehu's actions but living embodiments of the prophecies that had foretold them, their own vindication intertwined with the grander narrative of divine justice.

CHAPTER NINE:
Jehu: The Queen's Fall

The dust motes danced in the shafts of sunlight that pierced the gloom of the palace corridors, each one a tiny, shimmering testament to the chaos that had erupted. The clamor from the city, once a muffled murmur, now throbbed with a visceral intensity, a prelude to the storm that was gathering at the gates. Within the opulent chambers, however, a different kind of storm brewed – one of defiant resolve and a will as unyielding as the cedars of Lebanon. Jezebel, Queen of Israel, was not a woman to be erased without a final, incandescent flare.

She surveyed her reflection, not in the polished bronze mirrors that usually graced her chambers, but in the hushed stillness that preceded the end. The crimson of her robes, the deep, rich hue of dried blood and ancient wine, seemed to absorb the light, giving her an almost spectral aura. Her hair, usually a cascade of raven waves, was intricately styled, woven with threads of gold and interspersed with precious stones that caught the faint light, scattering it like captured stars. Jewels, heavy with the weight of generations and the promise of untold wealth, adorned her neck, her wrists, her fingers. This was not mere vanity; it was armor. It was a statement. It was the last defiant banner of a fallen kingdom, a declaration that even in the face of annihilation, she would reign, if only in her final moments.

The whispers of her attendants, usually hushed with fear or awe, were now ragged with terror. They scurried about her, their faces pale and drawn, their hands trembling as they adjusted the fine linen of her stola. She knew the name that was being cried in the streets, the name that was now synonymous with the end of her reign, the end of her house. *Jehu.* The blood-soaked warrior, the instrument of a wrath she had long scorned, now stood poised to deliver the final, devastating blow.

Yet, to merely await his arrival, to be dragged from her chambers like a common criminal, was an indignity she would not countenance. Her pride, the very quality that had fueled her defiance and, perhaps, her downfall, now demanded a different kind of stage. She would not be a captive; she would be a queen, even as the ground beneath her crumbled into dust. She would present herself not as a vanquished foe, but as a force of nature, unbowed, unyielding, and utterly unforgettable. She moved towards the grand window that overlooked the eastern approach to the city, the very path Jehu's chariots would soon thunder along. The sunlight, no longer a timid guest, poured through the vast opening, illuminating her from behind, casting her form into stark relief against the brilliant sky. It was a calculated tableau, designed to project an image of unassailable power, a final, spectral queen surveying her domain even as it slipped away.

Her attendants followed, their apprehension a palpable presence. They saw her ascend the few steps that led to the window's balustrade, her movements deliberate and graceful, each step imbued with a lifetime of command. She paused, her head held high, her gaze fixed on the distant horizon. The wind, stirring from the east, caught the edges of her robes, making them billow like the sails of a ship navigating treacherous seas. It whispered around her, an unseen audience to her final act of defiance.

Below, in the sprawling city, the sounds began to shift. The anxious murmurs of the populace and the fearful whispers of the remaining defenders of Samaria coalesced into a rising tide of apprehension. Then came the rumble. At first, it was a low thrum, a vibration felt more than heard, as if the very earth were beginning to groan under an immense pressure. It grew, steadily, inexorably, until it became a deafening roar – the thunder of hooves, the clatter of iron-shod wheels, the war cries of an army that had already tasted victory and was now poised to claim its ultimate prize.

Jezebel remained at the window, an immovable silhouette against the blinding light. She did not flinch, did not betray any hint of fear. Her expression, from the vantage point of those below, was impossible to discern, lost in the glare of the sun. But those who stood within the chamber, her loyal, terrified attendants, saw the tightening of her jaw, the almost imperceptible clench of her fist against the cool stone of the balustrade. She was a lioness at bay, cornered but still formidable, her defiance a silent roar that echoed the fury of the approaching army.

The first of Jehu's chariots appeared on the horizon, a glint of bronze and steel against the ochre landscape. Then another, and another, an unstoppable wave of destruction bearing down on the city. The air thrummed with the raw power of their advance, a palpable force that seemed to shake the very foundations of the palace. Jezebel watched them, her eyes narrowed, not in fear, but in a grim assessment, a final act of regal vigilance. She was the queen, and this was her court, even if it was now a court of judgment.

Her attendants, their faces etched with a mixture of horror and morbid fascination, could only watch as their queen prepared to face her fate. They had seen the destruction that had already befallen the house of Ahab, the brutal efficiency with which Jehu had carved a path through its male lineage. They knew the grim reputation of the new king, the relentless zeal that drove him. Yet, Jezebel, the foreign queen, the architect of so much of Israel's spiritual wandering, chose not to hide. She decided to stand at her window, arrayed in the full panoply of her queenship, a beacon of defiance against the encroaching darkness.

The chariots drew closer, their momentum carrying them forward with a terrifying inevitability. The dust they kicked up rose like a dark cloud, obscuring the sun for a fleeting moment and plunging the room into deeper shadow. Jezebel, however, remained in the light, a defiant figure bathed in the golden glow of the morning sun. She was not merely a queen observing an approaching enemy; she was a queen presenting herself to her conqueror, a final, audacious challenge hurled in the face of oblivion.

There was a moment, suspended in time, as the first chariot reached the foot of the palace walls, its horses snorting, their flanks lathered with sweat. The driver, a soldier grim and unyielding, looked up towards the grand window, his gaze sweeping across the facade. He saw a solitary figure at the highest window, a silhouette against the blinding sun, adorned in the trappings of royalty.

A hush fell over the approaching army, a brief, almost imperceptible pause in their triumphant advance. It was as if even they, hardened warriors accustomed to violence and bloodshed, were momentarily struck by the sheer audacity of the scene. Here was Jezebel, the queen they had been sent to destroy, presenting herself not in fear, but in regal splendor — a queen facing her fate with a pride that seemed to defy death itself.

Jezebel did not speak. Her silence was more potent than any cry, any curse. It was the silence of absolute self-possession, the silence of one who understood the gravity of the moment and chose to meet it with an unshakeable resolve. Her eyes, even from this distance, seemed to bore into the very soul of the approaching army, a silent challenge to their king, to their gods, to their very purpose.

The wind picked up again, tugging at the banners that now flew from Jehu's chariots, whipping them violently. It seemed to carry with it the murmurs of prophecy, the echoes of ancient warnings, and the chilling certainty of divine retribution. Jezebel stood bathed in the sunlight, a queen in her final, magnificent performance. She had orchestrated her life, her reign, and now, it seemed, she would orchestrate her end, a defiant queen facing the hunter, armed with nothing but her pride and the regalia of her fallen crown.

The attendants watched, their hearts pounding in unison with the thunder of the approaching chariots. They saw her lift a hand, not in supplication, but in a gesture that could be interpreted as anything from a regal acknowledgment to a final, contemptuous dismissal. It was a gesture that spoke of a queen who had ruled, who had loved and lost, who had wielded power and faced down opposition, and who would not, in her final breath, relinquish the dignity of her station.

The moment stretched, taut and fragile, as Jehu's chariot, leading the vanguard, drew to a halt directly below her window. The king himself, mounted on a magnificent warhorse, dismounted and looked up. The distance between them was not great, perhaps thirty cubits. Yet, in that space, a universe of history, of conflict, and of defiance seemed to reside. Jezebel's gaze met his, a silent, charged exchange across the gulf that separated them. She could see the hard lines of his face, the glint of triumph in his eyes, the grim satisfaction of a man who had executed his divinely appointed task with brutal efficiency. He saw her, too, not as a cowering woman, but as the formidable queen who had held Israel in her sway for so long, a queen whose legend was woven with threads of power, sorcery, and an unshakeable devotion to her foreign gods. Her lips moved, not in speech, but in a silent exhalation, a final breath of defiance. And now, she would face the ultimate consequence of her actions, not in shame, but in a blaze of regal glory. She had prepared herself not for death, but for a final, grand exit, a queenly farewell to a world that had long since ceased to be hers.

Jehu, from below, saw the subtle shift in her posture, the almost imperceptible tilt of her head. He recognized the unyielding spirit that had defined her reign, the very spirit that had made her such a formidable adversary. And perhaps, in that moment, he felt a flicker of something other than triumph – a grudging respect for the sheer, unadulterated audacity of her final stand.

But respect or not, his mission was clear. The prophets had spoken, and their prophecies were now being fulfilled with a terrible, inexorable logic. Jezebel, the queen who had dared to usurp the worship of Yahweh, the queen who had persecuted His prophets, was now to face the ultimate judgment. And she would face it not in hiding, not in fear, but at her window, adorned in her queenly splendor, a final, unforgettable image of defiance etched against the backdrop of a nation's violent rebirth. She was a queen who chose her own stage, even for her final scene, and that stage was the gaze of her conqueror, the eyes of her people, and the judgment of her God. Her pride, her ultimate undoing, was also, in this final moment, her crown.

Jehu, his gaze locked on the solitary figure silhouetted against the glare of the morning sun, felt a tremor of recognition, sharp and undeniable. There, at the highest window of the palace, stood Jezebel, the Queen of Israel, a monarch whose very name had become synonymous with defiance, idolatry, and the blood of the prophets. She was a vision of regal splendor, her form framed by the vast opening, adorned in the rich hues of her royal office, her hair a dark, intricate crown against the blinding light. It was a deliberate presentation, a final act of queenly theatre, and Jehu, the instrument of divine judgment, saw not a woman cowering in fear—still, a queen making her last, defiant stand.

The prophecies, whispered by Elijah and Elisha, echoed in his mind, each word a hammer blow against the edifice of her power. He remembered the searing pronouncements against her, the chilling predictions of her ultimate fate. The blood of Naboth, the innocent vineyard owner unjustly slain for his ancestral land, cried out from the earth, a stain that any earthly ritual would not cleanse. The countless prophets of Yahweh, whom she had hunted and slaughtered with ruthless efficiency, their blood spilled upon the stones of Samaria, also clamored for vengeance. These were not mere threats; they were pronouncements of a wrath that had been patient, a judgment that had been long in the making.

"Look!" Jehu's voice, rough with emotion and the dust of battle, cut through the hushed anticipation of his men. His finger, steady and unwavering, pointed towards the window where Jezebel stood. "Behold Jezebel, the daughter of Ethbaal, the queen who has defiled this land with her abominations and her shedding of innocent blood."

His men, clustered around him, followed his gaze. They saw her, a figure of terrible beauty, a queen in her final, defiant pose. They had witnessed the swift and brutal purging of Ahab's house, the extermination of his seventy sons, a massacre that had left the royal lineage of Israel utterly broken. They had seen the idols of Baal and Asherah toppled, their sacred groves desecrated. But Jezebel, the architect of so much of this spiritual corruption, remained. And now, she presented herself not as a fugitive but as a monarch facing her final audience.

Jehu's heart, though hardened by years of warfare and the grim necessity of his mission, was not unmoved. The prophecies were clear, and the time for their fulfillment had arrived. He turned to the men nearest him, the trusted eunuchs who served as his most loyal attendants, their faces a study in grim anticipation. These were men of efficiency, of unquestioning obedience, men who understood the weight of his commands. "Listen to me," Jehu commanded, his voice resonating with the authority of his new kingship, an authority forged in blood and validated by the ancient pronouncements of the prophets. "The word of the Lord spoken through His servant Elijah has come to pass."

He paused, letting the weight of his words settle upon them. The cheers of his victorious army, the rhythmic pounding of hooves, the metallic clang of armor – all seemed to fade into a distant hum, a backdrop to the gravity of this singular moment. "The Lord declared," Jehu continued, his voice gaining a resonant power, "that the dogs would devour Jezebel by the wall of Jezreel. And I, Jehu, the son of Nimshi, am the instrument of that prophecy."

His gaze swept across the faces of the eunuchs, seeking their complete understanding, their unwavering commitment to his decree. "She stands there," he gestured again towards the window, "a symbol of her iniquity, a monument to her wickedness. She has lived as a queen, adorned in her finery, and she shall meet her end in like manner, a final, terrible spectacle for those who still cling to her legacy."

A shiver ran through the ranks of the eunuchs. They knew the grim implications of Jehu's words. They had seen the swiftness with which he carried out his judgments, the unswerving zeal with which he pursued his divine mandate. Jezebel, the queen who had once commanded armies and seduced kings, was now to be subjected to a fate more ignominious than any common criminal.

"Go now," Jehu commanded, his voice firm, leaving no room for doubt or hesitation. "Go to the queen. Do my bidding. Let her not escape the judgment that awaits her. She is to be cast down from the window. She is to be trampled under the hooves of horses. She is to be torn asunder by the very creatures she so often favored, the beasts that were the emblems of her foreign gods."

The eunuchs exchanged grim glances. The task was straightforward, and the decree, once issued, was absolute in its effect. They understood the prophecies, the divine pronouncements that had sealed Jezebel's fate long before Jehu had even taken up his sword. This was not a moment of personal malice; it was the execution of a divine sentence, a fulfillment of ancient warnings.

"And when you have done this," Jehu added, his voice dropping to a low, resonant growl, "when her blood has stained the earth, and her flesh has become prey to the dogs, you shall leave no trace of her. No bone, no fragment, no remnant that might recall her reign or her abominations. Let her remembrance be as fleeting as the morning mist, dissolved by the unyielding light of truth and the cleansing power of Yahweh's justice."

He watched as the eunuchs, their faces set in grim determination, turned and moved with silent efficiency towards the palace. They were men of action, accustomed to executing the king's will without question or delay. As they disappeared into the shadows of the palace entrance, Jehu remained at his post, his gaze still fixed on the window. He knew that this act, this brutal fulfillment of prophecy, was more than just the demise of a queen; it was the definitive end of an era, the purging of a spiritual corruption that had festered for decades.

The cheers of his army, which had momentarily subsided, now rose again, a triumphant roar that seemed to shake the very foundations of Samaria. They knew that Jehu had delivered a decisive blow, that the forces of idolatry and foreign influence were being eradicated with relentless efficiency. But for Jehu, standing there, the echoes of the prophets' words were louder than any human acclaim. He saw in Jezebel's defiant posture not just the pride of a mortal queen, but the ultimate rebellion against the divine order.

The moments that followed stretched, taut and pregnant with anticipation. The air seemed to grow heavy, thick with the unspoken tension of a scene about to unfold. The sun climbed higher, its rays now beating down with fierce intensity, illuminating the scene with an almost unbearable clarity. Jehu knew that his eunuchs would be swift. He knew that Jezebel, despite her queenly composure, could not escape the grim reality of her situation.

He recalled the specific words of Elijah, delivered to him on the road to Damascus, the divine commission that had set him on this path of righteous destruction. "You shall strike the house of Ahab your master," the prophet had declared, "that I may avenge the blood of my servants the prophets, and the blood of all the servants of the Lord, at the hand of Jezebel. For all the house of Ahab shall perish: and I will cut off from Ahab every male, and him that is shut up and left in Israel." Jehu had fulfilled the latter part of that prophecy with devastating efficiency, leaving no male heir to the house of Ahab. Now, the final, personal judgment upon Jezebel herself was at hand.

Elijah had confronted Ahab on the very land, pointing out the sin, the stolen inheritance, and pronouncing the doom of their house. "In the place where dogs licked the blood of Naboth," Elijah had declared, "shall dogs lick your blood, even yours." And now, Jezebel herself was to fulfill that prophecy in its most chilling detail. Jehu felt the weight of this historical justice pressing down upon him. He was not merely a conqueror; he was an agent of retribution, a divinely appointed instrument to cleanse Israel of its deep-seated corruption.

The minutes ticked by, each one a drumbeat of anticipation. The sounds from the city grew more distant as the immediate aftermath of the battle gave way to a tense quiet. All eyes, it seemed, were focused on the palace, on the window where Jezebel still stood, a solitary, defiant figure. Jehu waited, his mind a storm of prophecy and consequence. He knew that the eunuchs would be discreet, efficient, and without mercy. Then, a subtle change occurred. A flicker of movement at the window, a brief interruption of the stark silhouette. It was impossible to discern the exact details from his vantage point, but there was a sudden, almost violent shift in her posture, a sense of something giving way. A cry, thin and piercing, seemed to slice through the air, quickly stifled, as if by a hand clamped over a mouth.

Jehu did not need to see the act itself. He understood. The eunuchs had acted. The decree had been carried out. Jezebel, the queen who had dared to defy the God of Israel, was no more. The prophecy, delivered decades ago, was now fulfilled in its terrible, unyielding truth. The dogs would indeed lick her blood by the wall of Jezreel.

A profound silence descended upon Jehu and his men. The triumphant shouts of the army seemed to die on their lips, replaced by a collective, awe-struck stillness. They had witnessed not just a battle or a conquest, but the unfolding of divine judgment —a moment when the heavens themselves seemed to have intervened. Jehu, the king who had seized the throne with ruthless efficiency, now stood humbled by the immense power of the prophecies he had fulfilled.

The eunuchs, their faces etched with a grim resolve that belied the horror of their task, moved with a practiced, silent efficiency. Jehu's command had been explicit, and the swiftness with which they responded was a testament to their years of service and their unquestioning obedience to the crown, even in its violent transition.

They reached the queen's chambers, the very locus of her power and influence. Jezebel, as Jehu had observed, stood framed against the immense window, a figure of almost defiant grandeur. Her regal attire, the silks and embroidered fabrics that had always proclaimed her status, now seemed like a shroud, a stark contrast to the brutal reality that was about to unfold. Her posture, though outwardly composed, betrayed a coiled tension, a queen bracing herself for an inevitable, yet still unimaginable, end. The sunlight, a relentless spotlight, seemed to mock the darkness that was about to engulf her.

As the eunuch entered the chamber, their presence, though silent, was an invasion. Jezebel turned, her gaze meeting theirs. There was no plea in her eyes, no desperate attempt to bargain or to flee. Perhaps she understood that her fate was sealed, that the prophecies, like relentless hounds, had finally cornered her. Or possibly, in her final moments, she embraced the queenly persona to its ultimate conclusion, facing death with the same unyielding spirit she had displayed throughout her life. Her expression was a complex tapestry of pride, defiance, and perhaps, a flicker of something akin to weariness – the weariness of a long and bloody struggle against a destiny she could no longer evade.

One of the eunuchs, the unspoken leader among them, approached her. His face was impassive, a mask honed by years of suppressing emotion in service to the throne. He spoke no words, for words were no longer necessary. Jehu's decree had been delivered, and their duty was clear. He gestured, a subtle, almost imperceptible nod towards the window. It was a silent command, a final confirmation of what was to come.

Jezebel, with a dignity that was both chilling and mesmerizing, did not resist. She moved towards the window, her steps measured, her head held high. As she reached the edge, she paused, her silhouette once again stark against the blinding expanse of the sky. It was a moment suspended in time, a final, dramatic tableau. She might have seen the vastness of the world beyond the palace walls, the land she had sought to dominate, the people she had ruled and often tormented. Perhaps in that fleeting instant, the entirety of her reign – the alliances forged, the battles waged, the idols erected, the prophets silenced – flashed before her eyes.

Then, with a swift, decisive motion that spoke of practiced, ruthless execution, they moved, not with brute force, but with a calculated efficiency that underscored the chilling nature of their task. They did not push her violently, but instead guided her, a grim escort to her ultimate destination. She was not thrown; she was *delivered* to the abyss. The eunuchs, their hands briefly touching her regal robes, propelled her forward.

The air caught her, a brief, fleeting resistance, before she began to fall. It was a descent that was both terrifyingly swift and, to those watching from below, agonizingly slow. The silks of her garments billowed around her like dark wings, a macabre parody of flight. The sunlight, which had illuminated her defiance moments before, now seemed to pursue her downwards, a mocking testament to the earthly life she was leaving behind. A strangled cry, a sharp, abrupt sound that was quickly swallowed by the distance and the chaos of the courtyard below, escaped her lips. It was a sound of surprise, perhaps, or of the sudden, brutal realization of the physical reality of her end.

Jehu, his gaze fixed on the window, saw only the swift departure. He did not witness the impact, nor the immediate aftermath. His command had been to cast her down, and that, he knew, had been fulfilled. The prophecies, however, were more detailed. He knew what awaited her in the courtyard below. The "dogs," the scavengers of the city, would fulfill the second part of Elijah's chilling pronouncement.

Down in the courtyard, the scene was one of stunned disbelief. The eunuchs had done their work with such speed that there was little room for reaction. The sudden appearance of the falling figure, a dark streak against the azure sky, had sent a ripple of shock through the assembled soldiers and servants who had gathered, drawn by the grim spectacle. There was no orderly procession, no dignified farewell—just the sudden, brutal arc of a falling body.

The immediate aftermath was a tableau of grim reality. The rich fabrics of her gown, once symbols of her status, were now torn and soiled. The sunlight, which had adorned her in life, now starkly illuminated the brutal truth of her demise. The first to react were the scavengers, the stray dogs that perpetually roamed the city, drawn by the scent of death. They were the inevitable executors of the prophecy, the unclean beasts that would fulfill the grim denouement of Jezebel's story.

They moved with a primal urgency, their presence a stark reminder of the ignominious fate that awaited all flesh, regardless of rank or title. The eunuchs, their duty done, had withdrawn, leaving the scene to the natural, unvarnished order of things. Jehu's final command had been clear: "Let her remembrance be as fleeting as the morning mist... Let no bone, no fragment, no remnant be found." And so, they had ensured that the dogs would fulfill that part of the prophecy, leaving no trace of the queen who had once commanded such immense power.

The prophecy concerning Jezebel had been delivered by Elijah decades earlier, a pronouncement of divine judgment against her wicked deeds, particularly the murder of Naboth. "In the place where dogs licked the blood of Naboth," Elijah had declared to Ahab, "shall dogs lick your blood, even yours." And now, by the wall of Jezreel, the prophecy was being fulfilled in its most literal and brutal sense. The blood that had been spilled in injustice was now to be avenged by the very creatures that symbolized impurity and ignominy.

From Jehu's vantage point, the scene in the courtyard was obscured by distance and the palace architecture. Yet, the knowledge of what was happening was more potent than any visual confirmation could be. He understood the significance of the moment. It was not just the end of Jezebel; it was the culmination of a spiritual war that had raged for years. It was the vindication of the prophets, the restoration of the covenant, the cleansing of Israel from the stain of Baal worship and foreign abominations.

The death of Jezebel was a brutal testament to the unyielding nature of divine judgment. She had been a force of nature in her own right, a woman of formidable will and ambition, who had left an indelible mark on the history of Israel. Her reign had been a period of intense spiritual turmoil, a time when the worship of Yahweh had been challenged and suppressed. Her demise marked the definitive end of that era, a violent severing of the ties to idolatry and foreign influence that had plagued the land.

The eunuchs, tasked with ensuring no trace remained, meticulously followed Jehu's orders. They ensured that the dogs had their fill, that any remains were disposed of in a manner that left no lingering symbol of her reign. This final act of erasure was as crucial to the prophecy as the fall itself. Jezebel was to be defeated and utterly forgotten, her legacy erased by the very dirt and the very beasts she had so despised.

The narrative of Jezebel's life, so filled with drama, power, and ultimately, destruction, concluded not in a glorious battle or a dignified passing, but in a swift, ignominious plunge from a high window. It was a death that was as stark and uncompromising as the prophecies that had foretold it. The queen who had presented herself as a defiant goddess had, in her final moments, become a mere mortal, subject to the same brutal finality as any other person. The legacy of Jezebel would forever be intertwined with her violent end. She would be remembered not for her beauty or her power, but for her wickedness, her idolatry, and the bloody consequences that followed her actions. The fall from the window was the ultimate symbol of her downfall, a physical manifestation of her spiritual and political ruin.

The swiftness of Jezebel's descent from the royal window was matched only by the brutal efficiency of her end. The prophecy of Elijah, a pronouncement that had hung over her reign like a perpetual storm cloud, was not merely spoken; it was to be enacted with chilling literalness in the very dust of the palace courtyard. The eunuchs, their grim task completed with the act of propulsion, had vanished back into the shadows of the palace, leaving the scene to the indifferent sky and the burgeoning scavengers of Jezreel.

Down below, where the crowds of soldiers and courtiers had gathered, a morbid fascination had replaced the initial shock. They watched, a collective breath held, as the queen's form met the unforgiving earth. It was not a gentle landing. The trajectory of her fall, combined with the unforgiving nature of the ground, ensured a violent, jarring impact. The silks that had billowed in her descent now lay matted and torn, clinging to a body that was already beginning to surrender its regal form to the indignity of death.

And then, the prophecy began its final, gruesome fulfillment. The dogs, attracted by the sudden disturbance and the undeniable scent of mortality, emerged from the nooks and crannies of the city. They were not noble beasts; these were the strays, the feral inhabitants of any urban center, driven by instinct and a constant hunger. Their arrival was not an act of malice, but an inevitable consequence of nature's unforgiving order, a stark reminder that even queens, in their demise, were reduced to mere sustenance.

They converged on the fallen queen with a primal urgency. Their initial approach was cautious, a sniffing, a circling, a silent assessment of the feast laid before them. But caution quickly gave way to a ravenous hunger. The first dogs, bolder than the rest, lunged forward, their teeth tearing into the rich fabrics that still partially concealed the queen's broken form. The sounds that followed were not the cries of a queen in pain, but the tearing of cloth, the snapping of jaws, and the guttural growls of a territorial dispute over the spoil.

Elijah's prophecy concerning the blood of Naboth had been specific: "In the place where dogs licked the blood of Naboth shall dogs lick your blood, even yours." And here, by the walls of Jezreel, in the very heart of the kingdom she had so ruthlessly controlled, the prophecy was being fulfilled with horrifying accuracy. The blood that had been shed unjustly, the life that had been extinguished for the sake of a vineyard, was now demanding a grim reckoning. The dogs, the instruments of this retribution, were systematically erasing any physical trace of the queen who had sanctioned such an act.

The sheer completeness of the destruction underscored the immensity of her downfall. There was no dignified burial, no grand mausoleum. Instead, there was the gnawing of flesh, the rending of sinew, the scattering of bone. The dogs showed no reverence, no recognition of the power she had once wielded. They saw only prey, and their actions were as unfeeling as the decrees she had so often issued. The queen who had once commanded armies and influenced kings was now at the mercy of beasts, her fate sealed by the very forces she had sought to defy.

As the dogs continued their grim work, the physical remnants of Jezebel's reign began to disappear. The rich fabrics were torn to shreds, the jewels that might have adorned her were likely lost in the ensuing chaos, swallowed by the dust, or carried away by the opportunistic scavengers. The very essence of her royal identity was being systematically dismantled, piece by piece, by the indifferent jaws of the dogs.

The eyewitness accounts, when they eventually filtered back to the ears of those who had not been present, were graphic and unsettling. They spoke of a scene of utter chaos, of the frenzied activity of the dogs, of the swift and brutal disintegration of what had once been the formidable queen of Israel. These accounts, filled with gruesome detail, served to reinforce the magnitude of the event, solidifying it in the collective memory as a pivotal moment in Israel's history. It was a day when the divine judgment was not just a spoken word, but a brutal, visible reality.

The completeness of Jezebel's destruction was perhaps the most profound aspect of her end. It was a deliberate and systematic unmaking, a purging of her very essence from the land. The prophecy had ensured that her demise would be a public spectacle, a demonstration of divine power that would resonate for generations to come. The dogs, in their unthinking role as agents of this judgment, ensured that the humiliation and the utter finality of her fate were fully realized. She had defied the prophets, promoted idolatry, and shed innocent blood. Her punishment was to be as profound and absolute as her transgressions. The scattered remnants of her body, consumed by the dogs, were the final, undeniable proof that the word of the Lord, once declared, would always find its fulfillment, however brutal.

The cessation of the dogs' activity was a gradual process, as their hunger was sated and their feast concluded. The dust of Jezreel, once stirred by the hooves of chariots and the clamor of royal processions, settled slowly, a pall over the grim spectacle that had unfolded. Jezebel was gone. Not merely dead, but utterly erased, a queen whose reign had been as vibrant and consuming as a desert fire, now reduced to scattered fragments by the very creatures the Law deemed unclean.

Her life, a tapestry woven with threads of audacious ambition and a fierce, misguided devotion, was now laid bare in its starkest form. Jezebel, the Phoenician princess, wife of Ahab, had arrived in Samaria like a tempest, bringing with her the opulent rituals and fervent worship of Baal. She had not merely tolerated this foreign god; she had championed him with an unyielding zeal, making his worship the state religion and actively persecuting the prophets of Israel. The memory of Naboth, whose vineyard was unjustly seized and whose life was forfeited for the king's fleeting desire, would forever be stained by her complicity, her cunning manipulation sealing his doom and her own. Her devotion was not a gentle reverence, but a consuming fire that demanded allegiance, burning away any trace of loyalty to the God of Israel.

The ambition that had fueled her every move was undeniable. She had been more than a queen consort; she had been a political force, an active participant in the machinations of power. Her influence over Ahab was legendary, a testament to a will as strong, if not stronger, than his own. Together, they had steered Israel down a path of spiritual corruption, alienating them from their covenant with the Almighty. Her beauty and her charm were weapons, wielded with the precision of a seasoned warrior, bending kings and courtiers to her will. Yet, this same brilliance, this same drive, when misdirected, became a tool of oppression, a force that crushed dissent and trampled upon righteousness.

The reign of Ahab and Jezebel had been a period of outward prosperity, marked by grand building projects and a flourishing of the arts. But beneath the gilded surface, a spiritual rot had set in. Baal worship, with its fertility rites and sensual worship, had seeped into the very fabric of Israelite society, eclipsing the reverence due to the God of their fathers. The altars to Yahweh were torn down, his prophets hunted and killed, their voices silenced by the executioner's sword or the ravenous jaws of Jezebel's favored beasts. The land itself seemed to cry out under the weight of this spiritual infidelity, a spiritual drought that mirrored the barrenness of a heart devoid of true faith.

Elijah, the stern and unyielding prophet of God, stood as a solitary beacon against the rising tide of idolatry. His confrontations with Jezebel were legendary, a clash of wills between divine authority and human pride. On Mount Carmel, he had exposed the impotence of Baal, calling down fire from heaven to consume his sacrifice, a dramatic vindication of Yahweh's power. Yet, even this miracle had not tempered Jezebel's wrath. Her pursuit of Elijah, her relentless vendetta, underscored the depth of her conviction in her own cause, a conviction that ultimately led to her own undoing.

Her final moments, from the royal window, were a desperate, defiant act. Cast out by Jehu, the usurper who had been anointed to cleanse Israel of Ahab's lineage, she had faced her end not with pleading but with the regal composure she had always maintained. Adorned in her royal attire, she had sought to meet her fate with the dignity of a queen, a final, futile attempt to assert her authority even in the face of annihilation. But the prophecy, spoken by Elijah, was to be fulfilled with a brutal finality; her blood, shed unjustly in the past, demanded a gruesome retribution.

Her legacy, if one could call it that, is a chilling cautionary tale. It spoke of the seductive danger of misplaced devotion, of the devastating consequences when power is wielded without righteousness. Jezebel's passion, a quality that, in the service of truth, might have been admirable, had instead become a destructive force, leading her and her kingdom into spiritual ruin. Her influence had been a potent poison, corrupting the spiritual heart of Israel, leading many astray from the covenant relationship with their God.

The whispers of her life, now silenced by the finality of her death, had resonated throughout Israel for years. Tales of her beauty, extravagance, cruelty, and unwavering commitment to Baal worship were recounted in hushed tones, a mixture of fear and awe surrounding her name. She was a figure of immense charisma and immense wickedness, a queen who had left an indelible, albeit dark, mark on the history of God's chosen people. Her reign was a dark chapter, one that highlighted the constant struggle between faith and idolatry, between obedience and rebellion.

As the dust settled and the sounds of the city gradually returned, the absence of Jezebel was palpable. The oppressive shadow she had cast over Israel was lifted, replaced by the daunting task of rebuilding and restoring the spiritual integrity of the kingdom. Jehu's actions, though brutal, had initiated a cleansing, a necessary step in the long process of turning Israel back towards their God. The end of Jezebel's era was not merely a political upheaval; it was a spiritual watershed, a moment of reckoning that would resonate for generations.

Her story would be passed down, not as a tale of triumph, but as a somber warning. It was a testament to the fact that even the most influential and powerful individuals are subject to divine judgment. The end of an era, marked by such a violent and ignominious conclusion, was a stark indication of the profound importance of living a life aligned with divine will, for in that alignment, and only in that alignment, lies true and lasting victory. The choices made by Jezebel, the fierce queen who sought to impose her will upon a nation and its God, ultimately led to her utter undoing, her reign a stark illustration of how even the most formidable human power is ultimately subject to the unyielding justice of the Almighty.

In Conclusion:

Ahab and Jezebel were a lethal attraction of two individuals drowning in pride, self-reliance, control, stubbornness, and modern-day narcissism. The act that was the deciding factor in whether Jezebel would live or die was when she became so arrogant that she began to regard herself as a goddess. Every time someone in the Bible has attempted to elevate themselves to be immortal or a god, they have met their end.

Instead of helping each other to find victory and humility through Yahweh, the God of Israel, Ahab and Jezebel chose to feed each other's lusts, desires, and get whatever they wanted, regardless of who it hurt. This is the definition of an unhealthy love. It is not love "God's Way!"

Throughout this series, you will find books randomly placed on the list that are not "healthy" types of love. It is easy to learn the correct way to love, but sometimes, as a professor, I find that my students learn more from the "disaster stories or scenarios" that teach them what NOT to do. I pray that this book was a blessing to you and that all the books in this series you have read have ignited a fire within you to have a close relationship with God the Father and His Son, Jesus Christ, who died on a Roman cross and then rose from the grave. He loved you so much that he gave his life for you. There is no greater way to "Love God's Way" than to give your life to him and for him if necessary.

With love,
La Wanda Blackmon

References and Websites

If you would like to conduct further research on this topic, particularly if you are a minister or teacher, I have listed several websites for your review. Also listed below are the scriptures I used to develop my backstory. I hope you have enjoyed this book and it has created a desire inside of you to learn more about God's word, God's love, grace, mercy, and patience with us.

Definition of terms and explanation of characters

Ahab: King of Israel, husband of Jezebel, who followed her religious practices.

Baal: A principal god of the Phoenicians and Canaanites, worshiped by Jezebel.

Baal: A West Semitic title meaning "lord" or "master," commonly used as the name of the chief deity of the Phoenician pantheon, often associated with storm and fertility.

Baalism: The religious system and practices centered on the worship of Baal.

Deuteronomy: The fifth book of the Hebrew Bible, containing covenant laws and historical narratives, which strongly influenced the theological outlook of the Deuteronomistic Historians.

Elijah: A major prophet in the Hebrew Bible, who served only the God, Yahweh. Elijah was active during the reign of Ahab, king of Israel, and is known for his confrontation with the prophets of Baal on Mount Carmel. He championed the worship of the one true God.

Jezebel: Daughter of Ethbaal I, king of the Sidonians, and wife of King Ahab of Israel, known for her promotion of Baal worship in the Northern Kingdom.

Jehu: A military commander anointed to overthrow the house of Ahab and purge Baal worship from Israel.

Jezreel: A fertile valley and important city in Israel, the location of Naboth's vineyard.

Naboth: An Israelite whose vineyard was unjustly seized by King Ahab at Jezebel's instigation.

Prophetic Literature: The collection of books in the Hebrew Bible attributed to prophets, such as Isaiah, Jeremiah, and Ezekiel, as well as the Former Prophets (Joshua, Judges, Samuel, Kings).

Samaria: The capital city of the Northern Kingdom of Israel during the reigns of Ahab and Jezebel.

Syncretism: The merging or blending of different religious beliefs, practices, and cults.

Yahweh: The national God of Israel, whose worship was central to the Israelite covenant. The covenantal name of the God of Israel. The "I am."

Bible Scriptures dealing with various types of marriages

<u>Acquisition of wives</u>: Genesis 24 and 29

<u>Jesus' teachings about the Galilean Wedding</u>: The Gospels

---

The King James Version of the Holy Bible was used to create the backstory.

1. I Kings 16-22.

2. II Kings 9-10.

3. II Chronicles 17-21.

Phoenician Loanwords and Hebrew Cognates

The following is a selective list of Phoenician loanwords and their proposed Hebrew cognates, shedding light on the linguistic and cultural exchange during the period of Ahab's reign:

Phoenician: 'šrt *(goddess Asherah)* - **Hebrew:**'ăšērâ (sacred pole, Asherah).

Phoenician: mlk *(king)* - **Hebrew:**meleḵ (king).

Phoenician: 'rb *(ivory)* - **Hebrew:**šen *(tooth, ivory, from Akkadian* sinnu).

Phoenician: 'b *(father)* - **Hebrew:**'āḇ (father).

Phoenician: bmh *(high place)* - **Hebrew:**bāmâ (high place).

Research Information

Listed in the section are the references I used during my years of working on this manuscript in the 1990s to develop the backstory and add my literary liberties with as much accuracy as possible. I wanted my stories to be as biblically, culturally, and geographically accurate as we can know or imagine from the available old maps. I realize that novels typically do not include reference lists. However, my first few books have prompted people to contact me to ask where I obtained this information.

In addition to the stories shared with me by the three Jewish Rabbis and the two Muslim Imams, I gained knowledge from these resources. At the time I wrote these books, the internet and Google did not exist. If any of my writing appears to be similar to AI, Google, other search engines, or websites, it is truly a coincidence.

In preparation for the publication of this book, given that the Dead Sea scrolls were discovered in 1947, my editor and I have researched topics that could have possibly changed (e.g., cultural issues or information on idols) to ensure that any discoveries had not rendered any of this book's claims invalid.

As a result, I found a couple of interesting websites that you might be interested in reading more about. For those books, we have listed the corresponding websites in this section as well. If no websites are listed for a book, it means we did not find any that we thought would help you research the book's topics in more depth.

I pray that my books cause you to want to "deep dive" even more as you study the Bible in its entirety—Old and New Testament.

References

Ahlström, Gösta W. (1998). *The History of Ancient Palestine from the Paleolithic Period to Alexander's Conquest.* London, England: Sheffield Academic Press.

Barnes, William H. (1991). *Studies in the Chronology of the Divided Monarchy of Israel* (Atlanta: Scholars Press, 1991) 29-55.

Bright, John. (1981). *A History of Israel.* 3rd ed. Louisville, KY: Westminster John Knox Press.

Cogan, Mordechai, and Hayim Tadmor. (1988). *II Kings: A New Translation with Introduction and Commentary.* New Kensington, PA: Anchor Bible.

Cross, F. M. (1972). "An Interpretation of the Nora Stone," *Bulletin of the American Schools of Oriental Research* 208 (Dec. 1972) 17, n. 11.

Eissfeldt, Otto. (1965). *The Old Testament: An Introduction.* New York, NY: Harper & Row.

Gammie, John G. (1980). *The Theology of fulfillment: Prophecy and the Old Testament.* Chico, CA: Scholars Press.

Hallo, William W., and K. Lawson Younger, eds. (1997). *The Context of Scripture: Monument, Library, and Archive.* Leiden, Netherlands: Brill Press.

Holladay, William L. *The New Interpreter's® Bible Commentary, Vol. I: Genesis, Exodus, Leviticus, Numbers, Deuteronomy, Joshua, Judges, Samuel, Kings.* Nashville, TN: Abingdon Press.

Lapp, Paul W. (1997). *Biblical Archaeology and Bible.* Atlanta, GA: Society of Biblical Literature.

Peñuela, J. M. (1953). "La Inscripción Asiria IM 55644 y la Cronología de los Reyes de Tiro", *Sefarad* 13 (1953, Part 1) 217-37; 14 (1954, Part 2) 1-39.

Rendsburg, Gary A. (1986). *The Redaction of the Book of Judges.* Chico, CA: Scholars Press, 1986.

Sasson, Jack M. *The Civilizations of the Ancient Near East.* New York, NY: Scribner, 1995.

Wildberger, Hans. (1997). *Isaiah 13-27: A Commentary.* Minneapolis, MN: Fortress Press.

Wright, G. Ernest. (1959). *The Old Testament and World Archaeology.* Owings, MD: Westminster Press.

Website:

https://worldhistoryedu.com/major-ancient-phoenician-deities/

About the Author

LaWanda Blackmon is an ordained minister, missionary, and prolific author with over 35 years of experience in ministry. She has authored over 25 nursing books and more than 100 workbooks in five nursing genres. She currently has two religious series in production: *"The Redeeming Love Series"* (a 60-book series) and the *"Revelation: Made Simple Series"* (a five-book series), before adding this 45-book biblical romance series, *"Love God's Way."* As of the time of publishing this series, Mrs. Blackmon has over 122 books registered under her name (all genres combined). Most are still in print, published by various publishers.

Mrs. Blackmon has recently written three shorter books as an encouragement tool to help individuals who want to know more about spiritual warfare but find it too intimidating. She began preaching at the age of 16, became licensed in 1991, and was ordained 15 years ago. Her heart has always been devoted to medical missions, both domestically and internationally.

Her education includes a two-year registered nursing training program, a double major (Associate of Science and Associate of Arts degrees), two Bachelor of Science degrees (in Nursing and Liberal Arts), and two master's degrees (in Nursing and Education). Her doctoral work has been in medical research and education. Her work experience spans the full spectrum of nursing and nursing leadership, including consulting and freelance writing.

Books in this Series

1) **Issac and Rebekah**: *A Divine Love that defies all arranged marriage concepts!*
2) **Jacob, Leah, and Rachel**: *Navigating Two Wives & Two Concubines*
3) **Abraham, Sarah, and Hagar**: *The Love Triangle*
4) **Hadassah**: *The Unusual Bride and a King*
5) **Hosea and Gomer**: *The Beauty of Redeeming Love*
6) **King Solomon and the Shulamite Woman**: *A Pure Love That Offers Everything*
7) **King Solomon and the Queen of Sheba**: *A Love from Two Worlds*
8) **Boaz and Ruth**: *Love the Second Time Around*
9) **Samson and Delilah**: *A Love that Destroys*
10) **King David and Michal**: *The Beauty of First Love*

11) **King David and Bathsheba:** *The Unforbidden Love and Murder*

12) **King David and Abigail:** *A Love that Protects*

13) **King David and Abishag:** *A Love that is Patient and Warm*

14) **Hannah:** *The Love of a Second Wife*

15) **Ahab and Jezebel:** *An Unhealthy Love*

16) **King Jehoram and Athaliah:** *A Love that Destroys and Kills*

17) **Lapidoth and Deborah:** *A Love that Lets each other Grow*

18) **Adam and Eve:** *The First Arranged Marriage*

19) **Amram and Jochebed:** *A love that chooses the best route even when it hurts!*

20) **Job and Dinah:** *A Love that Stays Regardless*

21) **Moses and Zipporah:** *A Love that Accepts You Regardless*

22) **Moses and Thabisa:** *A Love that was Fought and Forbidden*

23) **Salmon and Rahab:** *A Love that Protects and Restores*

24) **Abraham and Keturah:** *A Love that Nurtures*

25) **Hur and Miriam:** *A Unique Love (Sister of Moses)*

26) **Zechariah and Elizabeth:** *A Love that Waits*

27) **Mary and Joseph:** *A Love Forged in Faith*

28) **Priscilla and Aquilla:** *A Love that is called for a purpose*

29) **Ananias and Saphirah:** *A love built on deceit*

30) **Zebedee and Salome:** *A Love for Ministry*

31) **Aaron & Elisheba:** *A Love that Serves*

32) **Joanna & Chuza:** *A Love that Disappoints*

33) **Peter & Ahava:** *A Love that Survives*

34) **Pontius Pilate and Claudia:** *A love that disappoints and condemns*

35) **Herod Antipas and Herodias**: *A love that steals, deceives, and cons*
36) **Lot and his wife**: A love that lusts for the things of Sodom
37) **Lot and his two daughters**: Incest—the forbidden love
38) **Samuel and Eliana**: A Love for the Chosen One
39) **Joseph and Asenath**: A love that heals and restores
40) **Tamar & Judah**: A revengeful love
41) **Noah and Emzara**: A love that supports
42) **Jesse and his two wives**: A Love that resulted in Shame
43) **King Saul and Abinonah:** *A Donkey Herder's Love*
44) **King Saul and Rizpah:** *A Love that Defies Death*
45) **Heber and Jael**: *The Love of a Warrior Wife*

HFT Publishing, Inc. will place two books from this series on Amazon each month. If they can convert the manuscripts to Amazon KDP and Kindle format earlier, the books would post as soon as they are ready.

If you are not certain which ones you want to read first, you can go to the author's YouTube channel and look at the AI-generated video products that HFT Publishing, Inc., has developed for each book.

La Wanda Blackmon
@LBlackmonBooks

URL for YouTube Channel
https://www.youtube.com/channel/UCTyg2bSbpXc8EsSi4tsCeQg

Additionally, the Author's Page for La Wanda Blackmon will feature all books from all series. You will be able to read about the book and the author on www.amazon.com

Although La Wanda wrote these books in the late 1980s and throughout the 1990s, they need to be converted to the new, updated book publishing software. (It was not used back then.) This requires significant formatting and some changes. These books have never been published in eBook format. New book covers are being designed that are more modern and will reflect the author's updated information.

Of course, to ensure validity, all books are fact-checked and researched by the editing department of HFT Publishing, Inc. to verify that the "manually done" research from the 1990s remains accurate and has not been superseded by advancements in 21st-century technology, archaeological findings, and artificial intelligence usage. It is impossible to convert the books within a shorter timeframe than 90 days for each book. This project had been underway for almost a year when the first book, ***"Isaac and Rebekah: A Divine Love that Defies all Arranged Marriage Concepts,"*** was submitted to Amazon in August 2025.

To know what is available on Amazon at the time you are reading this book, go to the YouTube channel and review the videos. If a book has a video, it has already been converted and published. All 45 books will have a video added to this channel.

As soon as the books are ready for publication and the book video is uploaded to the YouTube channel, they will be listed on Amazon for pre-publication sales, allowing you to receive the book on the day it becomes available. All books will be available in both paperback and Kindle eBook formats. Initially, these will be available on Kindle Select. HFT Publishing, Inc. is unsure how long this will last, as I will not receive any revenue from these Kindle Unlimited listings. However, until we have listed and marketed all the books, you will have free access through Kindle Unlimited if you are a member.

If you have not read the first book, then go to the next page and read about this series and how it was developed. Note that this information is repeated in each book. This is not new material. It is included for the benefit of the first-time reader of this series.

Information about "A Love God's Way" Book Series Development

NOTE: This is not new information. It was initially printed in the "Issac and Rebekah" Book #1 of this series. In the event you have not read that first book, this information is added here for your convenience. Considering this book was initially written in the 1990s, while I lived in the Middle East, I wanted to share the story of how this series began and what has changed in this manuscript over the past 30 years.

I was an energetic writer. My 29-year-old mind was full of ideas. I loved history and often found myself with a romance novel and a Coke in hand, except when I was at work. So, for me to write religious, historical romance novels was not a far stretch of the imagination of those who knew me.

However, during the first Gulf War and my years living in the Middle East, it was challenging to find a publisher willing to take on a new, unknown writer. For manuscript proposals, they requested the introduction and the first three chapters if fewer than five chapters were included in the book. If you had more chapters, you had to send half of your book. Several publishers, I dealt with required the whole book. That limited how many of those types of publishers I dealt with.

I almost as many manuscripts started as I had finished. When things got tough during the war, I found it easier to take a handheld pocket recorder that used tapes similar to those of an answering machine recorder (remember those popular little devices from the 1980s?).

I then started recording the books. I planned to transcribe them later. Then I ended up at a hospital with one of those old Dictaphone transcription systems. It used the same mini cassette tapes as my recorder. However, with the headset, I could get clearer recordings. They were no longer using them and had piled them in a storage closet. I asked for permission to take it to my flat and use it. This revolutionized my recording process, reducing my recording time. It used an electrical cord, saving me the cost of a battery. I was recording so much that I was going through about $20 worth of double-A batteries a month (for 1990s prices, that was a significant number of batteries).

Then a civil war broke out in the area where I was living (after the Gulf War ended). I stayed behind to help stabilize the region. However, the Islamic radicals were not happy with the westernization we were bringing to the area. At times, things would get confiscated and destroyed. Especially writings and binders containing papers. Not all of the soldiers could read English. So, if it were in English, it was considered to be religious writings or Western ideas that would corrupt the women of the area. So, they would burn it.

I boxed up my manuscripts in boxes of gifts I was shipping back to the United States for my family members. I put a letter in there with instructions for my mother to stack these binders in my old bedroom at her house. She and Dad were so busy with the church, I knew she would never read them. However, my dad would. Years later, I found out that he read every one that Momma unpacked. When I got married, and all of my boxes arrived, I found about eight boxes of stuff I had sent as cargo freight via air (from the Persian Gulf region to Pensacola, Florida) at the port. Then my dad claimed them for me and put them in storage.

After I sent out my binders containing the writings and books I used for research while writing those nursing books and romance novels, I began sending out the tapes. I was putting them in letters and mailing them. However, they never got to the United States. So, after a few test mailings, I realized I could not send the real tapes with hours of my work on them without a plan.

So, I began going through my clothes. I decided I would sew the tapes into the linings of jackets and lined dresses. I packed the clothes and sent them by Air Freight. When they opened the boxes (it was apparent when we unpacked them that they had been thoroughly searched, but they did not realize that there were things sewn into the linings of those clothes). Only the clothes on top were shuffled. I suppose God wanted these books to survive! But the story gets stranger.

I did not even find those tapes until this summer (2025). Momma never unpacked the boxes labeled 'clothes'. They were just stored. I was rummaging through old storage boxes and opening them to see if I could donate some items to Goodwill, and I found clothes with these dictated books on tape inside.

I have found numerous tapes of books that were never transcribed into the computer. I do not even have a recorder to play them on. I have notified the publisher of my find. They are going to try to find me one of the old dictation players used by medical transcriptionists in hospitals in the 1980s. Those are the tapes I used for the recordings.

Once they locate a system to play these tapes on, we will start sometime in 2026, the laborious task of transcribing those stories. These will be novels, but they are based on true stories that people I helped save their lives told me their "love story." I had asked Momma about those tapes, and she declared that they never came. She claims she forgot that I told her I was sending them in the lining of clothes. It is a miracle that I found them. I am now praying that the Holy Spirit has protected those tapes and the dictation on them. The shipping date on the last box with clothes and tapes was the summer of 1995. It is precisely 30 years later that I am finding them!

Now, let us return to the topic of the boxes shipped from the Middle East with book manuscripts and my laptop. My parents had never opened them, so when my husband tore these boxes open in 2012, we were shocked at what was inside. I had sent so many writings and books home that I had forgotten about them. I sat and cried as I read all of those manuscript rejection letters again.

As I read and reflected, the Holy Spirit spoke to me. "Well, my child, you know your future. Regardless of the wars, I always hold on to what is important to me. As I lead, you will finish these books. For those who have already been written about but were rejected, I will open a door for them to be published. I did not give you all of this for anything. I did not instill in you the love of history and the Bible, so it would not be lost. Have patience. The time is coming. Just keep writing. I am going to introduce you to some people who will change the way you write. You try to write like Max Lucado and Francine Rivers, your two favorite authors, but I am going to change your style—you have a message that needs to be preserved for the tribulation period."

I remember those words as if it were this morning that he spoke to me. It scared me so bad. At that time in my life, there was one word and one phrase that would send my heart rate to 150, make my mouth go dry, and a headache would ensue. I did not know why. I was a Christian, and I knew I was ready—but I thought this was fear. Later, I was to learn it was the anointing; I did not know how to harness it. That word was "Rapture," and the phrase was "being left to go through the tribulation!"

I became a nursing professor, and my writing for educational purposes tripled. I have published numerous research, nursing, academic, and JACHO prep nursing articles over my nursing career. My healthcare writing was blessed, but everything I wrote in the scriptural or romance genre was a total bust. Then something terrible happened, which became my catalyst for change.

The COVID-19 pandemic hit in 2020 here in southern Alabama. God changed my ministry by combining my writing with my sermon preparation. I have continued with the healthcare writing. Teaching nursing is my career. Education is my heart. But preaching is my lifeline. I love to preach. I love to fast and pray. I love to spend time with Jesus. I would stay in my war room all day if hunger and the need for a restroom did not drive me out. It has not always been that way. COVID changed that. Something took hold of me during that pandemic. I could not spend enough time with God.

I even found that my hobby of restoring antiques was taking a back seat to my writing. That was not me. God was speaking. I was having dreams and visions. The more I fasted, the more he revealed himself to me. The visions were so real. I would be transported to a place that seemed so real. I do not know how to tell you without sounding delusional. So, I will say—the anointing is a fantastic thing—especially when you let go and let God anoint you!

In the midst of the COVID pandemic, I ended up with three large Christian publishers competing for my manuscripts. They were each trying to convince me that they were the best. I did not know what to do. God had anointed, and I knew I was on the right track. But I went from receiving hundreds of rejection letters to these three companies competing for the same manuscripts that had been rejected twenty years before.

But, "God is funny!" (I love this phrase by Eli's wife in the TV series *"The House of David"* that came out on Amazon Prime Video in February 2025). When I was praying and asking God which one of the three to go with, He said, 'None!' That is right. God did not select one of the top three. He did not choose a company that I had never written to or heard of—God selected a company that I did not even know existed!

So, "God is funny!" He does not see what we see. When he tells us what he sees, we think God is old and senile or at least out of touch with the 21st Century. But if you can get over that fact and let go and let God, he will transport you to a place that you have never reached, no matter who backed you! The center of his perfect will for your life and for what is coming!

Now, enough about how I got to this point with the writing. Let us talk about what I changed in this manuscript from its original writing date. I began writing about Isaac, Rebekah, and Queen Esther when I was 21. I wrote the introduction and one chapter. Then, in 1991, I added another chapter. Finally, in 1993, I had it basically written.

However, as I traveled and began writing about my experiences, my books were no longer in chronological order, following the Bible. The books are numbered in the order I wrote them. God would give me an idea, and I would start the book. Then I would end up traveling to a different location before I completed the book. So, I would start a new book. I did not want to miss the opportunity to capture what God had for me in each area where I was. So, the list is not in geographical order either. I hope this does not confuse you. Please note that I wrote them in the order they are numbered. Some locations we went to many times. Each time, I would come up with a new book idea.

You may read about pure love, fun love, and then caring love. Just as you start to feel good about the love lessons, an evil love jumps in. Now that the books are all being loaded on Amazon, I have noticed a pattern. God was putting the "corrective—ways not to love" books scattered throughout the series. To help you keep track of which books are being posted next on Amazon, check my YouTube Page, Facebook page, or drop me an email. (The publisher is not printing them in order. They are printing them in the order of likes from the test audiences.) Some of these books, I need to finish the last chapter and summarize, along with designing new book covers for each one. We anticipate that two books per month will be added to Amazon in paperback and eBook-Kindle versions until all 45 books have been loaded. Some books may have three or four loaded. Keep an eye on my YouTube channel: @LBlackmonBooks.

After HFT Publishing's unrelenting insistence this summer that I give them some Christian romance novels, I decided I had better do some more research and fact-checking. I decided to "Google" a few things to make sure I had them correct. My historical information primarily came from the locals and scholars I encountered in the Middle East. Some of the things I wrote them were more myth than historical facts. That was the best I could get during a war.

I realized that I would not have to do much editing on the first ten books to get them to press. The worst part would be the conversion from the 1990 Macintosh software to the Windows Office Professional 2021 software that my publisher used. I immediately signed a contract in June 2025 for ten books in this series, which was subsequently increased to 25 in July and 45 in August 2025, following the results from the target audiences that they had been researching.

I have written approximately 50 romance books. The latter ones have not been completed. I will not finish them at this time—maybe later. I feel an overwhelming urge to release the *"Revelation Made Simple"* series to the market before Christmas 2025. I make no promises, except to say that there will be at least 45 books in this series over the next two years.

HFT Publishing's goal is to release one title per month through the end of the year. Could you read, enjoy, and write to me? Send a letter to me through the publisher, or email me at the following email address:

lawanda@minister.com

Regular Mail: La Wanda Blackmon, Author
HFT Publishing, Inc.
P. O. Box 1863
Brewton, AL 36427-1863

(All books will range from 190 pages to 260 pages)